CURE

"A fascinating tale that never slows down." —*Library Journal*

INTERVENTION

"Cook can write up a storm and spin a taut tale, every chapter of which ends on a cliffhanger all the way up to an unforeseen conclusion. In the hands of a master, in other words, such confections have real possibilities—and Cook more than delivers. Just the book for the beach bag—or a transatlantic flight to Rome or Jerusalem." —*Kirkus Reviews*

FOREIGN BODY

"The topic of medical tourism is a timely one and raises questions of safety and standards of care outside the U.S. The non-stop action and format of the book make it one that you'll read quickly just to see what happens next."
—Bookreporter.com

"India's fledgling medical outsourcing industry could soon be taking a body blow from an upcoming medical mystery thriller by Robin Cook, the acknowledged maestro of the genre, which is set partly in New Delhi . . . thrills, chills and spills." —*The Times of India*

CRITICAL

"*Critical* is a top-notch thriller with the freshness and impact of his earlier efforts . . . Jack and Laurie . . . make ideal vehicles for Cook's campaign to raise public consciousness about medicine's pitfalls . . . *Critical* is tightly written, and each supporting character is vivid and memorable. The novel is a credit to the medical thriller genre, which Cook is generally thought to have created and made popular." —*San Francisco Chronicle*

"Cook's work is best-selling fiction girded by science fact. His novels have dissected a host of hot-button issues in medical practice, among them stem-cell research, organ donation and genetic decoding. With his 26th book, *Critical*, Cook . . . examine[s] a fresh controversy: specialty hospitals and the impact they will have on the health care industry."
—*The Post and Courier* (Charleston, SC)

CRISIS

"Cook packs a quality punch."   *—New York Daily News*

"Quick moving and suspenseful."   *—Panache*

"Robin Cook's *Crisis* mixes relevant social issues with murder and mayhem . . . The violence-wracked race to prove Bowman's complicity sparks car chases, gunfights, the disinterring of a corpse and a completely unexpected ending."
—USA Today

MARKER

"*Marker* is a perfect page-turner, and a perfect airplane novel. There's just enough information about hospital politics and medical language in the story to let us know this doctor knows the ins and outs of that world. And there's just enough to allow us to infer his meaning without keeping a medical dictionary beside the book. The finale is most inventive, and it's a perfect, explosive ending for what could be a nail-biting *ER*-type TV series, as well as a great horror film."   *—Boston Globe*

"Cook richly develops characters, allowing us to share their most personal thoughts and professional concerns. Add to these likeable heroes a compelling medical mystery and growing suspense, and the result is a highly entertaining read. By throwing in scientific and medical procedures as well as philosophical and moral dilemmas, the book also takes on the persona of a social commentary . . . Cook . . . offers readers a smart dissection of contemporary issues that affect us all. Who says science can't be fun?"   *—USA Today*

"The bestselling physician/author is in top form as he revisits the love/hate relationship between New York City medical examiners Laurie Montgomery and her lover, Jack Stapleton . . . the plot thickens before the denouement crackles to an electric edge-of-the-seat finale."
—Publishers Weekly (starred)

Titles by Robin Cook

BRAIN

Robin Cook

G. P. Putnam's Sons
New York

PUTNAM

G. P. Putnam's Sons
Publishers Since 1838
An imprint of Penguin Random House LLC
375 Hudson Street
New York, New York 10014

Copyright © 1979 by Robin Cook
Penguin supports copyright. Copyright fuels creativity, encourages diverse voices,
promotes free speech, and creates a vibrant culture. Thank you for buying an au-
thorized edition of this book and for complying with copyright laws by not repro-
ducing, scanning, or distributing any part of it in any form without permission.
You are supporting writers and allowing Penguin to continue to publish books for
every reader.

First Signet edition / May 1980
First G. P. Putnam's Sons mass-market edition / November 2016
G. P. Putnam's Sons premium edition ISBN: 9780451157973

Printed in the United States of America
41 40 39 38

From the brain, and from the brain only, arise our pleasures, joys, laughter, and jests, as well as our sorrows, pains, griefs and tears . . .

—Hippocrates
  The Sacred Disease
  Sect. XVII
  translated by W.H.S. Jones

BRAIN

1

March 7

Katherine Collins mounted the three steps from the sidewalk with a fragile sense of resolve. She reached the combination glass and stainless steel door and pushed. But it didn't open. She leaned back, gazed up at the lintel, and read the incised inscription, "Hobson University Medical Center: For the Sick and Infirm of the City of New York." For Katherine's way of thinking it should have read, "Abandon All Hope Ye Who Enter Here."

Turning around, her pupils narrowed in the morning March sunlight; her urge was to flee and return to her warm apartment. The last place in the world that she wanted to go was back into the hospital. But before she could move, several patients mounted the steps and brushed past her. Without pausing they opened the door to the main clinic and were instantly devoured by the ominous bulk of the building.

Katherine closed her eyes for an instant, marveling

1

at her own stupidity. Of course, the doors to the clinic opened outward! Clutching her parachute bag to her side, she pulled open the door and passed into the netherworld within.

The first thing that assaulted Katherine was the smell. There was nothing like it in her twenty-one years of experience. The dominant odor was chemical, a mixture of alcohol and sickeningly sweet deodorant. She guessed the alcohol was an attempt to check the disease that lurked in the air; she knew the deodorant was to cover the biological smells that hovered around illness. Any remnants of denial that Katherine had been using to help herself make this visit evaporated under the onslaught of the smell. Until her first visit to the hospital a number of months previously she had never considered her own mortality and had accepted health and well-being as her due. Now it was different and as she entered the clinic with its smell, the thought of all her recent health problems flooded into her consciousness. Biting her lower lip to keep her emotions under control, she pushed her way toward the elevators.

The hospital crowds were troublesome for Katherine. She wanted to draw into herself like a cocoon to avoid being touched, breathed or coughed on. She had difficulty looking at the distorted faces, scaly rashes and oozing eruptions. It was worse in the elevator, where she was pressed up against a group of humanity that reminded her of the crowds in a painting by Brueghel. Keeping her eyes glued to the floor indicator, she tried to ignore her surroundings by rehearsing the speech she was going to give to the receptionist at the GYN clinic. "Hello, my name is Katherine Collins. I'm a university student and I've been here four times. I'm about to go home to have my medical problems handled by my family internist and I'd like a copy of my gynecology records."

It sounded simple enough. Katherine allowed her eyes to wander to the elevator operator. His face was tremendously broad, but when he turned sideways, his head was flat. Katherine's eyes involuntarily fixed on the distorted image and when the operator turned to announce the third floor, he caught Katherine's stare. One of his eyes looked down and to the side. The other bore into Katherine with an evil intensity. Katherine averted her gaze, feeling her face redden. A large hairy man pushed past her to disembark. Steadying herself with her hand against the side of the elevator, she looked down at a blond five-year-old girl. One green eye returned her smile. The other was lost beneath the violaceous folds of a large tumor mass.

The elevator door closed and the car lifted. A dizzy sensation swept over Katherine. It was different from the dizziness that had presaged the two seizures she'd experienced the month before, but still it was frightening within the closed environment of the stuffy elevator. She shut her eyes and battled against the sense of claustrophobia. Someone coughed behind her and she felt a fine mist on her neck. The car jolted, the doors opened, and Katherine emerged on the fourth floor of the clinic. She moved over to the wall and leaned against it, letting the people behind her push by. Her dizziness cleared rapidly. Once she felt back to normal she turned left down a hall that had been painted light green twenty years before.

The corridor expanded into the waiting area for the GYN clinic. It was dense with patients, children, and cigarette smoke. Katherine crossed this central area and entered a cul-de-sac to the right. The university's

GYN clinic, which served all the colleges as well as the hospital employees, had its own waiting area, although the decor and furniture were the same as the main room. When Katherine entered there were seven women sitting on tubular steel and vinyl seats. All were nervously flicking the pages of outdated magazines. The receptionist sat behind a desk, a bird-like woman of about twenty-five with bleached hair, pale skin, and narrow features. Her name tag pinned firmly to her flat chest proclaimed her name to be Ellen Cohen. She looked up as Katherine approached the desk.

"Hello, my name is Katherine Collins . . ." She noticed that her voice lacked the assertiveness she had intended. In fact, when she got to the end of her request she realized that she sounded as if she were pleading.

The receptionist looked at her for a moment. "You want your records?" she asked. Her voice reflected a mixture of disdain and incredulity.

Katherine nodded and tried to smile.

"Well, you have to talk with Ms. Blackman about that. Please have a seat." Ellen Cohen's voice became brusque and authoritarian. Katherine turned and found a seat near to the desk. The receptionist went to a file cabinet and pulled Katherine's clinic chart. She then disappeared through one of the several doors leading to the examining rooms.

Unconsciously, Katherine began smoothing her shiny brown hair, pulling it down over her left shoulder. It was a common gesture for Katherine, particularly when she was under strain. She was an attractive young woman with bright attentive gray-blue eyes. Her height was five-two-and-a-half, but her energetic personality made her seem taller. She was well liked by her friends at college, probably because of her openness, and deeply loved by her parents, who worried about the vulnerability of their only daughter in the jungle of New York City. Yet it had been Katherine's parents' concern and overprotectiveness that had led to Katherine choosing a college in New York, believing the city would help her demonstrate her innate strength and individuality. Up until the current illness, she had been successful, scoffing at her parents' warnings. New York had become her city and she loved its throbbing vitality.

The receptionist reappeared and sat down to her typing.

Katherine's eyes surreptitiously swept around the waiting room, recording the bowed heads of the young women waiting their turns like unknowing cattle. Katherine was immensely thankful she was not waiting for an exam herself. She loathed the experience, which she had endured four times: the last just four weeks ago. Coming to the clinic had been her most difficult act of independence. In reality she would have much preferred to return to Weston, Massachusetts, and see her own gynecologist, Dr. Wilson. He'd been the first and only other doctor to examine her. Dr. Wilson was older than the residents who staffed the clinic and he had a sense of humor, which had defused the humiliating aspects of the experience, making it at least tolerable. Not so here. The clinic was impersonal and cold, and combined with the city hospital environment, each visit became a nightmare. Yet Katherine had persisted. Her sense of independence demanded it, at least until her illness.

The nurse practitioner, Ms. Blackman, emerged from one of the rooms. She was a stocky forty-five-year-old woman with jet black hair pulled back into a tight bun on the crown of her head. She was dressed in a spotless white uniform, starched to a professional crispness. Her attire reflected the way she liked to run the clinic: with cool efficiency. She'd worked for the Med Center for eleven years.

The receptionist spoke to Ms. Blackman, and Katherine heard her name mentioned. The nurse nodded, turning to look in Katherine's direction for a moment. Belying her crisp exterior, Ms. Blackman's dark brown eyes gave an impression of great warmth. Katherine suddenly thought that outside of the hospital, Ms. Blackman was probably a good deal nicer.

But Ms. Blackman did not come over to talk with Katherine. Instead she whispered something to Ellen Cohen, then returned to the examination area. Katherine felt her face redden. She guessed she was being deliberately ignored; it would be a way for the clinic personnel to show their displeasure about her wish to see her own doctor. Nervously she reached for a coverless year-old copy of *Ladies' Home Journal*, but she couldn't concentrate.

She tried to pass the time thinking about her arrival home that night; how surprised her parents would be. She could imagine herself walking into her old room. She hadn't been there since Christmas, but she knew it would look exactly as she'd left it. The yellow bedspread, the matching curtains, all the mementos of her adolescence carefully preserved by her mother. The reassuring image of her mother made Katherine question again if she should call and tell her parents she was coming home. The plus was that they would meet her at Logan Airport. The minus was that she'd probably be coerced into an explanation about why she was coming home, and Katherine wanted to discuss her illness face to face, not over the telephone.

Ms. Blackman reappeared after twenty minutes and again conversed with the receptionist in muted tones. Katherine pretended to be absorbed in her magazine. Finally the nurse broke off and came over to Katherine.

"Miss Collins?" said Ms. Blackman with subtle irritation.

Katherine looked up.

"I've been told you have requested your clinic records?"

"That's correct," said Katherine, putting the magazine down.

"Have you been unhappy with our care?" asked Ms. Blackman.

"No, not at all. I'm going home to see our family internist and I want a complete set of my medical records to take with me."

"This is rather irregular," said Ms. Blackman. "We're accustomed to sending records only when they are requested by a physician."

"I'm leaving for home tonight and I want the records with me. If my doctor needs them, I don't want to have to wait for them to be sent."

"This just isn't the way we do things here at the Med Center."

"But I know it's my right to have a copy of my records if I want it."

For Katherine an uncomfortable silence followed her last comment. She was not accustomed to such assertiveness. Ms. Blackman stared at her like an exasperated parent with a recalcitrant child. Katherine stared back, transfixed by Ms. Blackman's dark and fluid eyes.

"You'll have to speak to the doctor," said Ms. Blackman abruptly. Without waiting for a response she walked away from Katherine and stepped through one of the nearby doors. The latch engaged after her with mechanical finality.

Katherine drew in a breath and looked around her. The other patients were regarding her warily as if they shared the clinic personnel's disdain for her wish to upset the normal protocol. Katherine struggled to maintain her self-control, telling herself that she was being paranoid. She pretended to read her magazine, feeling the stares of the other women. She wanted to pull inside herself like a turtle or get up and leave. She couldn't do either. Time inched painfully forward. Several more patients were called for their exams. It was now obvious she was being ignored.

It was three-quarters-of-an-hour later when the clinic physician, dressed in rumpled white jacket and trousers, appeared with Katherine's chart. The receptionist nodded in her direction, and Dr. Harper sauntered over to stand directly in front of her. He was bald save for a frieze of hair that started over each ear and dipped down to meet in a wiry bush at the nape of his neck. He'd been the doctor who'd examined Katherine on two previous occasions, and Katherine had distinctly remembered his hairy hands and fingers, which had had an alien appearance when matted with the semi-transparent latex rubber gloves.

Katherine glanced up into the man's face, hoping for a glimmer of warmth. There wasn't any. Instead he silently flipped open her chart, supporting it with his left hand and following his reading with his right index finger. It was as if he were about to give a sermon.

Katherine let her glance drop. Along the front of his left pant leg was a series of minute bloodstains.

Hooked onto his belt on the right was a piece of rubber tubing, on the left a beeper.

"Why do you want your gynecology records?" he said without looking at her.

Katherine reiterated her plans.

"I think it's a waste of time," said Dr. Harper, still flipping through the pages. "Really, this chart has almost nothing in it. A couple of mildly atypical Pap smears, some gram positive discharge explainable by a slight cervical erosion. I mean, this isn't going to help anybody. Here you had an episode of cystitis, but it had been undoubtedly caused by sex the day before the symptoms started, which you had admitted to . . ."

Katherine felt her face flush with humiliation. She knew everyone in the waiting room could hear.

". . . look, Miss Collins, your seizure problem has nothing to do with Gynecology. I'd suggest you head up to Neurology clinic . . ."

"I've been to Neurology," interrupted Katherine. "And I have those records already." Katherine fought back the tears. She wasn't usually emotional, but the rare times she felt like crying, she had great difficulty controlling herself.

Dr. David Harper raised his eyes slowly from the chart. He took a breath and expressed it noisily through partially pursed lips. He was bored. "Look, Miss Collins, you've received excellent care here . . ."

"I'm not complaining about my care," said Katherine without looking up. Tears had filled her eyes and threatened to run down her cheeks. "I just want my records."

"All I'm saying," continued Dr. Harper, "is that you don't need any second opinions about your gynecological status."

"Please," said Katherine slowly. "Are you going to give me my records, or do I have to go to the administrator?" Slowly she looked up at Dr. Harper. With her knuckle she caught the tear that had spilled over her lower lid.

The doctor finally shrugged and Katherine could hear him curse beneath his breath as he tossed the chart onto the receptionist's desk, telling the woman to make a copy. Without saying goodbye or even looking back, he disappeared into the examining area.

As Katherine put on her coat she realized she was trembling and again felt light-headed. She walked over to the receptionist's desk and grasped the outer edge, leaning on it for support.

The bird-like blonde chose to ignore her while she completed typing a letter. When she put the envelope into the machine, Katherine reminded the receptionist of her presence.

"All right, just a moment," said Ellen Cohen with irritated emphasis on each word. Not until she'd typed the envelope, stuffed, sealed and stamped it, did she get to her feet, take Katherine's chart, and disappear around the corner. During the entire time she avoided Katherine's eyes.

Two more patients were called before Katherine was handed a manila envelope. She managed to thank the girl, but wasn't given the courtesy of a response. Katherine didn't care. With the envelope under her arm and her bag over her shoulder, she turned and half-ran, half-walked out into the confusion of the main GYN waiting room.

Katherine paused in the heavy air as a smothering wave of dizziness descended over her. Her fragile emotional state combined with the sudden physical effort of rapid walking had been too much. Her vision clouded and she reached out and groped for the back of a waiting-room chair. The manila envelope slipped from under her arm and fell to the floor. The room spun and her knees buckled.

Katherine felt strong hands grasp her upper arms, supporting her. She heard someone try to reassure her and tell her that everything was going to be all right. She wanted to say that if she could sit down for just a moment she'd be fine, but her tongue wouldn't cooperate. Vaguely she was aware she was being carried upright down a corridor, her feet, like those of a marionette, bumping ineffectually along the floor.

There was a door, then a small room. The awful spinning sensation continued. Katherine was afraid she might be sick, and cold perspiration appeared on her forehead. She was conscious of being lowered to the floor. Almost immediately her vision began to clear and the whirling of the room stopped. She was with two doctors dressed in white and they were helping her. With some difficulty they got one of her arms out of her coat and had applied a tourniquet. She was glad she was away from the crowded waiting room so that she was not a spectacle for everyone to stare at.

"I think I feel better," said Katherine, blinking her eyes.

"Good," said one of the doctors. "We're going to give you a little something."

"What?"

"Just something to calm you down."

Katherine felt a needle pierce the tender skin on the inside of her elbow. The tourniquet was pulled off and she could feel her pulse in her fingertips.

"But I feel much better," she protested. She turned

her head to see a hand depressing the plunger of a syringe. The doctors were bent over her.

"But I feel okay," said Katherine.

The two doctors didn't respond. They just looked at her, holding her down.

"I really feel better now," said Katherine. She looked from one doctor to the other. One of them had the greenest eyes Katherine had ever seen, like emeralds. Katherine tried to move. The doctor's grip tightened.

Abruptly Katherine's vision dimmed and the doctor appeared far away. At the same time she heard a ringing in her ears and her body felt heavy.

"I feel much . . ." Katherine's voice was thick and her lips moved slowly. Her head fell to the side. She could see she was on the floor of a storeroom. Then darkness.

2

March 14

Mr. and Mrs. Wilbur Collins supported each other while they waited for the door to be opened. At first the key wouldn't go into the lock, and the superintendent pulled it out and examined it to make sure it was the key to 92. He tried it again, realizing he'd had it upside down. The door opened and he moved aside to allow the Women's Dean of the university to step inside.

"Cute apartment," said the Dean. She was a petite woman, about fifty, with very nervous and quick gestures. It was apparent she felt under pressure.

Mr. and Mrs. Wilbur Collins and two uniformed New York City policemen followed the Dean into the room.

It was a small one bedroom apartment, advertised to have a river view. It did, but only from a tiny window in the closet-like bathroom. The two policemen stood aside with their hands clasped behind their backs. Mrs. Collins, a fifty-two-year-old woman, hesitated near the entrance as if she were afraid of what she might find. Mr. Collins, on the other hand, limped directly to the center of the room. He'd had polio in 1952 and it had affected his right lower leg, but not his shrewd ability in business. At fifty-five he was the number two man in the First National City Bank of Boston empire. He was a man who demanded action and respect.

"Since it's been only a week," offered the Dean, "maybe your concern is premature."

"We never should have allowed Katherine to come to New York," said Mrs. Collins, fidgeting with her hands.

Mr. Collins ignored both comments. He headed for the bedroom and looked in. "Her suitcase is on the bed."

"That's a good sign," said the Dean. "A lot of students react to pressure by leaving school for a few days."

"If Katherine had left, she would have taken her suitcase," said Mrs. Collins. "Besides, she would have called us on Sunday. She always calls us on Sunday."

"As Dean, I know how many students suddenly need a breather, even good students like Katherine."

"Katherine is different," said Mr. Collins disappearing into the bathroom.

The Dean rolled her eyes for the benefit of the policemen, who remained impassive.

Mr. Collins limped back into the living room. "She didn't go anyplace," he said with finality.

"What do you mean, dear?" asked Mrs. Collins with mounting anxiety.

"Just what I said," returned Mr. Collins. "She wouldn't go anywhere without these." He tossed a

14

half-empty packet of birth control pills onto the seat of the couch. "She's here in New York and I want her found." He looked at the policemen. "Believe me, I intend to see action on this case."

3

April 15

Dr. Martin Philips leaned his head against the wall of the control room; the coolness of the plaster felt good. In front of him four third-year medical students were pressed against the glass partition, watching in total awe as a patient was being prepared for a CAT scan. It was the first day of their radiology elective; they were starting with neuroradiology. Philips had brought them to see the CAT scanner first because he knew it would impress and humble them. Sometimes medical students tended to be smart-alecky.

Within the scanner room the technician was bending over, checking the position of the patient's head in respect to the gigantic doughnut-shaped scanner. He straightened up, peeled off a length of adhesive tape, and bound the patient's head to a Styrofoam block.

Reaching over to the counter, Philips took the req-

uisition form and the patient's chart. He scanned both
for clinical information.

"The patient's name is Schiller," said Philips. The
students were so absorbed in the preparations that
they did not turn to face him while he spoke. "Chief
complaint is weakness of the right arm and right leg.
He's forty-seven." Philips looked at the patient. Experience told him that the man was probably tremendously frightened.

Philips replaced the requisition form and chart
while inside the scanner room the technician activated the table. Slowly the patient's head slid into
the orifice of the scanner as if he were to be devoured. With a final glance at the position of the head,
the technician turned and retreated to the control
room.

"Okay, step back from the window for a moment,"
said Philips. The four medical students obeyed instantly, moving to the side of the computer, whose
lights were blinking in anticipation. As he had sur-
mised, they were impressed to the point of submis-
sion.

The technician secured the communicating door
and took the mike from its hook. "Stay very still, Mr.
Schiller. Very still." With his index finger the technician depressed the start button on the control panel.
Within the scanning room the huge doughnut-shaped
mass surrounding Mr. Schiller's head began abrupt,
intermittent rotational movements like the action of
the main gear of a gigantic mechanical clock. The
clunking sound, loud to Mr. Schiller, was muffled for
those on the other side of the glass.

"What's happening now," said Martin, "is that the
machine is making two hundred and forty separate

X-ray readings for each single degree of rotational movement."

One of the medical students made a face of total incomprehension to his colleague. Martin ignored the gesture and placed his face in his hands with his fingers over his eyes, rubbing carefully and then massaging his temples. He hadn't had his coffee yet and felt groggy. Normally he'd stop in the hospital cafeteria, but this morning he hadn't had time because of the medical students. Philips, as Assistant Chief of Neuroradiology, always made it a point to handle the medical students' introduction to neuroradiology. His compulsiveness in this regard had become a pain in the ass because it cut into his research time. The first twenty to thirty times he had enjoyed impressing the students with his exhaustive knowledge of the anatomy of the brain. But the novelty had worn off. Now it was enjoyable only if a particularly smart student came along, and in neuroradiology that didn't happen very often.

After a few minutes the doughnut-shaped scanner halted its rotational movement, and the computer console came alive. It was an impressive setup like a control panel in a science-fiction movie. All eyes switched from the patient to the blinking lights, except for Philips, who glanced down at his hands and tried to dislodge a small tab of dead skin alongside the nail of his index finger. His mind was wandering.

"In the next thirty seconds the computer simultaneously solves forty-three-thousand-two-hundred equations of tissue-density measurements," said the technician, eager to take over Philips' role. Philips encouraged this. In fact he merely gave the students their formal lectures, allowing the practical teaching to be done by the neuroradiology fellows, or the superbly trained technicians.

Lifting his head, Philips watched the medical students, who were transfixed in front of the computer console. Turning his gaze to the leaded window, Philips could just see Mr. Schiller's bare feet. Momentarily the patient was a forgotten participant in the unfolding drama. For the students the machine was infinitely more interesting.

There was a small mirror over a first-aid cabinet, and Philips looked at himself. He hadn't shaved yet and the day-old stubble stood out like bristles on a brush. He always arrived a good hour before anyone else in the entire department, and he'd developed the habit of shaving in the surgical locker room. His routine was to get up, jog, shower and shave in the hospital and stop for coffee in the cafeteria. This usually gave him two hours to work in his research interests without interruption.

Still looking in the mirror, Philips ran a hand through his thick sandy hair, pushing it back. There was such a difference between the lightness of the ends and the darker blond of the roots that some of the nurses kidded Philips about highlighting it. Nothing could have been further from the truth. Philips rarely thought about his looks, occasionally butchering his hair himself when he didn't have time to go to the hospital barber. But despite his inattention, Martin was a handsome man. He was forty-one and the recent lines that had formed about his eyes and mouth only enhanced his appearance, which earlier had seemed a bit boyish. Now he looked harder, and a recent patient had remarked that he seemed more like a cowboy on TV than a doctor. The comment had pleased him and it wasn't altogether without basis. Philips was just under six feet tall with a slight but athletic build, and his face did not give the impression of an academician. It was angular, with a ruler-straight nose and expressive mouth. His eyes were a lively light blue, and they, more than anything else, reflected his basic intelligence. He'd graduated summa cum laude from Harvard, class of 1961.

The cathode-ray tube on the output console came to life as the first image appeared. The technician hastily adjusted the window width and the density to give the best image. The medical students crowded around the small TV-like screen as if they were about to see the Super Bowl, but the picture they saw was oval with a white border and a granular interior. It was a computer-constructed image of the inside of the patient's head, positioned as if someone was looking down on Mr. Schiller after the top of his skull had been removed.

Martin glanced at his watch. It was a quarter to eight. He was counting on Dr. Denise Sanger to arrive at any moment and take over shepherding the medical students. What really was on Philips' mind this morning was a meeting with his research collaborator, William Michaels. Michaels had called the day before, saying that he was coming over early in the morning with a little surprise for Philips. By now Martin's curiosity had been honed to a razor's edge, and the suspense was killing him. For four years the two men had been working on a program to enable a computer to read skull X rays, replacing the radiologist. The problem was in programming the machine to make qualitative judgments about the densities of specific areas of X rays. If they could succeed, the rewards would be incredible. Since the problems of interpreting skull X rays were essentially the same as interpreting other X rays, the program would be eventually adaptable to the entire field of radiology. And if they accomplished that . . . Philips occasionally let himself dream of having his own research department, and even the Nobel Prize.

The next image appeared on the screen bringing Philips' mind back to the present.

"This slice is thirteen millimeters higher than the previous image," intoned the technician. With his finger, he pointed to the bottom section of the oval. "Here we have the cerebellum and . . ."

"There's an abnormality," said Philips.

"Where?" asked the technician, who was seated on a small stool in front of the computer.

"Here," said Philips, squeezing in so that he could point. His finger touched the area the technician had just described as the cerebellum. "This lucency here in the right cerebellar hemisphere is abnormal. It should have the same density as the other side."

"What is it?" asked one of the students.

"Hard to say at this point," said Philips. He leaned over to look at the questionable area more closely. "I wonder if the patient has any gait problem?"

"Yes, he does," said the technician. "He's been ataxic for a week."

"Probably a tumor," said Philips, standing back up.

The faces of all four medical students immediately reflected dismay as they stared at the innocent lucency on the screen. On the one hand they were thrilled to see a positive demonstration of the power of modern diagnostic technology. On the other hand, they were frightened by the concept of a brain tumor; the idea that anybody could have one; even they.

The next image began to wipe off the previous one.

"Here's another area of lucency in the temporal

lobe," said Philips, quickly pointing to an area already being replaced by the next image. "We'll see it better on the next slice. But we are going to need a contrast study."

The technician got up and went in to inject contrast material into Mr. Schiller's vein.

"What does the contrast material do?" asked Nancy McFadden.

"It helps outline lesions like tumors when the blood brain barrier is broken down," said Philips, who had turned to see who was coming into the room. He'd heard the door to the corridor open.

"Does it contain iodine?"

Philips hadn't heard the last question because Denise Sanger had come in and was smiling warmly at Martin behind the backs of the engrossed medical students.

She slipped out of her short white coat and reached up to hang it next to the first-aid cabinet. It was her way of getting down to work. Its effect on Philips was the opposite. Sanger had on a pink blouse, pleated in the front and topped with a thin blue ribbon tied in a bow. As she extended her arm to hang her coat, her breasts thrust against her blouse, and Philips appreciated the image as a connoisseur appreciated a work of art, for Martin thought Denise was one of the most beautiful women he had ever seen. She said she was five-five, whereas actually she was five-four. Her figure was slight, one hundred and eight pounds, with breasts that were not large but wonderfully shaped and firm. She had thick shiny brown hair, which she usually wore pulled back from her forehead and clasped with a single barrette on the back of her head. Her eyes were lighter brown with flecks of gray, giving her a lively, mischievous appearance.

Very few people guessed that she had been first in her medical school graduating class three years previously, nor did many believe that she was twenty-eight years old.

With her coat taken care of, Denise brushed past Philips, giving his left elbow a furtive squeeze. It was so fast that Philips couldn't respond. She sat down at the screen, adjusted the viewing controls to her liking, and introduced herself to the students. The technician returned and announced that the contrast material had been given. He prepared the scanner for another run.

Philips leaned over so that he had to support himself on Denise's shoulder. He pointed to the image on the screen. "Here's a lesion in the temporal lobe, and at least one, maybe two, in the frontal." He turned to the medical students. "I noted in the chart that the patient is a heavy smoker. What does all this suggest to you?"

The students stared at the image afraid to make any gesture. For them it was like being at an auction without money; any slight movement could have been interpreted as a bid.

"Let me give you all a hint," said Philips. "Primary brain tumors are usually solitary, whereas tumors coming from other parts of the body, what we call metastasis, can be single or multiple."

"Lung cancer," blurted one of the students as if he were on a TV game show.

"Very good," said Philips. "At this stage you can't be one hundred percent sure, but I'd be willing to put money on it."

"How long does the patient have to live?" asked the student, obviously overwhelmed by the diagnosis.

"Who's the doctor?" asked Philips.

"He's on Curt Mannerheim's neurosurgical service," said Denise.

"Then he doesn't have long to live," said Martin. "Mannerheim will operate on him."

Denise turned quickly. "A case like this is inoperable."

"You don't know Mannerheim. He operates on anything. Especially tumors." Martin again bent over Denise's shoulder, smelling the unmistakable aroma of her freshly washed hair. It was as unique to Philips as a fingerprint, and despite the professional setting, he felt a faint stirring of passion. He stood up to break the spell.

"Doctor Sanger, can I speak to you for a moment," he said suddenly, motioning her over to a corner of the room.

Denise complied willingly, with a bewildered expression.

"It's my professional opinion . . ." said Philips in the same formal tone of voice. He then paused and when he continued he lowered his voice to a whisper ". . . that you look incredibly sexy today." Denise's expression was slow to change. It took a moment for the comment to register. When it did, she almost laughed. "Martin, you caught me off-guard. You sounded so severe I thought I'd done something wrong."

"You have. You've worn this sexy outfit purely to inhibit my powers of concentration."

"Sexy. I'm buttoned up to my larynx."

"On you, anything looks sexy."

"That's your dirty mind, old man!"

Martin had to laugh. Denise was right. Whenever he saw her he inadvertently remembered how wonderful she looked naked. He'd been dating Denise

Sanger for over six months, and he still felt like an excited teenager. At first they'd taken every precaution to keep the rest of the hospital from getting wind of their affair, but as they'd become more and more confident that their relationship was serious, they'd become less concerned with secrecy, especially since the more they got to know each other, the narrower the difference in their ages became. And the fact that Martin was the Assistant Chief of Neuroradiology while Denise was a second-year resident in Radiology was a source of professional stimulus to them both, particularly after she began her rotation on his service, three weeks previously. Already Denise could match performance with the two fellows who had already finished their radiology residencies. And on top of that it was fun.

"Old man, huh?" whispered Martin. "For that comment, you're going to be punished. I'm leaving these medical students in your hands. If they start to get bored, send them over to the angiography room. We'll give them an overdose of the clinical before the theoretical."

Sanger nodded in resigned agreement.

"And when you finish the morning CAT schedule," continued Philips, still whispering, "come over to my office. Maybe we can steal away to the coffee shop!"

Before she could answer he took his long white coat, and left.

The surgical suites were on the same floor as Radiology, and Philips headed in that direction. Dodging a traffic jam of gurneys laden with patients waiting for fluoroscopy, Philips cut through the X-ray reading room. It was a large area with partitions formed by banks of X-ray viewing boxes, populated currently by a dozen or so residents chatting and having coffee.

The daily avalanche of X rays had yet to arrive, although the X-ray machines had been busy for about half an hour. First it would be a trickle of films, then a flood. Philips remembered all too well from his days as a resident. He'd trained at the Med Center and, responding to the tough atmosphere of one of the biggest and best radiology departments in the country, he had passed many twelve-hour days in that very room.

His reward for his effort had been an invitation to stay on for his fellowship in neuroradiology. When he'd finished, his performance had been so outstanding, he'd been offered a staff position with a joint appointment with the medical school. From that fledgling position he'd risen rapidly to his present status, Assistant Chief of Neuroradiology.

Philips stopped momentarily in the very center of the X-ray reading room. Its unique, low-level illumination, coming from the fluorescent bulbs behind the frosted glass of the X-ray viewing boxes, cast an eerie light over the people in the room. For a moment the residents looked like corpses with dead white skin and empty eye sockets. Philips wondered why he had never noticed this before. He looked down at his own hand. Its color was the same pasty hue.

He walked on feeling strangely unsettled. It was not the first time in the last year he had seen some familiar hospital scene through jaundiced eyes. Perhaps the reason was a slight but fomenting dissatisfaction with his job. His work was becoming progressively more administrative and, on top of that, he felt stagnated by circumstance. The Chief of Neuroradiology, Tom Brockton, was fifty-eight and was not considering retiring. Besides, the Chief of Radiology, Harold Goldblatt, was also a neuroradiologist.

Philips had to recognize that his meteoric rise within the department had ground to a halt, not for lack of ability on his part, but because the two positions over him were solidly occupied. For almost a year Philips had reluctantly begun to entertain the idea of leaving the Med Center for another hospital where he would have a shot at the top.

Martin turned down the corridor leading to surgery. He passed through the double swinging doors, whose sign warned visitors that they were entering a restricted area, and went through another set of swinging doors, to the patient-holding room. Here stood a swarm of gurneys filled with anxious patients awaiting their turn to be dissected. At the end of this large area was a long built-in white Formica desk guarding the entrance to the thirty operating rooms and to the recovery area. Three nurses in green surgical scrub dresses were busy behind the desk making sure the right patient got into the right room so he'd get the right operation. With almost two hundred operations in any twenty-four-hour period, this was a full-time job.

"Can someone tell me about Mannerheim's case?" asked Philips as he leaned over the desk.

All three nurses looked up and began to speak at once. Martin, being one of the few eligible doctors, was a welcome visitor to the OR. When the nurses realized what had happened, they laughed and then made an elaborate ceremony of deferring to one another.

"Maybe I should ask someone else," said Philips, pretending to leave.

"Oh, no," said the blond nurse.

"We can go back in the linen closet to discuss it," suggested the brunette. The OR was the one place in the hospital where inhibitions were relaxed. The atmosphere was totally different from any other service. Philips thought that perhaps it had something to do with everyone wearing the same pajama-like clothing, plus the potential for crisis, where sexual innuendos provided a relief valve. Whatever it was, Philips remembered it very well. He'd been a surgical resident for one year before deciding to go into radiology.

"Which one of Mannerheim's cases are you interested in?" asked the blond nurse. "Marino?"

"That's right," said Philips.

"She's right behind you," said the blond nurse.

Philips turned. About twenty feet away was a gurney supporting the covered figure of a twenty-one-year-old woman. She must have heard her name through the fog of her preoperative medication because her head slowly rolled in Philips' direction. Her skull was totally shaved in anticipation of her surgery, and the image reminded Philips of a small songbird without its feathers. He'd seen her briefly twice before when she was having her preoperative X rays, and Philips was shocked how different she looked now. He had not realized how small and delicate she was. Her eyes had a pleading quality like an abandoned child, and Philips had all he could do to turn away, directing his attention back to the nurses. One of the reasons he'd switched from surgery to radiology had been a realization he couldn't control his empathy for certain patients.

"Why haven't they started her?" he asked the nurse, angry the patient was being left to her fears.

"Mannerheim's been waiting for special electrodes from Gibson Memorial Hospital," said the blond nurse. "He wants to make some recordings from the part of the brain he's going to remove."

"I see . . ." said Philips, trying to plan his morning. Mannerheim had a way of upsetting everyone's schedules.

"Mannerheim's got two visitors from Japan," added the blond nurse, "and he's been putting on a big show all week. But they'll be starting in just a couple of minutes. They've called for the patient. We just haven't had anybody to send with her."

"Okay," said Philips, already starting back across the patient-holding area. "When Mannerheim wants his localization X rays, call my office directly. That should save a few minutes."

As he retraced his steps, Martin remembered he still had to shave and headed for the surgical lounge. At eight-ten it was almost deserted since the seven-thirty cases were all under way and the "to follow" cases could not hope to begin for some time. Only one surgeon was there talking on the telephone to his stockbroker while absentmindedly scratching himself. Philip passed into the changing area and twirled the combination to his foot-square locker, which Tony, the old man who took care of the surgical area, had allowed him to keep.

As soon as he had his face completely lathered, Philips' beeper went off making him jump. He hadn't realized how taut his nerves were. He used the wall phone to answer, trying to keep the shaving cream from the receiver. It was Helen Walker, his secretary, informing him that William Michaels had arrived and was waiting for him in his office.

Philips went back to his shaving with renewed enthusiasm. All his excitement about William's surprise came roaring back. He splashed himself with cologne and struggled back into his long white coat. Passing back through the surgical lounge, he noticed the surgeon was still on the phone with his broker.

When Martin reached his office he was at a half run. Helen Walker looked up from her typing with a start as the blurred image of her boss passed by her. She began to get up, reaching for a pile of correspondence and phone messages, but stopped when the door to Philips' office slammed shut. She shrugged and went back to her typing.

Philips leaned against the closed door, breathing heavily. Michaels was casually leafing through one of Philips' radiology journals.

"Well?" said Philips excitedly. Michaels was dressed as usual in his ill-fitting, slightly worn tweed jacket, which had been purchased during his third year at M.I.T. He was thirty but looked twenty, with hair so blond that it made Philips' look brown by comparison. He smiled, his small impish mouth expressing satisfaction, his pale blue eyes twinkling.

"What's up?" he said, pretending to go back to the magazine.

"Come on," said Philips, "I know you're just trying to rile me. The trouble is that you're being too successful."

"I don't know what . . ." began Michaels, but he didn't get any further. In one swift motion, Philips stepped across the room and tore the magazine from his hands.

"Let's not play dumb," said Philips. "You knew that telling Helen you had a 'surprise' would drive me crazy. I almost called you last night at four A.M. Now I wish I had. I think you deserved it."

"Oh, yeah, the surprise," teased Michaels. "I almost forgot." He leaned over and rummaged in his briefcase. A minute later he had pulled out a small package wrapped with dark green paper and tied with a thick yellow ribbon.

Martin's face fell. "What's that?" He'd expected some papers, most likely computer print-out paper, showing some breakthrough in their research. He never expected a present.

"It's your surprise," said Michaels, reaching toward Philips with the package.

Philips' eyes moved back to the gift. His disappointment was so acute it was almost anger. "Why the hell did you buy me a present?"

"Because you've been such a wonderful research partner," said Michaels, still holding the package toward Philips. "Here, take it."

Philips reached out. He had recovered from the shock enough to be embarrassed about his reaction. No matter how he felt he didn't want to hurt Michaels' feelings. After all, it was a nice gesture.

Philips thanked him while feeling the weight of the package. It was light and about four inches long and an inch high.

"Aren't you going to open it?" asked Michaels.

"Sure," said Philips, studying Michaels' face for an instant. Buying a present seemed so out of character for this boy genius from the Department of Computer Science. It wasn't that he wasn't friendly or generous. It was just that he was so completely involved with his research that he usually overlooked amenities. In fact, during the four years they'd been working together, Philips had never seen Michaels socially. Philips had decided that Michaels' incredible mind never turned off. After all, he had been singled out to head the newly created Division of Artificial Intelligence for the university at twenty-six. He'd completed his Ph.D. at M.I.T. when he was only nineteen.

"Come on," said Michaels impatiently.

Philips pulled off the bow and dropped it ceremoniously among the debris on his desk. The dark green paper followed. Beneath was a black box.

"There's a little symbolism there," said Michaels.

"Oh?" said Philips.

"Yeah," said Michaels. "You know how psychology treats the brain: like a black box. Well, you get to look inside."

Philips smiled weakly. He didn't know what Michaels was talking about. He pulled off the top of the box and separated some tissue. To his surprise he extracted a cassette case labeled *Rumors* by Fleetwood Mac.

"What the hell," smiled Philips. He hadn't the foggiest idea why Michaels would buy him a recording by Fleetwood Mac.

"More symbolism," explained Michaels. "What's inside is going to be more than music to your ears!"

Suddenly the whole charade made sense. Philips flipped open the case and pulled out the cassette. It wasn't a musical recording. It was a computer program.

"How far did we get?" asked Philips almost in a whisper.

"It's the whole thing," said Michaels.

"No!" said the incredulous Martin.

"You know the last material you gave me? It worked like a charm. It solved the problem of density and boundary interpretation. This program incorporates everything you've included in all your flow sheets. It will read any skull X ray you give it, provided you put it into that piece of equipment over there." Michaels pointed to the back of Philips' office. There on the top of Philips' worktable was a TV-sized electrical apparatus. It was obvious that it was built as a prototype rather than production model. The front was made of a plain stainless steel plate and its attaching bolts protruded. In the upper left-hand corner was a slot that was made to take the program cassette. Two electrical trunks protruded from its sides. One trunk fed into a typewriter input/output device. The other came from a rectangular stainless steel box about four feet square and one foot high. On the front of this metal apparatus was a long shot with visible rollers for the insertion of an X-ray film.

"I don't believe it," said Philips, afraid that Michaels was teasing him again.

"Neither do we," admitted Michaels. "Everything just suddenly fell together." He walked over and patted the top of the computer unit. "All the work you'd done in breaking down the problem-solving and pattern-recognition aspects of radiology not only made it apparent we needed new hardware but also suggested the way to design it. This is it."

"Looks simple from the outside."

"As usual, appearances are deceptive," said Michaels. "The innards of this unit are going to revolutionize the computer world."

"And think what it's going to do to the field of radiology if it can really read X rays," said Martin.

"It will read them," said Michaels, "but there could still be bugs in the program. What you have to do now is run the program against as many skull X rays as you can find that you have read in the past. If there are problems, I think they will be in the area of false negatives. Meaning the program will say the X ray is normal when pathology is really present."

"That's the same problem with radiologists," said Philips.

"Well, I think we'll be able to eliminate that in the program," said Michaels. "It's going to be up to you. Now to work this thing, first turn it on. I think even a doctor of medicine will be able to do that."

"Without doubt," said Philips, "but we'll need a Ph.D. to plug it in."

"Very good," Michaels laughed. "Your humor is improving. Once the unit is plugged in and turned on, you insert the cassette program into the central unit. The output printer will then inform you when to insert the X-ray film into the laser scanner."

"What about the orientation of the film?" asked Philips.

"Doesn't matter, except the emulsion side has to be down."

"Okay," said Philips, rubbing his hands together and eyeing the unit like a proud parent. "I still can't believe it."

"I can't, either," said Michaels. "Who would have guessed four years ago that we could have made this kind of progress? I can still remember the day you arrived unannounced in the Department of Computer Science, plaintively asking if anyone was interested in pattern recognition."

"It was just pure luck that I bumped into you," returned Philips. "At the time I thought you were one of the undergraduates. I didn't even know what the Division of Artificial Intelligence was."

"Luck plays a role in every scientific breakthrough," agreed Michaels. "But after the luck, there's lots of hard work, like what's facing you. Remember the more skull films you run with the program, the better it will be, not only to debug the program, but also because the program is heuristic."

"Let's not pull any big words on me," said Philips. "What do you mean 'heuristic'?"

"So you don't like some of your own medicine," laughed Michaels. "I never thought I'd hear a doctor complain about incomprehensible words. A heuristic program is one that is capable of learning."

"You mean this thing will get smarter?"

"You got it," said Michaels, moving toward the door. "But it's up to you now. And, remember, the same format will be applicable to other areas of radiology. So in your spare time, as if you're going to have any, start the flow sheet for reading cerebral angiograms. I'll talk to you later."

Closing the door behind Michaels, Philips went over to the worktable and eyed the X-ray-reading apparatus. He was eager to begin to work with it immediately, but he knew the burden of his daily routine proscribed it. As if in confirmation, Helen walked in with a pile of correspondence, telephone messages, and the cheerful news that the X-ray machine in one of the cerebral angiography rooms wasn't functioning properly. Reluctantly Philips turned his back on the new machine.

4

"Lisa Marino?" asked a voice, causing Lisa to open her eyes. Leaning over her was a nurse named Carol Bigelow, whose dark brown eyes were the only portion of her face visible. A flower-print hat contained her hair. Her nose and mouth were covered by a surgical mask.

Lisa felt her arm lifted and rotated so the nurse could read her identification bracelet. The arm was replaced and patted. "Are you ready for us to fix you up, Lisa Marino?" asked Carol, releasing the brake mechanism on the gurney with her foot, and pulling the bed out from the wall.

"I don't know," admitted Lisa, trying to see up into the nurse's face. But Carol had turned away saying, "Sure you are," as she pushed the bed past the white Formica desk.

The automatic doors closed behind them as Lisa began her fateful journey down the corridor to OR #21. Neurosurgery was usually done in one of four rooms: Number 20, 21, 22, or 23. These rooms were fitted out with the special needs of brain surgery in mind. They had overhead mounted Zeiss operating microscopes, closed-circuit video systems with recording capabilities, and special OR tables. OR #21 also had a viewing gallery and was the favorite of Dr. Curt Mannerheim, Chief of Neurosurgery, and Chairman of the Department for the medical school.

Lisa had hoped that she'd be sleeping at this point, but such was not the case. If anything, she seemed particularly aware and all her senses sharp. Even the sterile chemical smell seemed exceptionally pungent to her. There was still time, she thought. She could get out of the bed and run. She didn't want to be operated on, especially not her head. In fact, anything but her head.

The movement stopped. Turning her gaze, she saw the nurse disappear around a corner. Lisa had been parked like a car at the side of a busy thoroughfare. A group of people passed her, transporting another patient who was retching. His chin was being held back by one of the orderlies pushing the bed, and his head was a bandaged nightmare.

Tears began to run down Lisa's cheeks. The patient reminded her of her own upcoming ordeal. Her central being was going to be rudely cracked open and violated. Not just a peripheral part of her, like a foot or an arm, but her head . . . where her personality and very soul resided. Would she be the same person afterward?

When Lisa had been eleven she'd had acute appendicitis. The operation had certainly seemed scary at the time, but nothing like what she was experiencing now. She was convinced that she was going to lose her identity if not her life. In either case, she was fragmenting, and the pieces were there for people to pick up and examine.

Carol Bigelow reappeared.

"Okay, Lisa, we're ready for you."

"Please," whispered Lisa.

"Come now, Lisa," said Carol Bigelow. "You wouldn't want Dr. Mannerheim to see you crying."

Lisa didn't want anyone to see her crying. She shook her head in response to Carol Bigelow's question, but her emotion switched to anger. Why was this happening to her? It wasn't fair. A year ago she'd been a normal college girl. She'd decided to major in English, hopefully to prepare for law school. She loved her literature courses and had been a superior student, at least until she'd met Jim Conway. She knew she'd let her studies go, but it had only been a month or so. Before meeting Jim she'd had sex on several occasions, but it had never been satisfying and she'd questioned why there was so much fuss about it. But with Jim it had been different. She knew immediately that with Jim, sex was the way it was supposed to be. And she hadn't been irresponsible. She did not believe in the Pill, but she'd made the effort to be fitted with a diaphragm. She could remember very distinctly how hard it had been for her to find the courage to make that first GYN clinic visit and go back when it was necessary.

The gurney moved into the operating room. It was completely square, about twenty-five feet on a side. The walls were constructed of gray ceramic tile up to the glass-faced gallery above. The ceiling was dominated by two large stainless steel operating room lights shaped like inverted kettle drums. In the center of the room stood the operating table. It was a narrow, ugly piece of equipment, reminding Lisa of an altar for some pagan rite. At one end of the table was a round piece of padding with a hole in the center, which Lisa instinctively knew was to hold her head. Totally out of keeping with the environment, the Bee Gees crooned from a small transistor radio in the corner.

"There, now," said Carol Bigelow. "What I want you to do is slide over here onto the table."

"Okay," said Lisa. "Thank you." She was annoyed at her response. Thank you was the farthest thing from her mind. Yet she wanted the people to like her because she knew she depended on them to take care of her. Moving from the gurney to the operating table, Lisa held on to the sheet in a vain attempt to retain a modicum of dignity. Once on the table she lay still, staring up at the operating lights. Just to the side of the lights she recognized the glass partitions. Because of reflections, it was difficult to see through the glass, but then she saw the faces staring down at her. Lisa closed her eyes. She was a spectacle.

Her life had become a nightmare. Everything had been wonderful until that fateful evening. She had been with Jim and they both had been studying. Progressively, she had become aware that she was having difficulty reading, particularly when she came to a specific sentence beginning with the word "Ever." She was certain she knew the word but her mind refused to give it to her. She had to ask Jim. His response was a smile, thinking she was teasing. After she persisted, he told her "ever." Even after Jim had told her the word, when she looked at its printed form, it wouldn't come to her. She remembered feeling a powerful sense of frustration and fear. Then she began to smell the strange odor. It was a bad smell, and although she sensed she'd smelled it before, she could not say

40

what it was. Jim denied smelling anything and that was the last thing Lisa remembered. What had followed was her first seizure. Apparently it had been awful, and Jim was shaking when she regained consciousness. She had struck him several times and scratched his face.

"Good morning, Lisa," said a pleasant male voice with an English accent. Looking up behind her, Lisa met the dark eyes of Dr. Bal Ranade, an Indian doctor who had trained at the university. "You remember what I told you last night?"

Lisa nodded. "No coughing or sudden movements," said Lisa, eager to please. She remembered Dr. Ranade's visit vividly. He'd appeared after her dinner, announcing himself as the anesthesiologist who was going to take care of her during her operation. He had proceeded to ask her the same questions about her health she'd answered many times before. The difference was that Dr. Ranade did not seem to be interested in the answers. His mahogany face did not change its expression, except when Lisa described her appendectomy at age eleven. Dr. Ranade nodded when Lisa said she'd had no trouble with the anesthesia. The only other information that interested him was her lack of allergic reaction. He nodded then too.

Usually Lisa preferred outgoing people. Dr. Ranade was the opposite. He expressed no emotion, just a quiet intensity. But for Lisa, under the circumstances this cool affectation was appropriate. She was glad to find someone for whom her ordeal was routine. But then Dr. Ranade had shocked her. In the same precise Oxford accent he said: "I presume that Dr. Mannerheim has discussed with you the anesthetic technique which will be used."

"No," said Lisa.

41

"That's odd," said Dr. Ranade at length.

"Why?" asked Lisa, sensing trouble. The idea that there could be any breakdown in communication was alarming. "Why is that odd?"

"We usually use a general anesthesia for craniotomy," said Dr. Ranade. "But Dr. Mannerheim has informed us that he wants local anesthesia."

Lisa had not heard her operation described as a craniotomy. Dr. Mannerheim had said he was going to "turn a flap" and make a small window in her head so that he could remove the damaged part of her right temporal lobe. He'd told Lisa that somehow, a part of Lisa's brain had been damaged, and it was that section that was causing her seizures. If he could take just the damaged part out the seizures would stop. He'd done almost a hundred such operations with wonderful results. At the time Lisa had been ecstatic because up until Dr. Mannerheim all she could get from her doctors was compassionate head shaking.

And the seizures were horrible. Usually she knew when they were coming because she would smell the strangely familiar odor. But sometimes they came without warning, descending on her like an avalanche. Once in a movie theater, after she'd been given a long course of heavy medication and assurances that the problem was under control, she smelled the horrid odor. In a panic she'd jumped up, stumbled to the aisle, and ran back toward the lobby. At that point she became unaware of her actions. Later she "came to" propped up against the lobby wall by the candy machine, with her hand between her legs. Her clothes were partially off, and like a cat in heat, she'd been masturbating. A group of people was staring at her as if she were a freak, including Jim, whom she'd punched and kicked. Later she learned she'd assaulted two girls, injuring one enough to be hospitalized. At the time she'd "come to" all she could do was close her eyes and cry. Everyone was afraid to come near her. In the distance she remembered hearing the sound of the ambulance. She thought that she was going insane.

Lisa's life had come to a standstill. She wasn't insane, but no medication controlled her seizures. So when Dr. Mannerheim appeared, he seemed like a savior. It wasn't until Dr. Ranade's visit that she began to comprehend the reality of what was going to happen to her. After Dr. Ranade, an orderly had arrived to shave her head. From that moment on, Lisa had been frightened.

"Is there some reason why he wants local anesthesia?" asked Lisa. Her hands had begun to tremble. Dr. Ranade had thought carefully about his answer.

"Yes," he said finally, "he wants to locate the diseased part of your brain. He needs your help."

"You mean, I'll be awake when . . ." Lisa didn't finish her sentence. Her voice had trailed off. The idea seemed preposterous.

"That's correct," said Dr. Ranade.

"But he knows where the diseased part of my brain is," protested Lisa.

"Not well enough. But don't worry. I'll be there. There'll be no pain. All you have to remember is no coughing and no sudden movements."

Lisa's reverie was cut short by a feeling of pain in her left forearm. Looking up she could see tiny bubbles rising up in a bottle over her head. Dr. Ranade had started the IV. He did the same thing in her right forearm, threading into her a long thin plastic tube. Then he adjusted the table so that it tilted slightly downward.

"Lisa," said Carol Bigelow. "I'm going to catheterize you."

Picking up her head, Lisa looked down. Carol was busy unwrapping a plastic covered box. Nancy Donovan, another scrub nurse, pulled back Lisa's sheet exposing her from the waist down.

"Catheterize?" questioned Lisa.

"Yes," said Carol Bigelow, pulling on loose rubber gloves. "I'm going to put a tube into your bladder."

Lisa allowed her head to fall back. Nancy Donovan grasped Lisa's legs and positioned them so that the soles of her feet were together while her knees were widely apart. She lay exposed for the world to see.

"I'm going to be giving you a medicine called mannitol," explained Dr. Ranade. "It causes you to make a lot of urine."

Lisa nodded as if she understood while she felt Carol Bigelow begin to scrub her genitals.

"Hi, Lisa, I'm Dr. George Newman. Do you remember me?"

Opening her eyes, Lisa gazed into another masked face. These eyes were blue. On the other side of her was another face with brown eyes.

"I'm the Chief Resident in Neurosurgery," said Dr. Newman, "and this is Dr. Ralph Lowry, one of our Junior Residents. We'll be helping Dr. Mannerheim as I explained to you yesterday."

Before Lisa could respond she felt a sudden sharp pain between her legs, followed by a curious fullness in her bladder. She took a breath. She felt tape being placed on the inner part of her thigh.

"Just relax now," said Dr. Newman without waiting for her to respond. "We'll have you fixed up in no time." The two doctors directed their interest to the series of X rays that lined the back walls.

The pace in the OR quickened. Nancy Donovan appeared with a steaming stainless steel tray of instruments, and with a loud crash she heaved it on top of a nearby table. Darlene Cooper, another scrub nurse, who was already gowned and gloved, reached into the sterile instruments and began to arrange them on a tray. Lisa turned her head when she saw Darlene Cooper lift out a large drill.

Doctor Ranade wrapped a blood pressure cuff around Lisa's right upper arm. Carol Bigelow exposed Lisa's chest and taped on EKG leads. Soon the sonar-like beeps from the cardiac monitor competed with John Denver on the transistor.

Dr. Newman came back from studying the X rays and positioned Lisa's shaved head. With his pinky on her nose and his thumb on the top of her head, he drew a line with a marking pen. The first line went from ear to ear over the top of her head. The second line bisected this one, starting at the middle of the forehead and extending back to the occipital area.

"Now, Lisa, turn your head to the left," said Dr. Newman.

Lisa kept her eyes closed. She felt a finger palpate the ridge of bone that ran back from her right eye toward her right ear. Then she felt the marking pen trace a looping line that began at her right temple and arched upward and backward ending behind her ears. The line defined a horseshoe-shaped area with Lisa's ear at its base. This was to be the flap that Dr. Mannerheim had described.

An unexpected drowsiness coursed through Lisa's body. It felt like the air in the room had become viscous and her extremities leaden. It took great effort for her to open her eyelids. Dr. Ranade smiled down at her. In one hand was her IV line; in the other hand a syringe.

"Something to relax you," said Dr. Ranade.

Time became discontinuous. Sounds drifted in and out of her consciousness. She wanted to fall asleep but her body involuntarily fought against it. She felt herself being turned half on her side with her right shoulder elevated and supported by a pillow. With a sense of detachment she felt both wrists bound to a board that stuck out at right angles from the operating table. Her arms felt so heavy she couldn't have moved them anyway. A leather cinch went around her waist securing her body. She felt her head scrubbed and painted. There were several sharp needles accompanied by fleeting pain before her head was clamped in some sort of vise. Despite herself, Lisa fell asleep.

Sudden intense pain awoke her with a start. She had no idea how much time had passed. The pain was located above her right ear. It occurred again. A cry issued from her mouth and she tried to move. Except for a tunnel of cloth directly in front of her face, Lisa was covered with layers of surgical drapes. At the end of the tunnel, she could see Dr. Ranade's face.

"Everything is fine, Lisa," said Dr. Ranade. "Don't move now. They are injecting the local anesthetic. You'll only feel it for a moment."

The pain occurred again and again. Lisa felt like her scalp was going to explode. She tried to lift her arms only to feel the cloth restraints. "Please," she shouted, but her voice was feeble.

"Everything is fine, Lisa. Try to relax."

The pain stopped. Lisa could hear the doctors breathing. They were directly over her right ear.

"Knife," said Dr. Newman.

Lisa cringed. She felt pressure, like a finger being pressed against her scalp and rotated around the line drawn by the marking pen. She could feel warm fluid on her neck through the drapes.

"Hemostats," said Dr. Newman. Lisa could hear sharp metallic snaps.

"Raney clips," said Dr. Newman. "And call Mannerheim. Tell him we'll be ready for him in thirty minutes."

Lisa tried not to think about what was happening to her head. Instead she thought about the discomfort in her bladder.

She called to Dr. Ranade and told him she had to urinate.

"You have a catheter in your bladder," said Dr. Ranade.

"But I have to urinate," said Lisa.

"Just relax, Lisa," said Dr. Ranade. "I'll give you a little more sleep medicine."

The next thing Lisa was conscious of was the high-pitched whine of a gas-powered motor combined with a sense of pressure and vibration on her head. The noise was frightening because she knew what it meant. Her skull was being opened by a saw; she didn't know it was called a craniotome. Thankfully there was no pain, although Lisa braced for it to occur at any moment. The smell of scorched bone penetrated the gauze drapes over her face. She felt Dr. Ranade's hand take hers, and she was thankful for it. She pressed it as if it were her only hope of survival.

The sound of the craniotome died. The rhythmic beeping of the cardiac monitor emerged from sudden stillness. Then Lisa felt pain again, this time more like the discomfort of a localized headache. Dr. Ranade's face appeared at the end of her tunnel of vision. He watched her as she felt the blood pressure cuff inflate.

"Bone forceps," said Dr. Newman.

Lisa heard and felt bone crunching. It sounded very close to her right ear.

"Elevators," said Dr. Newman.

Lisa felt several more twinges, followed by what seemed to her a loud snap. She knew her head was open.

"Damp gauze," said Dr. Newman, in a matter-of-fact voice.

While still scrubbing his hands, Dr. Curt Mannerheim leaned over to look through the door into OR#21 and see the clock on the far wall. It was almost nine o'clock. At that moment, he saw his chief resident, Dr. Newman, step back from the table. The resident crossed his gloved hands on his chest, and walked over to study the X rays arranged on the view box. That could mean only one thing. The craniotomy was done and they were ready for the Chief. Dr. Mannerheim knew he didn't have much time to spare. The investigative committee from the N.I.H. was due to arrive at noon. What was at stake was a twelve-million-dollar research grant that would support his research activities for the next five years. He had to get that grant. If he didn't, he might lose his entire animal lab, and with it, the results of four years of work. Mannerheim was certain he was on the brink of finding the exact spot in the brain responsible for aggression and rage.

Rinsing the suds, Mannerheim caught sight of Lori

McInter, the Assistant Director of the OR. He shouted her name and she stopped in her tracks.

"Lori, dear! I've got two Jap doctors here from Tokyo. Could you send someone into the lounge to make sure they find scrub clothes and all that?"

Lori McInter nodded, although she indicated she wasn't pleased at the request. Mannerheim's shouting in the corridor irritated her.

Mannerheim caught the silent rebuke and cursed the nurse under his breath. "Women," he muttered. To Mannerheim, nurses were becoming more and more a pain in the ass.

Mannerheim burst into the OR like a bull into the ring. The congenial atmosphere changed instantly. Darlene Cooper handed him a sterile towel. Drying one hand, then the other, and working down his forearms, Mannerheim bent over to look at the opening in Lisa Marino's skull.

"God damn it, Newman," snarled Mannerheim, "when are you going to learn to do a decent craniotomy? If I've told you once, I've told you a thousand times to bevel the edges more. Christ! This is a mess."

Under the drapes Lisa felt a new surge of fear. Something had gone wrong with her operation.

"I . . ." began Newman.

"I don't want to hear a single excuse. Either you do it properly or you'll be looking for another job. I got some Japs coming in here and what are they going to think when they see this?"

Nancy Donovan was standing at his side to take the towel, but Mannerheim preferred to throw it on the floor. He liked to create havoc and, like a child, demanded total attention wherever he was. And he got it. He was considered technically one of the best neurosurgeons in the country, if not the fastest. In his own terms he said, "Once you get into the head, there's no time to pussyfoot around." And with his encyclopedic knowledge of the intricacies of human neuroanatomy, he was superbly efficient.

Darlene Cooper held open the special brown rubber gloves that Mannerheim demanded. As he thrust in his hands, he looked into her eyes.

"Ahhh," he cooed, as if he were experiencing orgastic pleasure from inserting his hands. "Baby, you're fabulous."

Darlene Cooper avoided looking into Mannerheim's gray-blue eyes, as she handed him a damp towel to wipe off the powder on the gloves. She was accustomed to his comments, and from experience she knew that the best defense was to ignore him.

Positioning himself at the head of the table with Newman on his right and Lowry on his left, Mannerheim looked down on the semi-transparent dura covering Lisa's brain. Newman had carefully placed sutures through partial thickness of the dura and had anchored them to the edge of the craniotomy site. These sutures held the dura tightly up to the inner surface of the skull.

"All right, let's get this show on the road," said Mannerheim. "Dural hook and scalpel."

The instruments were slapped into Mannerheim's hand.

"Easy, baby," said Mannerheim. "We're not on TV. I don't want to feel pain each time I ask for an instrument."

He bent over and deftly tented up the dura with the hook. With the knife he made a small opening. A pinkish gray mound of naked brain could be seen through the hole.

Once under way, Mannerheim became completely

professional. His relatively small hands moved with economical deliberation, his prominent eyes never wavering from his patient. He was a physical person with extraordinary eye-hand control. The fact that he was short, five-foot-seven-inches, was a constant source of irritation to him. He felt he'd been cheated of the extra five inches to match his intellectual height, but he kept in excellent condition and looked much younger than his sixty-one years.

With small scissors and cottonoid strips, which he inserted between the dura and the brain for protection, Mannerheim opened up the covering over Lisa's brain to the extent of the bony window. Using his index finger he gently palpated Lisa's temporal lobe. With his experience the slightest abnormality could be detected. For Mannerheim, this intimate interaction between himself and a live pulsating human brain was the apotheosis of his existence. During many operations, the sheer excitement made him sexually erect.

"Now let's have the stimulator and the EEG leads," he said.

Dr. Newman and Dr. Lowry wrestled with the profusion of tiny wires. Nancy Donovan, as his circulating nurse, took the appropriate leads when the doctors handed them to her and plugged them into the nearby electrical consoles. Dr. Newman carefully placed the wick electrodes in two parallel rows. One along the middle of the temporal lobe and the other above the Sylvian vein. The flexible electrodes with the silver balls went under the brain. Nancy Donovan threw a switch and an EEG screen next to the cardiac monitor came alive with fluorescent blips tracing erratic lines.

Dr. Harata and Dr. Nagamoto entered the OR.

Mannerheim was pleased not so much because the visitors might learn something, but because he loved an audience.

"Now look," said Mannerheim, gesturing, "there's a lot of bullshit in the literature about whether you should take the superior part of the temporal lobe out during a temporal lobectomy. Some doctors fear it might affect the patient's speech. The answer is, test it."

With an electrical stimulator in his hand like an orchestral baton, Mannerheim motioned to Dr. Ranade, who bent down and lifted up the drape. "Lisa," he called.

Lisa opened her eyes. They reflected the bewilderment from the conversation she'd been overhearing.

"Lisa," said Dr. Ranade. "I want you to recite as many nursery rhymes as you can."

Lisa complied, hoping that by helping the whole affair would soon be over. She started to speak, but as she did so Dr. Mannerheim touched the surface of her brain with the stimulator. In mid-word her speech stopped. She knew what she wanted to say, but couldn't. At the same time she had a mental image of a person walking through a door.

Noting the interruption in Lisa's speech, Mannerheim said, "There's your answer! We don't take the superior temporal gyrus on this patient."

The heads of the Japanese visitors bobbed in understanding.

"Now for the more interesting part of this exercise," said Mannerheim, taking one of the two depth electrodes he'd gotten from Gibson Memorial Hospital. "By the way, someone call X ray. I want a shot of these electrodes so we'll know later where they were."

The rigid needle electrodes were both recording

and stimulating instruments. Prior to having them sterilized, Mannerheim had marked off a point on the electrodes four centimeters from the needle tip. With a small metal ruler he measured four centimeters from the front edge of the temporal lobe. Holding the electrode at right angles to the surface of the brain, Mannerheim pushed it in blindly and easily to the four-centimeter mark. The brain tissues afforded minimal resistance. He took the second electrode and inserted it two centimeters posterior to the first. Each electrode stuck out about five centimeters from the surface of the brain.

Fortunately, Kenneth Robbins, the Chief Neuroradiology X-ray technician, arrived at that moment. If he had been late Mannerheim would have thrown one of his celebrated fits. Since the operating room was outfitted to facilitate X ray, the chief technician needed only a few minutes to take the two shots.

"Now," said Mannerheim, glancing up at the clock and realizing he was going to have to speed things up. "Let's stimulate the depth electrodes and see if we can generate some epileptic brain waves. It's been my experience that if we can, then the chances of the lobectomy helping the seizure disorder are just about one hundred percent."

The doctors regrouped around the patient. "Dr. Ranade," said Mannerheim. "I want you to ask the patient to describe what she feels and thinks after the stimulus."

Dr. Ranade nodded, then disappeared under the edge of the drapes. When he reappeared he indicated to Mannerheim to proceed.

For Lisa the stimulus was like a bomb blast without sound or pain. After a blank period that could have been a fraction of a second or an hour, a kaleidoscope of images merged into the face of Dr. Ranade at the end of a long tunnel. She didn't recognize Dr. Ranade nor did she know where she was. All she was aware of was the terrible smell that heralded her seizures. It terrified her.

"What did you feel?" asked Dr. Ranade.

"Help me," cried Lisa. She tried to move but felt the restraints. She knew the seizure was coming. "Help me."

"Lisa," said Dr. Ranade, becoming alarmed, "Lisa, everything is all right. Just relax."

"Help me," cried Lisa as she lost control of her mind. The fixation of her head held, as did the leather strap at her waist. All her strength concentrated into her right arm, which she pulled with enormous force and suddenness. The wrist restraint snapped and her free arm arched up through the drapes.

Mannerheim was mesmerized by the abnormal recordings on the EEG when he saw Lisa's hand out of the corner of his eye. If he had only reacted faster he might have been able to avoid the incident. As it was, he was so startled that for a moment he was incapable of reacting. Lisa's hand, flailing wildly to free her body imprisoned by the OR table, hit the protruding electrodes and drove them straight into her brain.

Philips was on the phone with a pediatrician named George Rees when Robbins knocked and opened the door. Philips waved the technician into his office while he finished his conversation. Rees was inquiring about a skull X ray on a two-year-old male child who was supposed to have fallen down stairs. Martin had to tell the pediatrician that he suspected child abuse because of the old rib fractures he'd seen on the patient's chest X ray. It was sticky business, and Philips was glad to hang up.

"What have you got?" Philips asked Robbins, swinging around on his seat. Robbins was the Chief Neuroradiology technician whom Philips had recruited, and there was a special rapport between the two men.

"Just the localization films you asked me to do for Mannerheim."

Philips nodded as Robbins snapped them up on Philips' viewer. Normally the chief technician didn't leave the department to take X rays, but Philips had asked him to attend personally to Mannerheim just to avoid any trouble.

Lisa Marino's operative X rays lit up on the screen. The lateral film showed a polyhedral lucency where the bone flap had been cut. Within this sharply defined area were the bright white silhouettes of the numerous electrodes. The long needle-like depth electrodes Mannerheim had pushed into Lisa Marino's temporal lobe were the most apparent, and it was the position of these instruments that interested Philips. With his foot, Philips activated the motor on a wall-sized X ray viewer called an alternator. As long as he held his foot on the pedal, the screen in front of him changed. The unit could be loaded with any number of films for him to read. Philips kept the machine running until he found the screen containing Lisa Marino's previous X rays.

By comparing the new films with the old, Philips could determine the exact location of the deep electrodes.

"Gees," said Philips. "You take beautiful X rays. If I could clone you, half of my problems would be over."

Robbins shrugged as if he didn't care, but the compliment pleased him. Philips was a demanding but appreciative boss.

Martin used a finely calibrated ruler to measure distances associated with minute blood vessels on the older X rays. With his knowledge of the anatomy of the brain and the usual location of these blood vessels, he could form in his mind a three-dimensional image of the area he was interested in. Translating this information to the new films gave him the position of the tips of the electrodes.

"Amazing," said Philips, leaning back. "Those electrodes are positioned perfectly. Mannerheim is fantastic. If only his judgment equaled his technical skill."

"Do you want me to take these films back to the OR?" asked Robbins.

Philips shook his head. "No, I'll take them myself. I want to talk to Mannerheim. I'm going to take some of these older films as well. The position of this posterior cerebral artery bothers me a little." Philips picked up the X rays and headed for the door.

Although the situation in OR #21 had returned to a semblance of normality, Mannerheim was furious about the accident. Even the presence of the foreign visitors did not temper his anger. Newman and Lowry suffered the greatest abuse. It was as if Mannerheim felt they had deliberately schemed to cause the problem.

He had started the temporal lobectomy as soon as Ranade had inducted Lisa under general endotracheal anesthesia. There had been a panic immediately after Lisa's seizure, although everyone acted superbly. Mannerheim had succeeded in grabbing Lisa's flailing hand before any more damage had been done. Ranade, the real hero, had reacted instantly, injecting a sleep dose of one hundred and fifty milligrams of thiopental IV, followed by a muscle paralyzer called d-tubocurarine. These drugs had not only put Lisa to sleep, but had also terminated the seizure. Within only a few minutes Ranade had placed the endotracheal tube, started the nitrous oxide, and positioned his monitoring devices.

Meanwhile, Newman had extracted the two inadvertently deeply embedded electrodes while Lowry removed the other surface electrodes. Lowry also had placed moist cottonoid over the exposed brain before covering the site with a sterile towel. The patient had been redraped and the doctors regowned and gloved. Everything had returned to normal except Mannerheim's mood.

"Shit," said Mannerheim, straightening up to relieve the tension in his back. "Lowry, if you'd rather do something else when you grow up, tell me. Otherwise hold the retractors so I can see." From Lowry's position the resident could not see what he was doing.

The door to the OR opened, and Philips entered, carrying the X rays.

"Watch out," whispered Nancy Donovan. "Napoleon is in a foul mood."

"Thanks for the warning," said an exasperated Philips. It irritated him that everyone tolerated Mannerheim's adolescent personality, no matter how good a surgeon he was. He put the X rays up on the viewer, aware that Mannerheim had seen him. Five minutes passed before Philips realized that Mannerheim was deliberately ignoring him.

"Dr. Mannerheim," Martin called over the sound of the cardiac monitor.

All eyes turned as Mannerheim straightened up,

shifting his head so that the beam of his miner-like head lamp fell directly on the radiologist's face.

"Perhaps you don't realize that we are doing brain surgery here and maybe you shouldn't interrupt," Mannerheim said with controlled fury.

"You ordered localization X rays," said Philips calmly, "and I feel it is my duty to provide the information."

"Consider your duty done," said Mannerheim, looking back into his expanding incision.

Philips' real concern was not the electrodes' positions, because he knew they were perfect. It was the orientation of the posterior or hippocampal electrode in relation to the formidable posterior cerebral artery. "There's something else," said Martin. "I . . ."

Mannerheim's head shot up. The beam of light from his head strafed the wall, then the ceiling, while his voice lashed out like a whip. "Dr. Philips, would you mind taking yourself and your X rays out of here so that we can finish the operation? When we need your help, we'll ask for it."

Then in a normal voice, he asked the scrub nurse for some bayonet forceps and went back to work.

Martin calmly took his X rays down and left the OR. Changing back to his street clothes in the locker room, he tried not to think too much; it was easier on his mood. Heading back to Radiology, he allowed himself to ponder about the conflict in his sense of responsibility that the incident evoked. Dealing with Mannerheim called on resources he never imagined he'd need as a radiologist. He hadn't resolved anything when he arrived back at the department.

"They are ready for you in the angiography room," said Helen Walker when he reached his office. She stood up and followed him inside. Helen was an extremely gracious thirty-eight-year-old black woman from Queens who had been Philips' secretary for five years. They had a wonderful working relationship. It terrorized Philips to think of her ever leaving, because like any good secretary she was instrumental in running Philips' day-to-day life. Even Philips' current wardrobe was the result of her efforts. He would have still been wearing the same boxy clothes he'd worn in college if Helen hadn't teased him into meeting her in Bloomingdale's one Saturday afternoon. The result had been a new Philips, and the contemporary fitted clothes suited his athletic body.

Philips tossed Mannerheim's X rays onto his desk, where they merged with the other X rays, papers, journals and books. It was one place Philips forbade Helen to touch. No matter what his desk looked like he knew where everything was.

Helen stood behind him reading a steady stream of messages she felt obligated to tell him. Dr. Rees had called asking about the CAT scan on his patient, the X ray unit in the second angiography room had been fixed and was functioning normally, the emergency room called saying that they were expecting a severe head injury that was going to need an emergency CAT scan. It was endless and it was routine. Philips told her to handle everything, which was what she'd planned to do anyway, and she disappeared back to her desk.

Philips removed his white coat and put on the lead apron he wore during certain X-ray procedures to protect himself from the radiation. The bib of the apron was distinguished by a faded Superman monogram, which had resisted all attempts at removal. It had been drawn there in jest two years previously by the neuroradiology fellows. Knowing the gesture had been made out of respect, Martin had not been annoyed.

As he was about to leave, his eyes swept across the surface of his desk for a reassuring glimpse of the program cassette, just to make certain he hadn't fantasized Michaels' news. Not seeing it, Martin walked over to shuffle through the more recent layers of debris. He found the cassette under Mannerheim's X rays. Philips started to leave, but again stopped. He picked up the cassette and Lisa Marino's latest lateral skull X ray. Yelling through the open door for Helen to tell the angio room he'd be right there, he walked over to his worktable.

He took off his lead apron and draped it over a chair. He stared at the computed prototype, wondering if it would really work. Then he held up Lisa Marino's operative X ray to the light that came from the banks of viewing screens. He wasn't interested in the electrode silhouettes and his mind eliminated them. What interested Philips was what the computer would say about the craniotomy. Philips knew they had not included the procedure in the program.

He flipped the switch on the central processor. A red light came on and he slowly inserted the cassette. He got it three-quarters of the way in, when the machine swallowed it like a hungry dog. Immediately the typewriter unit came alive. Philips moved over so he could read the output.

Hi! I am Radread, Skull I. Please enter patient name.

Philips pecked out "Lisa Marino" with his two index fingers and entered it.

Thank you. Please enter presenting complaint.

Philips typed: "seizure disorder," and entered that.

THANK YOU. PLEASE ENTER RELEVANT CLINICAL IN-
FORMATION.

Philips typed: "21-year female, one year history of
temporal lobe epilepsy."

THANK YOU. PLEASE INSERT FILM IN LASER SCANNER.

Philips went over to the scanner. The rollers within
the lips of the insertion slot were moving. Carefully
Philips lined up the X ray with its emulsion side
down. The machine grabbed it and pulled it inside.
The output typewriter activated. Philips walked over.
It said: THANK YOU. HAVE A CUP OF COFFEE. Philips
smiled. Michaels' sense of humor emerged when least
expected.

The scanner emitted a slight electrical buzz; the
output device stayed silent. Philips grabbed his lead
apron and left the office.

There was silence in OR #21 as Mannerheim mobi-
lized Lisa's right temporal lobe and slowly lifted it
from its base. A few small veins could be seen linking
the specimen to the venous sinuses, and Newman
skillfully coagulated and divided them. At last it was
free, and Mannerheim lifted the piece of the brain
out of Lisa's skull and dropped it into a stainless steel
dish held by Darlene Cooper, the scrub nurse. Mannerheim looked up at the clock. He was doing fine. As
the operation had progressed, Mannerheim's mood
had changed again. Now he was euphoric and justly
pleased with his performance. He'd done the procedure in half the usual time. He was certain he'd be
in his office at noon.

"We're not quite finished," said Mannerheim, taking
the metal sucker in his left hand and forceps in his
right. Carefully he worked over the site where the
temporal lobe had been, sucking out more brain tis-

sue. He was removing what he called the deeper nuclei. This was probably the riskiest part of the procedure, but it was the part Mannerheim liked the best. With supreme confidence he guided the sucker, avoiding vital structures.

At one point a large globule of brain tissue momentarily blocked the opening of the sucker. There was a slight whistling noise, before the piece of tissue whooshed up the tube. "There go the music lessons," said Mannerheim. It was a common neurosurgical quip, but coming from Mannerheim after all the tension he'd caused, it was funnier than usual. Everyone laughed, even the two Japanese doctors.

As soon as Mannerheim had finished removing brain tissue, Ranade slowed the ventilation of the patient. He wanted to let Lisa's blood pressure rise a little while Mannerheim inspected the cavity for any bleeding. After a careful check Mannerheim was satisfied the operative site was dry. Taking a needle holder he began to close the dura, the tough covering over the brain. At that point, Ranade began carefully to lighten Lisa's anesthesia. When the case was over he wanted to be able to remove the tube in Lisa's trachea without her coughing, or straining. This required a delicate orchestration of all the drugs he'd been using. It was imperative that Lisa's blood pressure not go up.

The dural closure went swiftly and with a deft rotation of his wrist, Mannerheim placed the last interrupted stitch. Lisa's brain was again covered, although the dura dipped down and was darker where Lisa's temporal lobe had been. Mannerheim cocked his head as he admired his handiwork, then stepping back, he snapped off his rubber gloves. The sound echoed in the room.

"All right," said Mannerheim, "close her up. But let's not make it your life's work."

Motioning for the two Japanese doctors to come with him, Mannerheim left the room.

Newman took Mannerheim's position at Lisa's head.

"Okay, Lowry," said Newman, echoing his boss, "let's see if you can help me rather than hinder me."

After dropping the bone flap into place like the top of a Halloween pumpkin and tying the sutures, Newman was ready to close. With a pair of rugged tooth forceps, he grabbed hold of the edge of Lisa Marino's wound and partially everted it. Then he plunged the needle deep into the skin of the scalp, making sure he picked up pericranium, and brought the needle out in the wound. Detaching the needle holder from its original position on the shank of the needle, he used the instrument to grab the needle tip, bringing the suture out into the wound. With essentially the same technique, he put the silk through the other side of the wound, trailing the suture off into Dr. Lowry's waiting hand so he could tie the stitch. They repeated this procedure until the wound was closed with black sutures, giving the impression of a large zipper on the side of Lisa's head.

During this part of the procedure, Dr. Ranade was still ventilating Lisa by compressing a breath bag. As soon as the last stitch was to be placed, he planned to give Lisa one hundred percent oxygen and reverse the remaining muscle paralyzer her body hadn't metabolized. On schedule his hand again compressed the breathing bag, but this time his experienced fingers detected a subtle change from the previous compression. Over the last few minutes Lisa had begun to make initial efforts to breathe on her own. Those ef-

forts had provided a certain resistance to ventilating
her. That resistance had been gone on the last compression. Watching the breathing bag and listening
with his esophageal stethoscope, Ranade determined
that Lisa had suddenly stopped trying to breathe. He
checked the peripheral nerve stimulator. It told him
the muscle paralyzer was wearing off on schedule.
But why wasn't she breathing? Ranade's pulse increased. For him anesthesia was like standing on a secure but narrow ledge on the side of a precipice.

Quickly, Ranade determined Lisa's blood pressure.
It had risen to 150 over 90. During the operation it
had been stable at 105 over 60. Something was
wrong!

"Hold up," he said to Dr. Newman, his eyes darting
to the cardiac monitor. The beats were regular but
slowing with longer pauses between the spikes.

"What's wrong?" asked Dr. Newman, sensing the
anxiety in Dr. Ranade's voice.

"I don't know." Dr. Ranade checked Lisa's venous
pressure while preparing to inject a drug called nitroprusside to bring down her blood pressure. Up to this
point Dr. Ranade believed the variation in Lisa's vital
signs was a reflection of her brain responding to the
insult of surgery. But now he began to fear hemorrhage! Lisa could be bleeding and the pressure in her
head could be going up. That would explain the sequence of signs. He took the blood pressure again. It
had risen to 170 over 100. Immediately he injected
the nitroprusside. As he did so, he felt that unpleasant
sinking feeling in his abdomen associated with terror.

"She might be hemorrhaging," he said, bending
down to lift Lisa's eyelids. What he saw was what
he'd feared. The pupils were dilating. "I'm sure she's
hemorrhaging," he yelled.

The two residents stared at each other over the patient. Their thoughts were the same. "Mannerheim's going to be furious," said Dr. Newman. "We better call him. Go ahead," he said to Nancy Donovan. "Tell him it's an emergency."

Nancy Donovan dashed over to the intercom and called out to the front desk.

"Should we open her back up?" asked Dr. Lowry.

"I don't know," said Newman nervously. "If she's hemorrhaging inside her brain it would be better to get an emergency CAT scan. If she's bleeding into the operative site, then we have to open her up."

"Blood pressure still rising," said Dr. Ranade with disbelief as he watched his gauge. He prepared to give her more medication to bring the blood pressure down.

The two residents remained motionless.

"Blood pressure still rising," shouted Dr. Ranade. "Do something, for Christ sake!"

"Scissors," barked Dr. Newman. They were slapped into his hand and he cut the sutures he'd just finished placing. The wound spontaneously gaped open as he got to the end of the incision. As he pulled the scalp flap back, the section of skull they'd removed for the craniotomy pushed up at them. It seemed to be pulsating.

"Let me have the four units of blood that's on call," shouted Dr. Ranade.

Dr. Newman cut the two hitch sutures holding the bone flap in place. The piece of bone fell to the side before Dr. Newman picked it up. The dura was bulging out with an ominous dark shadow.

The OR door burst open and Dr. Mannerheim came flying in, his scrub shirt was unbuttoned save for the bottom two.

"What the hell's going on?" he shouted. Then he caught sight of the pulsating and bulging dura. "Jesus Christ! Gloves! Let me have gloves!"

Nancy Donovan started to open a new pair of gloves, but Mannerheim snatched them away from her and pulled them on without scrubbing.

As soon as a few sutures were cut, the dura burst open, and bright red blood squirted out over Mannerheim's chest. It soaked him as he blindly cut the rest of the sutures. He knew he had to find the source of the bleeding.

"Sucker," yelled Mannerheim. With a rude sound, the machine began to draw off the blood. Immediately it became apparent that the brain had shifted or swelled because Mannerheim quickly encountered the brain itself.

"The blood pressure is falling," said Ranade.

Mannerheim yelled for a brain retractor to help him try to see the base of the operative site, but blood welled up the moment he took the sucker away.

"Blood pressure . . ." said Dr. Ranade, pausing. "Blood pressure unobtainable."

The sound of the cardiac monitor, which had been so constant during the operation, slowed to a painful pulse, then stopped.

"Cardiac arrest!" shouted Dr. Ranade.

The residents whipped up the heavy surgical drapes, exposing Lisa's body and covering her head. Newman climbed up on the stool next to the OR table and began cardiac resuscitation by compressing Lisa's sternum. Dr. Ranade, having obtained the blood, hung it up. He'd opened all his IV lines, running fluid into Lisa as fast as possible.

"Stop," yelled Mannerheim, who'd stepped back from the OR table when Dr. Ranade had shouted cardiac arrest. With a feeling of utter frustration, Mannerheim threw the brain retractor to the floor.

He stood there for a moment, his arms at his sides with blood and bits of brain dripping from his fingers. "No more! It's no use," he said finally. "Obviously some major artery gave way. It must have been from the God-damned patient pushing in those electrodes. Probably transected an artery and put it into spasm, which was camouflaged by the seizure. When the spasm relaxed it blew. There's no way you can resuscitate this patient."

Grabbing his scrub pants before they fell, Mannerheim turned to leave. At the door he looked back at the two residents. "I want you to close her up again as if she were still alive. Understand?"

5

"My name is Kristin Lindquist," said the young woman waiting at the university's GYN clinic. She managed a smile, but the corners of her mouth trembled slightly. "I have an appointment with Dr. John Schonfeld at eleven-fifteen." It was exactly eleven according to the wall clock.

Ellen Cohen, the receptionist, looked up from her paperback novel at the pretty face smiling down at her. Immediately she saw that Kristin Lindquist was everything Ellen Cohen was not. Kristin had real blond hair, which was as fine as silk, a small turned-up nose, big deep blue eyes, and long shapely legs. Ellen hated Kristin instantly, labeling her in her mind as one of those California sluts. The fact that Kristin Lindquist was from Madison, Wisconsin, would not have made any difference to Ellen. She took a long drag on her cigarette, blowing the smoke out her nose as she scanned the appointment book. She crossed off Kristin's name and told her to take a seat, adding that

Kristin would be seeing Dr. Harper, not Dr. Schonfeld.

"Why isn't Dr. Schonfeld going to see me?" asked Kristin. Dr. Schonfeld had been recommended by one of the girls in the dorm.

"Because he's not here. Does that answer your question?"

Kristin nodded, but Ellen didn't notice. She'd returned to her novel, although when Kristin walked away, Ellen watched her with jealous irritation.

It was at that moment that Kristin should have left. She thought about it, realizing that no one would have noticed if she just continued walking the way she'd come. She already disliked the hospital's dilapidated environment, which reminded her of disease and decay. Dr. Walter Peterson in Wisconsin had an office that was clean and fresh, and although Kristin still did not enjoy her semiannual exam, at least it hadn't been depressing.

But she did not leave. It had taken a significant amount of courage for her to make the appointment, and she was compulsive about finishing what she'd started. So she sat down on the stained vinyl waiting-room chair, crossed her legs, and waited.

The hands of the wall clock advanced painfully slowly and after fifteen minutes Kristin realized the palms of her hands were sweating. She recognized she was becoming more and more anxious, and wondered if there was something psychologically wrong with her. There were six other women in the small waiting room, all of whom seemed calm, a fact which magnified Kristin's distress. It made her sick to think about her internal structure, and coming to the gynecologist forced the whole issue at her in a brutal and unpleasant way.

Picking up a tattered magazine, Kristin tried to divert her mind. She was unsuccessful. Almost every advertisement reminded her of her upcoming ordeal. Then she saw a picture of a man and a woman, and a new concern entered her mind: how long after sex can sperm be found in the vagina? Two nights previously Kristin had seen her boyfriend, Thomas Huron, a senior, and they had slept together. Kristin knew that she'd be humiliated if the doctor could tell.

The relationship with Thomas was the reason Kristin had decided to make an appointment at the clinic. They'd been seeing each other steadily since the fall. As their relationship grew, Kristin realized that trying to decide when it was "safe" was no longer a reasonable method of birth control. Thomas refused to take any responsibility and continually pressured Kristin for more frequent sex. She'd inquired about birth control pills at the student dispensary and had been told she first had to have a gynecological exam at the Med Center. Kristin would have preferred to have gone to her old doctor at home, but her concern for privacy made that impossible.

Taking a deep breath, Kristin realized her stomach was now a knot and she could feel unsettling rumblings in her abdomen. The very last thing she wanted was to get so upset she got diarrhea. Even the thought mortified her. Looking up at the clock, she hoped she wouldn't have to wait much longer.

One hour and twenty minutes later Ellen Cohen called Kristin into one of the exam rooms. The linoleum floor felt cold to her feet as she undressed behind a small screen. There was one hook and she hung up all her clothes. As she had been directed, she put on a hospital gown, which came to mid-thigh and

71

tied at the front. Looking down she noticed her nipples were erect from the cold, poking out through the worn cotton fabric like two hard buttons. She hoped they'd go down before the doctor saw her.

Emerging from behind the curtain, Kristin saw the nurse, Ms. Blackman, arranging instruments on a towel. Kristin averted her eyes, but not before she'd caught an unwanted glimpse of a host of gleaming stainless steel instruments, including a speculum and some forceps. The mere sight of these devices made Kristin feel weak.

"Ah, very good," said Ms. Blackman. "You're quick, and we appreciate that. Come!" Ms. Blackman patted the exam table. "Climb up here now. The doctor will be in shortly." With her foot Ms. Blackman moved a small stool to a strategic position.

Using both hands to clutch at her flimsy gown, Kristin made her way to the examination table. With the metal stirrups jutting off at the end, the table looked like some medieval torture device. She stepped on the stool and sat down facing the nurse.

Ms. Blackman then took a detailed medical history, which impressed Kristin with its thoroughness. No one had ever taken the time to do such a complete job, which included careful inquiries into Kristin's family history. When Kristin had first seen Ms. Blackman, she'd been uneasy, fearing that the nurse was going to be as cold and harsh as her appearance suggested. But during the course of the history-taking, Ms. Blackman was so pleasant and so interested in Kristin as a person that Kristin began to relax. The only symptoms of note that Ms. Blackman wrote down were a mild discharge Kristin had noted over the last several months and occasional intermenstrual spotting, which she'd had as long as she could remember.

"All right, let's get ready for the doctor," said Ms. Blackman, putting aside the chart. "Lie down now and feet in the stirrups."

Kristin complied, vainly trying to hold the edges of her gown together. It was impossible and her composure began to fade once again. The metal stirrups felt like ice, sending a chill through her body.

Ms. Blackman shook open a freshly laundered sheet and draped it over Kristin. Lifting up the end, Ms. Blackman looked beneath. Kristin could almost feel the nurse's gaze on her totally exposed crotch.

"Okay," said Ms. Blackman, "move yourself down to the end of the table."

Using a kind of rotational movement of her hips, Kristin walked her backside toward her feet.

Ms. Blackman, still looking under the sheet, wasn't satisfied. "A little more."

Kristin moved farther until she felt her buttocks half off the end of the table.

"That's fine," said Ms. Blackman, "now relax before Dr. Harper comes in."

Relax! thought Kristin. How could she relax? She felt like a piece of meat in a rack waiting to be pawed over by customers. Behind her was a window and the fact that its drape was not completely closed bothered her immensely.

Without a knock, the door to the exam room opened and a hospital courier thrust his head in. Where were the blood samples that were going to the lab? Ms. Blackman said she'd show him and disappeared.

Kristin was left by herself in the sterile atmosphere, enveloped by the aseptic smell of alcohol. She closed her eyes and took deep breaths. It was the waiting that made it so bad.

The other door opened. Kristin raised her head, expecting to see the doctor, but instead saw the receptionist, who asked where Ms. Blackman was. Kristin only shook her head. The receptionist left, slamming the door. Kristin put her head back and closed her eyes again. She wasn't going to be able to take much more.

Just when Kristin thought she'd get up and leave, the door opened and the doctor strode in.

"Hi, dear, I'm Doctor David Harper. How are you today?"

"Fine," said Kristin limply. Dr. David Harper was not what Kristin had expected. He seemed to be too young to be a doctor. His face had stubby boyish features, which clashed with his almost bald head. His eyebrows were so bushy they didn't look real.

Dr. Harper went over to the small sink and quickly washed his hands. "You're a student at the university?" he asked, reading her chart on the counter.

"Yes," answered Kristin.

"What are you studying?"

"Art," said Kristin. She knew that Dr. Harper was just making small talk, but she didn't care. In fact, it was a relief to talk after the interminable wait.

"Art: Isn't that nice," said Dr. Harper indifferently. After drying his hands, he tore open a package of latex rubber gloves. In front of Kristin he thrust his hands into them, snapping them noisily back over his wrists, then adjusting each finger in turn. It was done meticulously, like a ritual. Kristin noticed that Dr. Harper had plenty of hair everywhere but on the top of his head. Seen through the sheer latex, the hair on the backs of his hands looked vulgar.

Walking down to the foot of the table, he quizzed Kristin about her mild discharge and her occasional spotting. Obviously he wasn't impressed by either symptom. Without any more delay, he sat down on the small stool, disappearing from Kristin's view. She felt a sense of panic when the bottom edge of the sheet was picked up.

"All right," said Dr. Harper casually. "I want you to scoot down here toward me."

As Kristin moved even farther down the table, the door to the exam room opened and Ms. Blackman entered. Kristin was glad to see her. She felt her legs being pushed apart, to their limit. She couldn't have been more exposed and vulnerable.

"Let's have the Graves' speculum," said Dr. Harper to Ms. Blackman.

Kristin couldn't see what was going on but she heard the sharp clink of metal hitting against metal and it gave her a sinking feeling in the pit of her abdomen.

"Okay," said Dr. Harper. "I want you to relax now."

Before Kristin could respond, a gloved finger spread the lips of her vagina and the muscles of her thighs contracted by reflex. Then she felt the cold intrusion of the metal speculum.

"Come on, relax! When was your last Pap smear?"

It took a few seconds for Kristin to realize the question was being directed at her. "About a year ago." There was a spreading sensation.

Dr. Harper stayed silent. Kristin had no idea what was happening. With the speculum inside of her, she was terrified to move a muscle. Why was it taking so long? The speculum moved slightly and she could hear the doctor murmuring. Was something wrong with her? Lifting her head, Kristin could see that he wasn't even looking at her. He had turned and was bending over the small table, doing something that required both hands. Ms. Blackman was nodding and whispering. Lying back down, Kristin wished he'd hurry and take the speculum out. Then she felt it move, followed by a strange deep sinking sensation in her abdomen.

"Okay," said Dr. Harper finally. The speculum came out as fast as it went in and with only a momentary twinge of pain. Kristin breathed a sigh of relief only to be assaulted by the rest of the examination.

"Your ovaries feel fine," Dr. Harper said finally as he pulled off his soiled gloves, dropping them into a covered pail.

"I'm glad," said Kristin, referring more to the termination of the experience.

After a quick breast exam, Dr. Harper told her she could get dressed. He acted curt and preoccupied. Kristin stepped behind the screen, pulling the curtain closed. She put her clothes on as quickly as possible, afraid the doctor might leave before she had the chance to talk with him. When she emerged from the dressing area she was still buttoning her blouse. It was good timing because Dr. Harper was just completing her chart.

"Dr. Harper," began Kristin. "I wanted to ask about birth control."

"What would you like to know?"

"I'd like to know what would be the best method for me to use."

Dr. Harper shrugged. "Each method has its good points and bad points. As far as you're concerned, I don't think there's any contraindication for using any of the methods. It's a personal choice. Talk to Ms. Blackman about it."

Kristin nodded. She wanted to ask more, but Dr. Harper's abrupt manner made her feel self-conscious.

"Your exam," continued Dr. Harper, as he put his pen back into his jacket pocket and stood up, "was essentially normal. I noticed a slight erosion of your cervix, which would explain your mild discharge. It's nothing. Perhaps we should check it again in a couple of months."

"What is an erosion?" asked Kristin. She wasn't sure she wanted to know.

"It's just an area devoid of the usual epithelial cells," said Dr. Harper. "Do you have any other questions?"

Dr. Harper made it apparent he was in a hurry to end the consultation. Kristin hesitated.

"Well, I've got more patients," said Dr. Harper quickly. "If you need more information on birth control, ask Ms. Blackman. She's very good on counseling. Also, you might bleed a little after the exam, but don't worry about it. See you again in a couple of months." With a final smile, and a pat on the top of Kristin's head, Dr. Harper left.

A moment later the door opened and Ms. Blackman looked in. She seemed surprised that Dr. Harper had left. "That was fast," said Ms. Blackman, picking up the chart. "Come on in the lab and we'll finish you up and get you on your way."

Kristin followed Ms. Blackman into another room with two examining tables as well as long counter tops with all sorts of medical paraphernalia, including a microscope. On the far wall was a glass-fronted instrument cabinet filled with an assortment of evil-appearing devices. Next to it hung an eye chart. Kristin noticed it because it was one of those charts composed only of the letter E.

"Do you wear glasses?" asked Ms. Blackman.

"No," said Kristin.

"Fine," said Ms. Blackman. "Now lie down and we'll draw your blood work."

Kristin did what she was told. "I get a little weak when blood is drawn."

"That's very common," said Ms. Blackman. "That's why we ask you to lie down."

Kristin averted her eyes so she didn't have to see the needle. Ms. Blackman was very fast and afterward she took Kristin's blood pressure and pulse. Then she darkened the room for a vision exam.

Kristin tried to get Ms. Blackman to discuss birth control, but it wasn't until she'd finished her routine that she responded to Kristin's questions. And then she just referred Kristin back to the Family Planning Center at the university, saying that she would have no problems now that she'd had her gynecological exam. Concerning the erosion, Ms. Blackman made a little sketch to be sure everything was clear. Then she took Kristin's phone number and told her that she'd be informed if there were any irregularities with her test results.

With great relief Kristin hurried from the clinic. At last it was over. After all the tension she'd experienced, she decided she'd skip her afternoon class. Reaching the center of the GYN clinic, Kristin felt a little disoriented, forgetting which way she'd come. Turning on her heels, she looked for a sign for the elevators. She spied it on the wall of the nearest corridor. But when the image of the word fell on her retina, something strange happened in Kristin's brain. She felt a peculiar sensation and a slight dizziness, followed by an obnoxious odor. Although she couldn't place the smell, Kristin felt it was strangely familiar.

With a sense of foreboding Kristin tried to ignore the symptoms and pushed her way down the crowded corridor. She had to get out of the hospital. But the dizziness increased and the corridor began to spin. Grabbing an edge of a doorway for support, Kristin closed her eyes. The spinning sensation stopped. At first she was afraid to open her eyes fearing the symptoms would return, and when she did so, she did it gradually. Thankfully the dizziness didn't recur, and in a few moments she was able to let go of the doorjamb.

Before Kristin could take a step, a hand grabbed her upper arm and she recoiled in fright. She was relieved when she saw that it was Dr. Harper.

"Are you all right?" he asked.

"I'm fine," said Kristin quickly, embarrassed to admit her symptoms.

"Are you sure?"

Kristin nodded and for emphasis, pulled her arm from Harper's grip.

"Sorry to bother you then," said Dr. Harper, who excused himself and walked away down the hall.

Kristin watched him merge with the crowd. She took a breath and started for the elevators, her legs rubbery.

6

Martin left the angiography room as soon as he was convinced the resident had everything under control and the catheter was out of the patient's artery. He walked briskly down the corridor. Approaching his office he hoped Helen had gone to lunch, but as he rounded the last corner, she saw him and bounded up like a cat with her omnipresent handful of urgent messages. It wasn't that Philips did not really want to see her, it was just that he knew she had all sorts of bad news.

"The second angiography room is again nonfunctional," she said the moment she caught his attention. "It's not the X-ray unit itself, but rather the machine that moves the film."

Philips nodded as he hung up his lead apron. He was aware of the problem and he trusted that Helen had already called the company with whom they had a service agreement. He eyed the print-out device on his worktable. He could see a whole page of computer-generated notes.

"Also there's a problem with Claire O'Brian and Joseph Abbodanza," said Helen. Claire and Joseph were two neuroradiology technicians they'd been training over the years.

"What kind of problem?" asked Philips.

"They've decided to get married."

"Well," laughed Philips. "Have they been doing unnatural acts in the darkroom?"

"No!" snapped Helen. "They've decided to get married in June, then take the whole summer off for a trip to Europe."

"Whole summer!" shouted Philips. "They can't do that! It will be hard enough letting them take their two week vacation at the same time. I hope you told them that."

"Of course I did," said Helen. "But they said they don't care. They're going to do it even if it means they get fired."

"Jesus Christ," said Philips, slapping his forehead. He knew that with their training Claire and Joseph could get work in any major medical center.

"Also," said Helen. "The Dean of the medical school called. He said they voted in a meeting last week to double the number of medical-student groups rotating in Neuroradiology. He said last year's students voted the service one of the best electives."

Philips closed his eyes and massaged his temples. More medical students! That was all he needed! Christ!

"And the last thing," said Helen, heading for the door. "Mr. Michael Ferguson called from Administration to say that the room we're using for supplies has to be vacated. They need it for social service."

"And what, pray tell, are we supposed to do with the supplies?"

"I asked the same question," said Helen. "He told me you knew all along that space wasn't allocated to Neuroradiology, and that you'd think of something. Well, I'm taking a quick break for lunch. I'll be back shortly."

"Sure," said Philips. "Enjoy your lunch."

Philips waited for a few minutes until his blood pressure fell to normal. Administrative problems were becoming increasingly less tolerable. He walked over to the print-out device and pulled out the report.

Radread, Skull I

Marino, Lisa

Clinical information
21-yr-old female with one-year history of temporal lobe epilepsy. A single left lateral projection presented from a portable X ray unit. The projection appears to be approximately eight degrees off from true lateral. There is a large lucency in the right temporal region representing an area devoid of bone. The edges of this area are sharp suggesting an iatrogenic origin. This impression is confirmed by a heavy soft tissue area below the bony defect suggesting a large scalp flap. X ray is most likely an operative X ray. Numerous metallic bodies are noted representing surface electrodes. Two narrow cylindrical metallic electrodes appear to be depth electrodes in the temporal lobe, most likely positioned in the amygdala and hippocampus. Brain densities show fine linear variations in the occipital, mid-parietal, and lateral temporal lobes.

Conclusion
Operative X ray with large bony defect in the right temporal region. Multiple surface electrodes and

two depth electrodes. Widespread density variations of an unprogrammed nature.

Recommendations
Anterio posterior and oblique projections as well as CAT scan recommended for better characterization of the linear density variations and for localization of depth electrodes. Angiographic data recommended to associate position of depth electrodes with major vessels.
****Program requests insertion in central memory unit of the significance of linear density variations.

Thank you and please
send check to
William Michaels, Ph.D.,
and Martin
Philips, M.D.

Philips couldn't believe what he'd just read. It was good; it was better than good, it was fantastic. And with the little piece of humor at the end, it was overwhelming. Philips went back over sections of the report. It was extraordinarily difficult for him to believe that he was reading a report that came from their machine and not another neuroradiologist. Even though the unit had not been programmed for craniotomies, it seemed to have been able to reason with the information it had and come up with the right answer. And then there was the part about density variations. Philips had no idea what that was.

Fetching Lisa Marino's X ray from the laser scanner, Philips put it up on a viewer. He began to feel a little alarmed when he didn't see the variations the printout suggested. Maybe their new method of dealing with densities, which had been the stumbling block from the beginning, was not any good after all.

Philips activated his alternator and X rays flashed by on the screen until he found Lisa Marino's angiogram study. He stopped the alternator and took off one of her earlier lateral skull films. Putting it up next to the operative X ray, he again looked for density variations as described in the printout. To his disappointment the X ray looked normal.

The door to his office opened and Denise Sanger walked in. Philips smiled but then went back to what he was doing. Folding a sheet of paper in half, he cut out a tiny piece. When he opened the paper, there was a small hole in the center.

"So," Denise said, putting her arms around him for a hug, "I see you've been busy in here making cut-outs."

"Science advances in strange and wondrous ways," said Philips. "A lot has happened since I saw you this morning. Michaels delivered our first skull-reading unit. Here's the first printout."

While Denise read it, Philips placed the sheet of paper with the hole in it against Lisa Marino's X ray on the viewer. What the paper did was eliminate all the other complicated aspects of the X ray film except the small section visible through the hole. Martin studied the tiny area very carefully. Taking the paper away he asked Denise if she could see anything abnormal. She couldn't. When he put the paper back she still couldn't, until he pointed to some minute white flecks oriented linearly. Taking the paper away, they could both see it now that their eyes were expecting it.

"What do you think it is?" asked Denise, while she examined the film very closely.

"I haven't the slightest idea." Philips walked over to the input/output console and prepared the small computer to accept Lisa Marino's earlier film. He hoped the program would see the same density variation. The laser scanner gobbled up the film with the same relish it had displayed earlier. "But it disturbs me," added Philips. He stepped back to the input/output unit as it chattered into activity.

"Why?" asked Denise, her face illuminated by the pale light from the X ray viewer. "I think this report is fantastic."

"It is," agreed Philips. "That's the point. It suggests that the program can read X rays better than its creator. I never saw those density variations. Reminds me of the Frankenstein stories." Suddenly Martin laughed.

"Now what's so funny?" asked Denise.

"Michaels! Apparently this thing is programmed so that each time I give it an X ray it tells me to relax while it works. The first time it said have a cup of coffee. This time it says to get a bite to eat."

"Sounds like a good suggestion to me," said Denise. "What about that romantic rendezvous you promised in the coffee shop? I don't have much time; I've got to get back to the CAT scanner."

"I can't leave right now," said Philips in an apologetic voice. He knew he'd suggested lunch and he didn't want to disappoint her. "I'm really excited about this thing."

"Okay," said Denise. "But I'm going to grab a sandwich. Can I bring you back something?"

"No thanks," said Philips. He noticed the output printer was coming alive.

"I'm really glad that your research is going so well," she said at the door. "I know how important it is for you." Then she was gone.

As soon as the output printer stopped, Philips

pulled out the sheet. Like the first one, the report was very complete, and to Philips' delight, the computer again described the density variation and recommended more X rays from different angles as well as another CAT scan.

Throwing his head back, Philips whooped with excitement, pounding the counter top as if it were a kettledrum. A few of Lisa Marino's X rays slipped out from under the retaining clips and fell from the viewer screen. As Philips turned and bent down to pick them up, he spotted Helen Walker. She was standing by the door, watching him as if he were crazy.

"Are you all right, Dr. Philips?" asked Helen.

"Sure," said Martin, feeling his face redden as he retrieved the X rays. "I'm fine. Just a little excited. I thought you were going to lunch?"

"I've been," said Helen. "I brought a sandwich back to eat at my desk."

"How about getting William Michaels on the phone for me."

Helen nodded and disappeared. Philips put the X rays back up. Looking at the subtle white flecks, he pondered what it could mean. It didn't look like calcium, and it was not oriented in a pattern like blood vessels. He wondered how he could go about determining if the changes were in the gray matter or cellular area of the brain called the cortex, or if they were in the white matter or fiber layer of the brain.

The phone buzzed and Philips reached over and picked up the extension. It was Michaels. Philips' excitement was obvious as he described the program's incredibly successful performance. He said it seemed able to pick up a type of density variation that had been previously missed. He spoke so quickly that Michaels had to ask him to slow down.

"Well, I'm glad it's working as well as we expected," said Michaels, when Martin finally paused.

"As well as expected? It's more than I ever hoped."

"Fine," said Michaels. "How many old X rays have you run?"

"Really only one," admitted Martin. "I ran two, but they were both from the same patient."

"You've only run two X rays?" said Michaels, disappointed. "I hope you didn't wear yourself out."

"All right, all right. Unfortunately I don't have much time during the day to spend on our project."

Michaels said he understood, but implored Philips to run the program against all the skull films he'd read in the last few years, rather than being sidetracked by one positive finding. Michaels emphasized anew that at this juncture of their work, eliminating false negative readings was the most important task.

Martin continued to listen, but he couldn't stop studying the spidery density changes on Lisa Marino's X ray. He knew she was a seizure patient and his scientific mind quickly asked if there could be an association between the seizures and these subtle findings on the X ray. Perhaps they represented some diffuse neurological disease . . .

Philips terminated the conversation with Michaels with a new sense of excitement. He'd remembered that one of Lisa Marino's tentative diagnoses was multiple sclerosis. What if he'd stumbled on a radiological diagnosis for the disease? It would be a fantastic find. Doctors had been looking for laboratory diagnosis of multiple sclerosis for years. Martin knew he had to get more X rays and a new CAT scan on Lisa Marino. It wasn't going to be easy since she'd

just been operated on, and he'd have to get Mannerheim's approval. But Mannerheim was research-oriented and Philips decided to approach him directly.

He yelled through the door for Helen to get the
neurosurgeon on the phone and went back to Lisa
Marino's X ray. In radiological terms the density
changes were called reticular although the fine lines
seemed to be parallel rather than net-like. Using a
magnifying glass, Martin wondered if nerve fibers
could be responsible for the pattern he was seeing.
That idea didn't make sense because of the relatively
hard X rays that had to be used to penetrate the
skull. His train of thought was interrupted by the
buzzer. Mannerheim was on the phone.

Philips began the conversation with some usual
pleasantries, ignoring the recent episode about the X
rays in the OR. With Mannerheim it was always better to let such encounters slide. The surgeon seemed
peculiarly silent so Martin continued, explaining that
he was calling because he'd noticed some peculiar
densities on Lisa Marino's X rays.

"I think these densities should be explored and I'd
like to get more skull films and another CAT scan as
soon as the patient can tolerate it. That is, of course,
if you agree."

An uncomfortable pause followed. Philips was
about to speak when Mannerheim snarled, "Is this
some kind of a joke? If it is, it's in very bad taste."

"It's no joke," said Martin, bewildered.

"Listen," shouted Mannerheim. His voice was rising, "It's a bit late for Radiology to be reading X rays
now. Christ!"

There was a click and a dial tone. Mannerheim's
egocentric behavior seemed to have reached new
heights. Martin hung up the phone, thinking. He

knew he couldn't let his emotions intervene; besides, there was another approach. He was aware that Mannerheim didn't follow his post-op patients that carefully, and that it really was Newman, the Chief Resident, who was responsible for their day-to-day management. Martin decided to get in touch with Newman and see if the girl was still in the recovery room.

"Newman?" asked the OR desk. "He's been gone for some time."

"Oh!" said Philips. He switched the phone to the other ear. "Is Lisa Marino still in the recovery room?"

"No," said the OR desk. "Unfortunately she never made it."

"Never made it?" Philips suddenly comprehended Mannerheim's behavior.

"Died on the table," said the nurse. "Tragedy, especially since it was Mannerheim's first."

Philips turned back to his viewer. Instead of seeing Lisa Marino's X ray, he saw her face as it had been that morning in the patient-holding area outside of surgery. He remembered his image of a bird without its feathers. It was disturbing and Philips forced his attention back to the X ray. He wondered what could have been learned. Impulsively Martin slid off his stool. He wanted to go over Lisa Marino's chart; he wanted to see if he could associate the pattern on the X ray with any clinical signs and symptoms of multiple sclerosis in Lisa Marino's neurological workup. It wouldn't take the place of more X rays, but it was something.

Passing Helen, who was eating a sandwich at her desk, he told her to call down to the angiography room and tell the residents to start without him and that he'd be there shortly. Helen swallowed rapidly and asked what she should tell Mr. Michael Ferguson about the supply room when he called back. Philips didn't respond. He'd heard her but he pretended he hadn't. "Fuck Ferguson," he said to himself as he turned down the main corridor toward surgery. He'd learned to despise hospital administrators.

There were still a few patients waiting in the holding area when Philips arrived in surgery, but it was nowhere near so chaotic as the morning. Philips recognized Nancy Donovan, who had just come out from the OR suites. He walked over and she smiled.

"Had some trouble with the Marino case?" asked Philips sympathetically.

Nancy Donovan's smile vanished. "It was awful. Just awful. Such a young girl. I feel so sorry for Dr. Mannerheim."

Philips nodded, although he found it astounding that Nancy could sympathize with a bastard like Mannerheim.

"What happened?" he asked.

"A major artery blew right at the end of the case."

Philips shook his head in understanding and dismay. He remembered the proximity of the electrode and the posterior cerebral artery.

"Where would the chart be?" asked Philips.

"I don't know," admitted Nancy Donovan. "Let me ask at the desk."

Philips watched as Nancy spoke to the three nurses at the OR desk. When she came back she said, "They think it's still in Anesthesia, adjacent to room number twenty-one."

Returning to the surgical lounge, which was now crowded, Philips changed into a scrub suit. Then he walked back to the OR area. The main corridor leading down between the OR rooms showed signs of the morning battles. Around each scrub sink were pools of water whose surfaces opalesced with a film of soap. Scrub sponges and brushes littered the edges of the sinks with a few scattered on the floors. On a gurney pushed to the side of the corridor was a sleeping surgeon. He'd probably been up all night operating and when he'd come out of his case, thought he'd use the gurney for a moment's respite. Instead he'd fallen fast asleep and no one disturbed him.

Philips reached the anesthesia room next to OR #21 and tried the door. It was locked. Stepping back he looked through the small window of the OR room. It was dark, but when he pushed the door, it opened. He flipped a switch and one of the huge kettledrum operating lights came to life with a low electrical hum. It cast a concentrated beam of light straight down on the operating table, leaving the rest of the room in relative darkness. To Philips' shock, OR 21 had not been cleaned since the Marino disaster. The empty operating table with its mechanical undercarriage had a particularly evil appearance. On the floor around the head of the table were pools of thickened blood. Bloodstained footprints radiated out in various directions.

The scene made Martin feel sick, reminding him of unpleasant episodes in medical school. He shuddered and the feeling passed. Purposefully avoiding the gore, he rounded the table and went through the swinging door into the anesthesia room. With his foot, he kept the door ajar so he could see to turn on the light. But the room wasn't so dark as he'd expected. The door into the hall was open about six inches, allowing some light to enter from the corridor. Surprised, Philips turned on the overhead fluorescent lights.

In the center of the room, which was half the size of the OR, was a gurney supporting a shrouded body. The corpse was covered by a white sheet, save for the toes, which stuck out obscenely. Philips would have been all right had it not been for the toes. They advertised that the covered mound was indeed a human body. On top of the body, casually placed, was the hospital chart.

Breathing shallowly, as if the presence of death was contagious, Philips skirted the gurney and fully opened the door to the corridor. He could see the sleeping surgeon and several orderlies. He glanced in both directions, wondering if he had tried the wrong door earlier. Unable to figure out the discrepancy, he decided to ignore it, and returned to the chart.

He was about to open it when he was seized by a compulsion to lift the shroud. He knew he did not want to look at the body, yet his hand reached out and slowly pulled back the sheet. Before the head was uncovered, Philips closed his eyes. When he opened them he found himself looking at the lifeless, porcelain face of Lisa Marino. One eye was partially open revealing a glazed and fixed pupil. The other was closed. On the right side of her shaved head was a carefully sutured horseshoe-shaped incision. She had been cleaned up from the operation and no blood was visible. Philips wondered if Mannerheim had done that so he could say she died after and not during surgery.

The cold finality of death swept Martin's mind like an arctic wind. Quickly he covered the hairless head and carried the chart over to the anesthesiologist's stool. Like most patients at a university's hospital, Lisa Marino already had a thick chart even though she'd been in the hospital for only two days. There were long workups by various levels of residents and medical students. Philips flipped past wordy consults from Neurology and Ophthalmology. He even found a note by Mannerheim but the scribble was totally illegible. What Martin wanted was the final summary by the Chief Neurosurgical resident, Dr. Newman.

In summary the patient is a twenty-one-year-old Caucasian female with a one-year history of progressive temporal lobe epilepsy, who entered the hospital for a right temporal lobectomy under local anesthesia. The patient's seizure disorder has been totally unresponsive to maximum medical therapy. The seizures have become more frequent, usually heralded by an aura of obnoxious odor, and characterized by increasing aggressiveness and sexual acting out. Seizure loci have been mapped in both temporal lobes but significantly more on the right by EEG.

There has been no history of trauma or known brain insult. The patient has enjoyed good health until present illness although several atypical Pap smears were reported.

Other than the abnormal EEG findings, the entire neurological workup has been normal.

All laboratory work, including cerebral angiography and CAT scan have been normal.

Subjectively the patient has reported some visual perceptual problems, but these have not been confirmed by either neurology or ophthalmology. The patient has also repeated transient paresthesias and muscle weaknesses, but these have not been documented. A diagnosis of multiple sclerosis with seizures is entertained but not confirmed. The patient was presented at Neurology/Neurosurgery grand rounds, and it was the combined opinion that she was a good candidate for a right temporal lobectomy.

[Signed] George Newman

Philips replaced the chart gingerly on top of Lisa Marino as if she still had sensation. Then he fled back to the lounge to change into his street clothes. He had to admit that the chart hadn't been as rewarding as he'd hoped. It had mentioned multiple sclerosis as he'd remembered, but offered no information that could take the place of additional X rays or another CAT scan. As Philips finished dressing he kept picturing Lisa's pale death mask. It reminded him that she would probably be autopsied, having died during surgery. Using the wall phone, he called Dr. Jeffrey Reynolds in Pathology, a friend and former fellow student, and told him about the case.

"Haven't heard about it yet," said Reynolds.

"She died in the OR around noon," said Philips. "Although they took the time to sew her up."

"Not uncommon," said Reynolds. "Sometimes they rush them down to the recovery room to pronounce them dead just so it doesn't mess up their operative statistics."

"Will you be doing a post?" asked Philips.

"Can't say," said Reynolds. "It's up to the examiner."

"If you did a post," continued Philips, "when would it be?"

"We're really busy right now. Probably early this evening."

"I'm very interested in this case," said Philips. "Look, I'll hang around the hospital until the autopsy is done. Could you leave word that I'm to be paged when they do the brain?"

"Sure," said Reynolds. "We'll order in and have a real party. And if there is no autopsy, I'll let you know."

Cramming everything into his locker, Philips ran out of the lounge. Ever since he'd been an undergraduate, he suffered from unreasonable anxiety whenever he was behind in his work. As he ran back through the busy hospital, he felt that same old unwelcome feeling. He knew he was overdue in the angiography room and that the residents would be waiting; he knew he had to call Ferguson as much as he'd like to ignore the son-of-a-bitch; he knew he'd have to talk to Robbins about the techs who wanted to take off the whole freakin summer; and he knew Helen had a dozen other emergencies waiting for him at the office.

As he ran past the CAT scanner, Philips decided to make a quick detour. After all, what was two more minutes when he was already so late. Entering the computer room, Philips welcomed the breath of cool air conditioning required to keep the computers functioning. Denise and the four medical students were grouped around the TV-like screen, totally absorbed. Standing behind them was Dr. George Newman. Philips came up to the group, unnoticed, and looked at the screen. Sanger was describing a large left subdural hematoma, and pointing out to the students how the blood clot had pushed the brain over to the right. Newman interrupted and suggested the blood clot might be intracerebral. He said he thought the blood was inside the brain and not on its surface.

"No! Dr. Sanger is right," said Martin. Everyone turned, surprised to see Philips in the room. He bent over, and using his finger, described the classical radiological features of a subdural hematoma. There was no question that Denise was correct.

"Well, that settles it," said Newman good-naturedly. "I'd better take this fellow to surgery."

"The sooner the better," agreed Philips. He also suggested where Newman should make the hole through the skull to facilitate removal of the clot. He was about to ask the Chief Resident some questions about Lisa Marino, but thought better of it and let the surgeon leave.

Before Martin rushed off himself he took Denise aside. "Listen. To make up for standing you up at lunch, how about a romantic dinner?"

Sanger shook her head and smiled. "You're up to something. You know I'm on call here at the hospital tonight."

"I know," admitted Martin. "I was thinking of the hospital cafeteria."

"Wonderful," said Denise, sarcastically. "What about your racketball?"

"I'm canceling it," said Philips.

"Then you're really up to something."

Martin laughed. It was true that he only canceled racketball for national emergencies. Philips told Denise to meet him in his office to go over the day's X rays after she'd finished the CAT scan schedule. She could bring the medical students if they wanted to come. Back in the hall, they said quick goodbyes, then Philips left. He again broke into a run. He wanted to get up a good head of steam so that when he passed Helen he'd be an unstoppable blur.

7

Waiting in a long line to check in, Lynn Anne Lucas wondered if it had been a good idea to come to the emergency room. Earlier she had called student health, hoping to be seen on campus, but the doctor had left at three, and the only place she could get immediate care was the emergency room at the hospital. Lynn Anne had debated with herself about waiting until the following day. But all she had to do was pick up a book and try to read to convince herself to go at once. She was scared.

The emergency room was so busy in the late afternoon that the queue just to check in moved at a snail's pace. It seemed as if all of New York were there. The man behind Lynn Anne was drunk, dressed in rags, and reeking of old urine and wine. Each time the line would move forward, he would stumble into Lynn Anne, grabbing at her to keep from falling. In front of Lynn Anne was a huge woman, carrying a child completely swathed in a dirty blanket. The woman and child were silent, waiting their turn.

Large doors sprang open to Lynn Anne's left, and the check-in line had to give way to a swarm of gurneys carrying the results of an auto accident that had occurred just minutes earlier. The injured and dead were whisked past the waiting area and taken directly into the emergency room proper. Those waiting to be seen knew it was going to take that much longer to be called. In one corner a Puerto Rican family was sitting around a Kentucky Fried Chicken bucket having dinner. They seemed unconcerned with what was happening in the emergency room and hadn't even noticed the arrival of the auto-accident victims.

Finally only the huge woman with the baby was ahead of Lynn Anne. Hearing the woman speak it was apparent she was foreign. She told the clerk that "the baby she no cry no more." The clerk told her that usually the complaint was the opposite, which the woman didn't understand. The clerk asked to see the baby. The woman pulled back the edges of the blanket, revealing a baby the color of the sky before a summer storm, a dark blue-gray. The baby had been dead so long it was stiff like a board.

Lynn Anne was so shocked that when it was her turn she couldn't speak. The clerk sympathized with her and told her that they have to be prepared to see anything and everything. Pushing her auburn hair from her forehead, Lynn Anne found her voice and gave her name, student I.D. number, and her complaint. The clerk told her to have a seat and that it would be a wait. He assured her they'd see her as soon as possible.

After waiting nearly two more hours, Lynn Anne Lucas was led down a busy hall and placed in a cubicle separated from a larger room by stained nylon curtains. An efficient LPN took an oral temperature and her blood pressure, then left. Lynn Anne sat on the edge of an old examining table and listened to the multitude of sounds around her. Her hands were wet from anxiety. She was twenty, and a Junior, and had been entertaining the idea of going to medical school by taking the required courses. But now when she looked around, she wondered. It was not what she'd expected.

She was a healthy young woman, and her only other experience with hospital emergency rooms had been a roller-skating mishap at age eleven. Strangely enough she'd been brought to the very same emergency room, since she and her family had lived nearby before moving to Florida. But Lynn Anne had not had a bad memory of the event. She guessed that the Med Center had changed as much as its neighborhood since she'd been there as a child.

The intern who appeared a half-hour later was youthful Dr. Huggens. Being from West Palm Beach he seemed to enjoy the fact that Lynn Anne was from Coral Gables, and he made small talk about Florida while he looked at her chart. It was also obvious that he was pleased Lynn Anne was a pretty all-American girl, something he hadn't seen in his last one thousand patients. Later he even asked for her phone number.

"What brings you to the ER?" he said, beginning his workup.

"It's hard to describe," said Lynn Anne. "I get episodes of not seeing right. It started about a week ago while I was reading. All at once I began to have trouble with certain words. I could see them but I couldn't be sure of their meaning. At the same time I would get a terrible headache. Here." Lynn Anne put her hand on the back of her head and ran it around the side of her head to a point above her ear. "It's a dull pain that comes and goes."

Dr. Huggens nodded.

"And I can smell something," said Lynn Anne.

"What was that?"

Lynn Anne acted a little embarrassed. "I don't know," she said. "It is a bad smell, and although I don't know what it is, it seems familiar."

Dr. Huggens nodded, but it was apparent that Lynn Anne's symptoms were not falling into any simple category. "Anything else?"

"Some dizziness, and my legs feel heavy, and it's happening more often now, almost every time I try to read."

Dr. Huggens put down the chart and examined Lynn Anne. He looked into her eyes and ears; he looked into her mouth and listened to her heart and lungs. He tested her reflexes, had her touch things, walk in a straight line, and remember sequences of numbers.

"You seem pretty normal to me," said Dr. Huggens. "I think maybe you should take two doctors and come back and see us in the aspirin." He laughed at his own joke. Lynn Anne didn't laugh. She had decided she wasn't going to be brushed off that easily, especially after waiting so long. Dr. Huggens noticed she wasn't responding to his humor. "Seriously. I think you should take some aspirin for symptomatic relief and come back to Neurology tomorrow. Maybe they'll be able to find something."

"I want to see Neurology now," said Lynn Anne.

"This is an emergency room, not a clinic," said Dr. Huggens firmly.

"I don't care," said Lynn Anne. She shielded her emotions with defiance.

"Okay, okay!" said Dr. Huggens. "I'll get Neurology. In fact I'll get Ophthalmology too, but it might be a wait."

Lynn Anne nodded. She was afraid to talk for the moment lest her defense dissolve to tears.

And a wait it was. It was after six when the curtain was pulled aside again. Lynn Anne looked up into the bearded face of Dr. Wayne Thomas. Dr. Thomas, a black from Baltimore, surprised Lynn Anne, who had never been treated by a black doctor. But she quickly forgot her initial reaction and responded to his exacting questions.

Dr. Thomas was able to uncover several more facts he felt were significant. About three days previously Lynn Anne had had one of her "episodes" as she called them, and had immediately jumped up from her bed where she had been reading. The next thing she remembered was that she "came to" on the floor, having fainted. Apparently she had hit her head, because she had suffered a large lump on the right side of her scalp. Dr. Thomas also learned that Lynn Anne had had two atypical Pap smear tests and was currently scheduled to return to GYN clinic in a week. She also had had a recent urinary-tract infection successfully treated with sulfur.

After finishing the history, Dr. Thomas called in an LPN and did the most complete physical examination Lynn Anne had ever had. He did everything Dr. Huggens did and more. Most of the tests were a total mystery to Lynn Anne, but his thoroughness encouraged her. The only test she disliked was the lumbar puncture. Curled up on her side with her knees to her

chin, she felt a needle pierce the skin of her lower
back, but it only hurt for a moment.

When he finished, Dr. Thomas told Lynn Anne that
he wanted to take some X rays to make sure she had
not fractured her skull when she had fallen. Just before he left her he told her that all he found during
the examination was that certain areas of her body
seemed to have lost sensation. He admitted that he
didn't know if it was significant or not.

Lynn Anne waited again.

"Can you believe it?" asked Philips while he shoved
more turkey tetrazzini into his mouth. He chewed
quickly and swallowed. "Mannerheim's first OR death
and it has to be a patient I wanted more film on."

"She was only twenty-one, wasn't she?" said Denise.

"That's right." Martin put more salt and pepper on
his food to give it some taste. "Tragedy, actually a
double tragedy since I can't get those films."

They had taken their hospital cafeteria trays to the
farthest corner from the steam table, trying to isolate
themselves as much as possible from the institutional
environment. It was difficult. The walls were painted
a dirty mustard; the floor was covered with gray linoleum; and the molded plastic chairs were an awful
yellow-green. In the background the hospital paging
system maintained a steady monotone of doctors'
names and the extension number they were to call.

"Why was she having the surgery?" asked Denise,
picking at her chef's salad.

"Seizure disorder. But the interesting thing was that
she might have had multiple sclerosis. After you left
this afternoon, it occurred to me that the density
changes we saw on her X ray might represent some

sort of widespread neurological disease. I checked her chart. Multiple sclerosis was being considered."

"Have you pulled any films of patients with known multiple sclerosis?" asked Denise.

"That starts tonight," said Philips. "In order to check Michaels' program I've got to run as many skull films as possible. It will be very interesting if I can find any other cases with the same radiologic picture."

"It sounds as if your research project has really taken off."

"I hope so." Martin took one bite of his asparagus and decided against taking any more. "I'm trying not to let myself get too excited this early, but, my God, it looks good. That's why I got so excited about this Marino case. It promised something immediately tangible. Actually there's still a chance. She's being autopsied tonight, so I'll try to correlate the radiological picture with the Path findings. If it is multiple sclerosis, we're back in the ball game. But I tell you, I've got to find something to get me away from this clinical rat race, even if it's only a couple of days a week."

Denise put down her fork and looked into Martin's restless blue eyes. "Get away from clinical? You can't do that. You're one of the best neuroradiologists there is. Think of all the patients that benefit from your skills. If you leave clinical radiology, that will be a real tragedy."

Martin put down his fork, and grasped her left hand. For the first time he didn't care who in the hospital might be watching. "Denise," he said softly. "At the present time in my life there are only two things I really care about: you and my research. And if there were some way I could make a living out of being with you, I might even forget the research."

Denise looked at Martin uncertain whether to be

flattered or wary. She'd become more and more confident of his affection but she had no idea that he had even the potential for commitment. From the beginning she'd been awed by his reputation and seemingly encyclopedic knowledge of radiology. He had been both a lover and professional idol and she hadn't allowed herself the thought that maybe their relationship had a future. She wasn't sure she was ready for it.

"Listen," Martin continued. "This is neither the time nor the place for this kind of conversation." He pushed his asparagus out of the way as if to make a point. "But it's important that you know where I'm coming from. You're at an early stage in your clinical training, which is very fulfilling. You spend all your time learning and dealing with patients. Unfortunately I spend the smallest part of my time doing that. The major part is spent trying to handle administrative headaches and bureaucratic bullshit. I've had it up to here."

Denise raised her left hand, which was still firmly grasped in his, and lightly brushed his knuckles with her lips. She did it quickly, then looked at him from under her dark eyebrows. She was being purposefully coquettish, knowing that it would defuse his sudden anger. It worked as it usually did and Martin laughed. He squeezed her hand before letting go, then glanced around to see if anyone had seen.

His beeper shocked them both as it went off. He got up immediately and strode over to the hospital phones. Denise watched him. She had been attracted to him since they met, but she found herself increasingly drawn by his humor and surprising sensitivity, and now his new admission of dissatisfaction and vulnerability seemed to heighten her feelings.

But was it true vulnerability? Was Philips' excuse about administrative burdens only a rationalization to explain a dissatisfaction with having to grow older, and having to admit that, professionally speaking, his life had become predictable? Denise didn't know. As long as she had known Martin, he'd always approached his work with such compulsion that she'd never considered the possibility of dissatisfaction, but she was moved that he would share his feelings with her. It must mean he believed their relationship was more important than she thought he had.

Watching Martin at the phone, she admitted one other point about their affair. He had given her the strength to finally end another relationship, which had been totally destructive. While Denise was still a medical student she had met and had been dazzled by a neurology resident who had skillfully manipulated her feelings. Because of the impersonal isolation of school, Denise was susceptible to the idea of commitment. There had never been any doubt in her mind that she would be able to mix a home and a career with someone who was intimately aware of the demands of medicine. Richard Druker, her lover, was astute enough to recognize her feelings and to convince her that he felt the same way. But he didn't. He led her on for years, avoiding any real commitment, but cleverly fostering her dependency. The result was that she could not break away from him, even after she recognized what he was and suffered the humiliation of several of his affairs. She kept returning like an old dog for more abuse, vainly hoping that he'd mend his ways and become the person he said he was. Hope became desperation as she began to question her own femininity rather than his immaturity.

She had not been able to let go until she met Martin Philips.

Now as Martin walked back to their table, Denise felt a rush of affection, and gratitude. At the same time she recognized he was a man, and she was afraid of assuming a commitment he did not feel.

"This is not my day," said Martin, sitting down across from her. "That was Dr. Reynolds. Marino is not being autopsied."

"I thought she'd have to be," said Denise, surprised and trying to switch her mind back to medicine.

"True. It was a medical examiner's case, but in deference to Mannerheim, the examiner released the body to our Path department. The Path department approached the family for permission, and the family refused. Apparently they were pretty hysterical."

"That's understandable," said Sanger.

"I suppose," said Philips, dejectedly. "Damn. . . . Damn!"

"Why not pull some X rays of patients with known multiple sclerosis and see if you can find similar changes."

"Yeah," said Philips with a sigh.

"You could think a little about the patient rather than your own disappointment."

Martin stared at Denise for several minutes, making her feel that she had overstepped an unspoken boundary. She hadn't meant to be moralizing. Then his face changed and he smiled broadly.

"You're right!" he said. "In fact you just gave me a fabulous idea."

Directly across from the emergency room desk was a gray door with a sign that read EMERGENCY ROOM STAFF. It was the lounge for the interns and residents, although it was rarely used for relaxation. In the back was a lavatory with showers for the men; the women doctors had to go upstairs to the Nurses' lounge. Along the side there were three small rooms with two cots each, but they weren't used much except for short naps. There was never time.

Dr. Wayne Thomas had taken the one comfortable chair in the lounge: an old leather monster with some of its stuffing extruding through an open seam like a dehisced wound.

"I think Lynn Anne Lucas is sick," he was saying with conviction.

Around him, either leaning against the desk or seated in one of the wooden chairs, were Dr. Huggens, Dr. Carolo Langone, Resident in Internal Medicine; Dr. Ralph Lowry, Resident in Neurosurgery; Dr. David Harper, Resident in Gynecology; and Dr. Sean Farnsworth, Resident in Ophthalmology. Separated from the group were two other doctors reading EKG's at a counter.

"I think you must be horny," said Dr. Lowry with a cynical smile. "She's the best-looking chick we've seen all day and you're trying to find some excuse to admit her on your service."

Everyone laughed but Dr. Thomas. He didn't move except for his eyes, which turned to Dr. Langone.

"Ralph has a point," admitted Langone. "She's afebrile, normal vital signs, normal blood work, normal urine, and normal cerebral spinal fluid."

"And normal skull X ray," added Dr. Lowry.

"Well," said Dr. Harper, getting up from his chair. "Whatever it is, it ain't GYN. She's had a couple of abnormal Pap smears, but that's being followed in the clinic. So I'm going to leave you to solve this problem without me. To tell you the truth, I think she's being hysterical."

"I agree," said Dr. Farnsworth. "She claims to have trouble seeing but her ophthalmology exam is normal and with this near vision card she can read the small row of numbers with ease."

"What about her visual fields?" asked Dr. Thomas.

Farnsworth got to his feet, preparing to leave. "Seem normal to me. Tomorrow we can have a Goldmann field done, but we don't do them on an emergency basis."

"And her retinas?" asked Dr. Thomas.

"Normal," said Farnsworth. "Thanks for the consult. It's been swell." Picking up his suitcase of instruments, the ophthalmologist left the room.

"Swell! Shit," said Dr. Lowry. "If I have one more Goddamn prissy eyeball resident tell me they don't do Goldmann fields at night, I think I'll punch him out."

"Shut up, Ralph," said Dr. Thomas. "You're starting to sound like a surgeon."

Dr. Langone stood up and stretched. "I got to be going too. Tell me Thomas, why do you think this girl is sick: just because of her decreased sensation? I mean, that's pretty subjective."

"It's a feeling I have. She's scared, but I'm sure she's not hysterical. Besides, her sensory abnormalities are very reproducible. She's not faking. There's something screwy going on in her brain."

Dr. Lowry laughed. "The only thing screwy about this case is what you'd like to be doing if you met her under more social circumstances. Come on, Thomas. If she were a dog, you woulda' just told her to come back to clinic in the A.M."

The whole lounge laughed. Dr. Thomas waved

them away as he pulled himself from the easy chair. "I give up with you clowns. I'll handle this case myself."

"Be sure to get her phone number," said Dr. Lowry as Thomas left. Dr. Huggens laughed, he'd already thought it wasn't a bad idea.

Back in the ER Thomas looked around. From seven to nine there was a relative respite, as if people took time out from misery, pain, and illness while they ate. By ten, the drunks, the auto accidents, and the victims of thieves and psychos would begin to arrive; by eleven it would be the crimes of passion. So Thomas had a little time to think about Lynn Anne Lucas. Something was nagging him about the case; he felt as if he were missing some important clue.

Stopping at the main desk, he asked one of the ER clerks if Lynn Anne Lucas's hospital chart had arrived from the record room. The clerk checked, said no, but then reassured him that he'd call again. Dr. Thomas nodded absently, wondering if Lynn Anne had taken any exotic drugs. Turning down the main corridor, he headed back to the examination room, where the girl was waiting.

Denise had no inkling what Martin's "fabulous idea" was. He had asked her to come back to his office around 9 P.M. It was about a quarter past when she had a break from reading trauma films in the emergency room. Using the stairs across from the closed hospitality shop, she reached the Radiology floor. The corridor seemed a different place from the commotion and chaos of the day. At the very end of the hall one of the janitors was using a power polisher on the vinyl floor.

The door to Philips' office was open, and Denise could hear his dictating monotone. When she entered, she found him finishing up the day's cerebral angiograms. In front of him on his alternator was a series of angiographic studies. Within each X ray of the skull the thousands of blood vessels showed up as white threads which appeared like an upside-down root system to a tree. While he spoke he pointed with his finger at the pathology for Denise's benefit. She looked and nodded, although it was incomprehensible how he knew the names and the normal size and position of each vessel.

"Conclusion:" said Philips, "Cerebral angiography shows a large arteriovenous malformation at the right basal ganglia in this nineteen-year-old male. Period. This circulatory malformation is supplied by the right middle cerebral artery via the lenticulostriate branches as well as from the right posterior cerebral artery via the thalamoperforate and the thalamogeniculate branches. Period." End of dictation. Please send a copy of this report to doctors Mannerheim, Prince, and Clauson. Thank you."

With a click, the recorder stopped, and Martin swung around in his chair. He was wearing a mischievous smile and he rubbed his hands together like a Shakespearean rogue.

"Perfect timing," he said.

"What's gotten into you?" she asked, pretending to be scared.

"Come," said Philips, leading her outside. Against the wall was a loaded gurney complete with IV bottles, linen, and a pillow. Smiling at her surprise, Martin began pushing the gurney down the hall. Denise caught up to him at the patient elevator.

"*I* gave you this fabulous idea?" she asked, helping guide the gurney into the car.

"That's right," said Philips. He hit the button for the subbasement and the doors closed.

They emerged in the bowels of the hospital. A tangle of pipes, like blood vessels, ran off in both directions, twisting and turning on one another as if in agony. Everything was painted gray or black, eliminating all sense of color. The light, which was sparse, came from wire-mesh encased fluorescent bulbs placed at distant intervals, causing contrasting patches of white glare to be separated by long stretches of heavy shadow. Across from the elevator was a sign: MORGUE: FOLLOW RED LINE.

Like a trail of blood, the line ran along the middle of the corridor. It traced a complicated route through the dark passages, winding sharply when the corridor branched. Ultimately it ran down a sloping incline, which nearly pulled the gurney from Martin's hands.

"What in God's name are we doing down here?" asked Denise, her voice echoing with their footsteps in the lifeless spaces.

"You'll see," said Philips. His smile had waned and his voice sounded tense. His original playfulness had given way to a nervous concern about the prudence of what he was doing.

The corridor abruptly opened up into a huge underground cavern. The lighting here was equally as meager as in the corridor, and the two-story-high ceiling was lost in shadow. On the left wall was the closed door to the incinerator, and the hiss of hungry flames could be heard.

Ahead were the double swinging doors leading into the morgue. In front of them the red line on the floor ended with abrupt finality. Philips left the gurney and advanced toward the entrance. Pushing open the door on the right he looked inside. "We're in luck," he said, returning to the gurney. "We have the place to ourselves."

Denise followed reluctantly.

The morgue was a large neglected room, which had been allowed to decay to the point that it resembled one of those unearthed porticoes of Pompeii. A multitude of hooded lights hung on bare wires from the ceiling, but only a few had bulbs. The floor was constructed of stained terrazzo, while walls were surfaced with cracked and chipped ceramic tile. In the center of the room was a partially sunken pit containing an old marble autopsy slab. It had not been used since the twenties, and standing amid the debris, it appeared like an ancient pagan altar. Autopsies were currently done in the department of Pathology on the fifth floor, in a modern stainless steel setting.

Numerous doors lined the walls of the room, including a massive wooden one that resembled a meat refrigerator in a butcher shop. On the far wall was an inclined corridor that led up in utter darkness to a door opening on a back alley of the hospital complex. It was deathly quiet. The only noise was an occasional drip from a sink and the hollow sounds of their own footsteps.

Martin parked the gurney and hung up the IV bottle.

"Here," he said, handing Denise a corner of one of the fresh sheets and directing her to tuck it around the pad on the gurney.

He went over to the large wooden door, pulled the pin from the latch, and with great effort opened it up.

An icy mist flowed out, layering itself on the terrazzo floor.

After finding the light switch Martin turned and noticed Denise had not budged.

"Come on! And bring the gurney."

"I'm not moving until you tell me what's going on," she said.

"We're pretending it's the fifteenth century."

"What do you mean?"

"We're going to snatch a body for science."

"Lisa Marino?" asked Denise incredulously.

"Exactly."

"Well I'm not going to have any part of this." She backed up as if about to flee.

"Denise, don't be silly. All I'm going to do is get the CAT scan and X rays I wanted. Then the body is coming right back. You don't think I'm going to keep it, do you?"

"I don't know what to think."

"What an imagination," said Philips as he grabbed the end of the gurney and pulled it into the antique walk-in refrigerator. The IV bottle clanked against its metal pole. Denise followed, her eyes rapidly exploring the interior which was completely tiled; walls, ceiling and floor. The tiles had once been white; now they were an indeterminate gray. The room was thirty feet long and twenty feet wide. Parked in rows on each side were old wooden carts with wheels the size of those on a bicycle. Down the center of the room was an open lane. Each cart supported a shrouded corpse.

Philips slowly moved down the center aisle, glancing from side to side. At the back of the room he turned around and began lifting the corner of each sheet. Denise shivered in the damp cold. She tried not to look at the bodies closest to her, which had been the gory result of one of the rush-hour traffic accidents. A foot, still wearing its shoe, stuck out at a crazy angle, advertising that the leg had been broken in mid-calf. Somewhere out of sight an old compressor chugged to life.

"Ah, here she is," said Philips, peering under one of the sheets. Thankfully, for Denise, he left the shroud in place and motioned for her to bring the gurney down. She did it like an automaton.

"Help me lift her," said Philips.

Denise grabbed Lisa Marino's ankles through the sheet to avoid touching the corpse. Philips hefted the torso. On the count of three, they moved the body, noticing that it had already become stiff. Then with Denise pulling, and Martin pushing, they guided the gurney back out of the refrigerator. Philips closed and secured the door.

"What's the IV for?" asked Sanger.

"I don't want people to think we're pushing around a corpse," said Philips. "And for that effect, the IV is the maestro's touch." He pulled the sheet down, exposing Lisa Marino's bloodless face. Denise looked away as Martin raised the head and shoved the pillow under it. Then he ran the blank IV line beneath the sheet. Stepping back, he checked the effect. "Perfect." Then he patted the corpse's arm, saying, "Are you comfortable now?"

"Martin, for God's sake, do you have to be so gruesome?"

"Well, to tell you the truth, it's a defense. I'm not sure we should be doing this."

"Now he tells me," moaned Denise as she helped guide the gurney through the double door.

They retraced their steps through the subterranean labyrinth and entered the patient's elevator. To their dismay, it stopped on the first floor. Two orderlies were standing with a patient in a wheelchair. Martin and Denise stared at each other for a moment, in fear. Then Denise looked away, castigating herself for becoming involved in this ridiculous caper.

The orderlies wheeled the patient onto the elevator so that he was facing the rear, which they weren't supposed to do. They were involved in a conversation about the upcoming baseball season, and if they had noticed Lisa Marino's appearance, they didn't mention it. But the patient was different. He looked over and saw the huge sutured horseshoe incision on the side of Lisa Marino's head.

"She have an operation?" he asked.

"Yeah," said Philips.

"She going to be alright?"

"She's a little tired," said Philips. "She needs some rest."

The patient nodded as if he understood. Then the doors opened on the second floor, and Philips and Sanger got off. One of the orderlies even helped pull the gurney out.

"This is ridiculous," said Sanger as they made their way up the empty hallway. "I feel like a criminal."

They entered the CAT scan room. The redheaded technician saw them through the leaded window from the control room, and came in to help. Philips told him it was an emergency scan. After the technician adjusted the table, he positioned himself behind Lisa Marino's head and put his hands under her shoulders, preparing to lift. Feeling the ice-cold, lifeless flesh, he jumped back.

"She's dead!" he said, shocked.

Denise covered her eyes.

"Let's say she's had a hard day," said Philips. "And you're not to talk about this little exercise."

"You still want a CAT scan?" asked the technician incredulously.

"Absolutely," said Philips.

Pulling himself together, the technician helped Martin lift Lisa onto the table. Since there was no need for immobilization restraints, he immediately activated the table and Lisa's head slid into the machine. After checking the position, he directed Philips and Sanger into the control room.

"She might be pale," said the technician, "but she looks better than some of the patients we get from neurosurgery." He pushed the button to start the scanning process and the huge doughnut-shaped machine abruptly came to life and began its rotation around Lisa's head.

Grouping themselves in front of the viewing screen, they waited. A horizontal line appeared at the top of the screen, then moved down the face, seemingly unveiling the first image. The bony skull was apparent but no definition could be determined within. Inside the skull it was dark and homogeneous.

"What the hell?" said Martin.

The technician walked over to the control console and checked his settings. He came back, shaking his head. They waited for the next image. Again the skull outline was seen but the interior was uniform.

"Has the machine been working okay tonight?" asked Philips.

"Perfect," answered the technician.

Philips reached out and adjusted the viewing controls, called the window level and window width. "My God," he said after a minute. "You know what we're looking at? Air! There's no brain. It's gone!"

They stared at one another with a shared sense of surprise and disbelief. Abruptly Martin turned and ran back into the scanner room. Denise and the technician followed. Martin grasped Lisa's head with both hands and lifted. Owing to stiffness, the corpse's whole torso came up from the table. The technician lent a hand, enabling Philips to see the back of Lisa's head. He had to look closely at the livid skin, but he found it: a fine U-shaped incision extending around the base of her skull, which had been closed with a subcuticular stitch so that no sutures could be seen.

"I think we'd better get this body back to the morgue," said Martin uneasily.

The trip back was fast with very little talk. Denise did not want to go but she knew Martin would need help lifting Lisa from the gurney. When they reached the incinerator, he again checked to make sure the morgue was empty. Holding the doors open, he waved Denise in, helping push the gurney over to the refrigerator. Quickly he opened the massive wooden door. Denise watched his breath coming in short puffs in the cold air as he backed down the aisle, pulling on the stretcher. They aligned it with the old wooden cart and were about to lift the body when a shocking sound reverberated in the frigid air.

Denise and Martin felt their hearts jump, and it took them several seconds before they realized the noise was Denise's beeper. She switched it off hurriedly, embarrassed as if the intrusion were her fault, grabbed Lisa's ankles, and on the count of three helped lift her onto the cart.

"There's a wall phone out in the morgue," said Martin lifting the shroud. "Answer your page while I make sure the body looks the way we found it."

Needing no more encouragement, Denise hurried out. She was totally unprepared for what happened. As she turned toward the phone, she ran directly into a man who had been approaching the open refrigerator door. An involuntary whimper escaped from her, and she had to put her hands up to absorb the impact.

"What are you doing here?" snapped the man. His name was Werner and he was the hospital diener. He reached out and grabbed one of Sanger's upright wrists.

Hearing the commotion, Martin appeared at the refrigerator's threshold. "I'm Dr. Martin Philips and this is Dr. Denise Sanger." He wanted his voice to sound strong, instead it sounded hollow and dull.

Werner let go of Denise's wrist. He was a gaunt man with high cheekbones, and a cavernous face. The dim light made it impossible to see his deeply set eyes. The eye sockets were blank, like burnt holes in a mask. His nose was narrow and sharp, like a hatchet. He was dressed in a black turtleneck, fronted by a black rubber apron.

"What are you doing with my bodies?" asked Werner, pushing past the doctors and the gurney. Inside the refrigerator he counted the corpses. Pointing to Marino, he said, "Did you take this one out of here?"

Having recovered from his initial shock, Philips marveled at the diener's proprietary feeling toward the dead. "I'm not sure it's correct to say 'your bodies,' Mr. . . ."

"Werner," said the diener, walking back to Martin and poking a large index finger in Philips' face. "Until somebody signs for these corpses, they're my bodies. I'm responsible."

Philips thought it better not to argue. Werner's mouth with its narrow lips was set in a firm, uncompromising line. The man seemed like a coiled spring. Philips started to speak but his voice came out in an embarrassing squeak. Clearing his throat, he started again: "We want to talk to you about one of these bodies. We believe it's been violated."

Sanger's beeper went off for the second time. Excusing herself she hurried over to the wall phone and answered her page.

"Which body are you talking about?" snapped Werner. His gaze never left Martin's face.

"Lisa Marino," said Philips, pointing to the partially covered corpse. "What do you know about this woman?"

"Not much," said Werner, turning toward Lisa and relaxing to a degree. "Picked her up from surgery. I think she's going out later tonight or early in the morning."

"What about the body itself?" Martin noticed the diener wore his hair in a crew cut, brushed straight up along the sides.

"Nice," said Werner, still looking at Lisa.

"What do you mean, nice?" asked Philips.

"Best looking woman I've had for some time," said Werner. As he turned to face Martin, his mouth pulled back in an obscene smile.

Momentarily disarmed, Martin swallowed. His mouth was dry and he was glad when Denise returned saying, "I've got to go. I've been paged from the ER to check a skull film."

"All right," said Martin, trying to arrange his thoughts. "Meet me in my office when you're free."

Denise nodded, and with a sense of relief, she left.

Martin, distinctly ill-at-ease alone with Werner in the morgue, forced himself to walk over to Lisa Marino. Pulling back the sheet he rotated Lisa's corpse by pulling up her shoulder. Pointing to the carefully sutured incision, Philips said, "What do you know about this?"

"I don't know anything about that," said Werner quickly.

Philips wasn't even sure the diener had seen what Martin was pointing to. Letting Lisa's body roll back on the cart, Philips studied the man. His rigid countenance reminded Martin of a Nazi cliché.

"Tell me," said Philips. "Have any of Mannerheim's boys been down here today?"

"I don't know," said Werner. "I was told there was to be no autopsy."

"Well, that's no autopsy incision," said Philips. Grabbing the edge of the sheet, Philips pulled it over Lisa Marino. "Something strange is going on. Are you sure you don't know anything about this?"

Werner shook his head.

"We'll see," said Philips. He walked out of the refrigerator, leaving the gurney for Werner to deal with. The diener waited until he heard the outer doors close. Then he grabbed the cart and gave it a powerful shove. It shot out of the refrigerator, sped halfway across the morgue, and crashed into the corner of the marble autopsy table, tipping over with a tremendous clatter. The IV bottle smashed into a million shards.

Dr. Wayne Thomas leaned against the wall, his arms folded across his chest. Lynn Anne Lucas was sitting on the old examining table. Their eyes were on the same level; his, alert and contemplative; hers, drained and exhausted.

"What about this recent urinary infection?" said Dr. Thomas. "It cleared up on the sulfa drugs. Is there anything else about that illness that you haven't mentioned?"

"No," said Lynn Anne, slowly, "except they did send me to a urologist. He told me that I had a problem of too much urine being in my bladder after I'd gone to the bathroom. He told me to see a neurologist."

"Did you?"

"No. The problem cleared up on its own, so I didn't think it mattered."

The curtain parted and Dr. Sanger poked her head in.

"Excuse me. Someone called for a consult on a skull film."

Thomas pushed off from the wall, saying he'd just be a minute. As they walked back to the lounge he gave Denise a thumbnail sketch of Lynn Anne's case. He told her that he thought the X ray was normal but wanted confirmation about the pituitary area.

"What's the diagnosis?" asked Denise.

"That's the problem," said Thomas opening the door to the lounge. "The poor thing has been here for five hours, but I can't put it all together. I thought maybe she was a druggie but she's not. She doesn't even smoke grass."

Thomas snapped the film up on the viewer. Denise scanned it in an orderly fashion, starting with the bones.

"I've been getting some crap from the rest of the

ER staff," Thomas said. "They think I'm interested in the case because the patient is a piece of ass."

Denise broke off from studying the X ray to eye Thomas sharply.

"But that's not it," said Thomas. "There's something wrong with this girl's brain. And whatever it is, it's widespread."

Sanger redirected her attention to the film. The bony structure was normal, including the pituitary area. She looked at the vague shadows within the skull. For orientation purposes she checked to see if the pineal gland was calcified. It wasn't. She was about to declare the film normal when she perceived a very slight variation in texture. Forming a small open area with her two hands, she studied the particular section of the film. It was a trick similar to the one she saw Philips do with the hole in the paper. Taking her hands away she was convinced! She'd found another example of the density change Martin had shown to her earlier on Lisa Marino's film.

"I want someone else to see this film," said Denise, pulling it from the viewer.

"You find something?" asked Thomas, encouraged.

"I think so. Keep the patient here until I get back." Denise was gone before Thomas could reply.

Two minutes later she was in Martin's office.

"Are you sure?" he asked.

"I'm pretty sure." She handed the film to him.

Martin took the X ray but didn't put it up immediately. He fingered it, afraid he would be faced with another disappointment.

"Come on," said Denise. She was eager to have her suspicions confirmed.

The X ray slid under the clips. The light in the

viewer blinked, then came on. Philips' trained eye traced an erratic path over the appropriate area. "I think you're right," he said. Using the piece of paper with the hole in it, he examined the X ray more closely. There was no doubt that the same abnormal density pattern he'd seen on Lisa Marino's X ray existed on this film. The difference was that on the new one it was less pronounced and not so extensive.

Trying to control his excitement, Martin switched on Michaels' computer. He keyed in the name. Turning to Denise, he asked what the patient's present complaint was. Denise told him it was difficulty in reading associated with blackout spells. Philips entered the information, then stepped over to the laser reader. When the little red light came on, he pushed in the edge of the film. The output typewriter snapped into action. Thank you, it said. Take a Nap!

While they waited, Denise told Martin what else she'd learned about Lynn Anne Lucas, but he was most excited about the fact that the patient was alive and in the emergency room.

As soon as the typewriter ceased its rapid staccato, Philips tore off the report. He read it with Denise looking over his shoulder.

"Amazing!" said Philips when he'd finished. "The computor certainly agrees with your impression. And it remembered that it had seen the same density pattern on Lisa Marino's X ray, and on top of that it asks me to tell it what this density variation is! This thing is God-damn amazing. It wants to learn! It's so human it scares me. The next thing I know is that it will want to get married to the CAT scan computer and take the whole summer off."

"Married?" said Sanger, laughing.

Martin waved her off. "Administrative worries. Don't get me started! Let's get this Lynn Anne Lucas up here and do the CAT scan and X rays I couldn't do on Lisa Marino."

"You realize it is a bit late. The CAT scan technician closes the unit down at ten and leaves. We'd have to call him in. Are you sure you want to do all this tonight?"

Philips looked at his watch. It was ten-thirty. "You're right. But I don't want to lose this patient. I'm going to see that she's admitted at least for the night."

Denise accompanied Martin back down to the ER, leading him directly into one of the large treatment rooms. She motioned for him toward the right corner, and pulled back a curtain separating a small examining area. Lynn Anne Lucas looked up with bloodshot eyes. She'd been sitting next to the table, leaning on it, with her head on her arm.

Before Denise could introduce Philips, her beeper went off and she left Martin to talk with Lynn Anne by himself. It was immediately apparent to him that the woman was exhausted. He smiled at her warmly, then asked if she would mind staying overnight so that they could get some special X rays in the morning. Lynn Anne told him she didn't care, so long as she was taken out of the emergency room and could go to sleep. Philips gave her arm a gentle squeeze. He told her he'd arrange it.

At the main desk, Philips had to act like he was in a bargain basement, pushing, yelling and even hitting the countertop with an open palm to get the attention of one of the harried clerks. He asked about Lynn Anne Lucas, wanting to know who was in charge of the patient. The clerk checked the main roster and told him it was Dr. Wayne Thomas, who was currently down in room 7 with a stroke.

When Philips walked in he found himself in the middle of a cardiac arrest. The patient was an obese man who draped over the examining table like a huge pancake. A bearded black fellow, who Philips soon learned was Dr. Thomas, was standing on a chair giving the patient cardiac massage. With each compression Dr. Thomas' hands disappeared into folds of flesh. On the other side of the patient, a resident was holding defibrillator paddles while he watched the tracing on the cardiac monitor. At the patient's head, an anesthetist was ventilating him with an ambu bag, coordinating her efforts with Dr. Thomas.

"Hold up," said the resident with the defibrillator.

Everyone backed up while he positioned the paddles over the conductive grease on the patient's ill-defined thorax. When he compressed the button on top of the anterior chest lead, a surge of current raced through the patient's chest, spreading electrical havoc. The patient's extremities fluttered ineffectually like a fat chicken trying to fly.

The anesthetist immediately recommenced respiratory assistance. The monitor readjusted itself and a slow but regular tracing appeared.

"I got a good carotid pulse," said the anesthetist with her hand pressing on the side of the patient's neck.

"Good," said the resident with the defibrillator. He hadn't taken his eyes from the monitor, and when the first ectopic ventricular spike occurred, he ordered "seventy-five milligrams of Lidocaine."

Philips walked over to Thomas and got his attention by tapping his leg. The resident climbed down from his chair and stepped back, although he kept an eye on the table.

"Your patient, Lynn Anne Lucas," said Philips. "She has some interesting X-ray findings in her occipital area extending foward."

"I'm glad you found something. My intuition has been telling me there's something wrong with the girl but I don't know what it is."

"I can't help with the diagnosis yet," said Philips. "What I'd like to do is take more films tomorrow. How about admitting her for the night."

"Sure," said Thomas. "I'd love to but I'm going to take a lot of flak from the boys if I don't have even a provisional diagnosis."

"How about multiple sclerosis?"

Thomas stroked his beard. "Multiple sclerosis. That's a little out on a limb."

"Is there any reason it couldn't be multiple sclerosis?"

"No," said Thomas. "But there isn't much reason to suggest it either."

"How about very early in its course."

"Possibly, but multiple sclerosis is usually diagnosed later when its characteristic pattern becomes apparent."

"That's just the point. We're suggesting the diagnosis earlier rather than later."

"All right," said Thomas, "but I'm going to specifically say in my admitting note that Radiology suggested that diagnosis."

"Be my guest," said Philips. "Just be sure to write on the order sheet that CAT scan and polytomography are to be done tomorrow. I'll take care of scheduling it from Radiology."

Back at the desk Philips endured the crowd long enough to obtain Lynn Anne Lucas's emergency room chart and hospital record. He took both into the deserted lounge and sat down.

First he read Dr. Huggens' and Dr. Thomas' workups. There was nothing exciting. Next he looked at the chart. By the color coding on the edge of the pages, he noticed there was a radiology report. He opened the chart to that page, which described a skull X ray at age eleven secondary to a roller-skating mishap. The X ray had been read by a resident Philips knew. He'd been several years behind Philips and now was in Houston. The X ray was described as normal.

Working backward through the chart, Philips read entries over the last two years related to upper respiratory infections treated at the dispensary on campus. He also glanced over a series of GYN clinic visits where mildly atypical Pap smears had been noted. Philips had to admit to himself that the information was not so informative as it should have been because of the embarrassing amount of general medicine he'd forgotten since his house staff days. From 1969 to 1970 there were no entries on the chart.

Philips returned the chart to the ER desk before starting back to his office. He took the stairs by twos, his energy level spurred by a wonderful sense of investigative excitement. After the disappointment with Marino, the discovery of Lucas was that much more titillating. Back in his office, he pulled down the dusty internal medicine textbook and looked up multiple sclerosis.

As he had remembered, the diagnosis of the disease was circumstantial. There was no consistent laboratory aid save for autopsy. The obvious and immense value of a radiological diagnosis again occurred to Philips. He read on, noticing that the classic features of the disease included abnormalities in vision as well as bladder dysfunction. After reading the first two sentences of the next paragraph, Philips stopped. He went back and read them aloud:

Diagnosis may be uncertain in the early years of the disease. Long latent periods between a minor initial symptom, which may not even come to medical attention, and the subsequent development of more characteristic ones may delay the final diagnosis.

Philips grabbed the phone and punched out Michaels' home number. With a sensitive radiological diagnosis, delay of the final diagnosis would be avoided.

It was only after the phone had already started to ring that Martin glanced at his watch. He was shocked to realize it was after eleven. At that moment Michaels' wife, Eleanor, whom Philips had never met, answered the phone. Philips immediately launched into a lengthy apology for calling so late although she did not sound as if she'd been asleep. Eleanor assured him that they never retired before midnight and put her husband on the line.

Michaels laughed at what he called Philips' adolescent enthusiasm, when he learned that Martin was still in his office.

"I've been busy," explained Philips. "I've had a cup of coffee, something to eat, and taken a nap."

"Don't let everybody see those printouts," said

Michaels, laughing anew. "I programmed some obscene suggestions as well."

Philips went on to tell Michaels excitedly that the reason he was calling was that he'd found another patient in the ER, named Lynn Anne Lucas, who had the same abnormal density pattern he'd seen on the Marino film. He told Michaels that he had not been able to follow up on Marino, but was going to get definitive films in the morning. He added that the computer had actually asked him to tell it what the abnormal density changes were. "The Goddamn thing wants to learn!"

"Remember," said Michaels, "the program approaches radiology the same way you do. It's your techniques that it utilizes."

"Yeah, but it's already better than me. It picked up this density variation when I didn't see it. If it uses my techniques, how do you explain that?"

"Easy. Remember, the computer digitizes the image into a two-hundred-fifty-six by two-hundred-fifty-six grid of pixel points with gray values between zero and two hundred. When we tested you, you only could differentiate gray values of zero to fifty. Obviously the machine is more sensitive."

"I'm sorry I asked," said Philips.

"Have you run the program against any old skull X rays?"

"No," admitted Philips, "I'm about to start."

"Well, you don't have to do everything in one night. Einstein didn't. Why not wait until morning?"

"Shut up," said Philips good-naturedly and hung up.

Armed with Lynn Anne Lucas's hospital number, Philips found her X ray file with relative ease. It contained only two recent chest films and the skull series taken after the roller-skating accident when she was eleven. He put one of the old lateral skull films up on the viewer next to the X ray taken that evening. Comparing them, Philips ascertained that the abnormal density had developed since age eleven. To be perfectly certain, Philips fed one of the older films into the computer. It concurred.

Philips put Lynn Anne's old X rays back into the envelope and put the new ones on top. Then he put the package on his desk, where he knew Helen wouldn't touch it. Until Lynn Anne had her new studies, there was nothing else to be done on her case.

Martin wondered what he should do. Despite the hour he knew he was still too excited to sleep and besides he wanted to wait for Denise. He was hoping she'd come by his office when she finished whatever she was doing. He thought about paging her, but then thought better of it.

He decided to pass the time by getting some old skull X rays from the file room. He thought he might as well start the process of checking the computer program. In case Denise came back before he did he left a note for her on the door. "I'm in Central Radiology."

At one of the terminals of the hospital's central computer he painfully typed out what he wanted: a printout of the names and unit numbers of all patients having had skull X rays in the last ten years. When he was finished he pushed the "enter" button and swung around in the chair to face the output printer. There was a short delay. Then the machine spewed out paper at an alarming rate. When it finally stopped, Philips found himself holding a list of thousands of names. Just looking at it made him feel tired.

Undaunted, he sought out Randy Jacobs, one of the department's evening employees, hired to file the day's X rays and pull the films needed for the following day. He was a full-time pharmacy student, a talented flautist, and an out-of-the-closet gay. Martin found him sharp-witted, ebullient, and a fabulous worker.

To start, Martin asked Randy to pull the X rays on the first page of the list. That represented about sixty patients. With his usual efficiency, Randy had twenty lateral skull films on Philips' alternator in as many minutes. But Philips did not run the films on the computer as Michaels had asked. Instead he began to examine them closely, unable to resist the temptation to look for more of the abnormal densities he had discovered on Marino and Lucas's X rays. Using his paper with the hole as a screening device, he began to go from one film to another, advancing the viewing screens as needed by depressing the electrical lever with his foot. He'd processed about half of the X rays when Denise arrived.

"All your big talk about wanting to leave clinical radiology and you're looking at X rays when it's almost midnight."

"It is a bit silly," said Martin, leaning back in his chair and rubbing his eyes with his knuckles, "but I had these old films pulled and I thought I'd check to see if I could find another case like Lucas or Marino."

Denise came up behind him and rubbed his neck. His face looked tired.

"Have you found any?" she asked.

"No," said Philips. "But I've only looked at a dozen or so films."

"Have you narrowed down your field?"

"What do you mean?"

"Well, you've seen two cases. Both are recent, both are women, and both are about twenty."

Philips looked at the row of films in front of him and grunted. It was his way of acknowledging that Denise had a good point without saying so. He wondered why he hadn't thought of it himself.

She followed him back to the main computer terminal maintaining a steady stream of commentary about the busy evening in the ER. Philips listened with half an ear while he made his entry. He asked for the names and unit numbers of female patients, aged fifteen to twenty-five, who'd had skull films within the last two years. When the output printer came alive it only typed one line. It told Philips that the data bank was not keyed to retrieve skull films by sex. Philips adjusted his demand on the keyboard. When the printer reactivated, it typed at a vicious rate, but only for a short interval. The list comprised only a hundred and three patients. A quick scan suggested that somewhat less than half were female.

Randy liked the new list. He said the size of the other was demoralizing. While they waited, he pulled seven envelopes saying it would give them something to start with while he gathered the others.

Back in his office, Martin admitted that he was beat and that fatigue was beginning to erode his enthusiasm. He dropped the X rays in front of his alternator and put his arms around Denise, pressing her against him. His head dropped over her shoulder. She hugged him back, her hands just beneath his shoulder blades. They stood there for a moment supporting each other, not speaking.

Finally Denise looked up into Martin's face and

pushed his blond hair from his forehead. His eyes were closed.

"Why not call it a day," she said.

"Good idea," said Philips, opening his eyes. "Why don't you come on back to my apartment? I'm still a bit manic; I need to talk."

"Talk?" asked Denise.

"Whatever."

"Unfortunately, I'm certain I'll be called back to the hospital."

Philips lived in an apartment building called the Towers, which had been built by the Med Center and was contiguous with the hospital. Although it had been designed with very little creativity, it was new, safe, and superbly convenient. It was also built on the river and Martin had one of the riverside units. Denise, on the other hand, lived in an old building on a cluttered side street. Her apartment was on the third floor and its windows faced a forever dark air shaft.

Martin pointed out that his apartment was as close to the hospital as the on-call room in the nurses' quarters, which was available for Denise's use, and three times closer than her own apartment. "If you get called, you get called," he said.

She hesitated. Seeing each other while she was on call was a new experience and Denise was afraid that escalating the relationship was going to force a decision.

"Maybe," she said. "First, let me check the ER and make sure there aren't any problems brewing."

While he waited for her, he began putting some of the new X rays on his viewer. He had three of them up before his eyes were pulled back to the first. Leaping from his chair, he put his nose to the film.

Another case! There was the same speckling starting in the very back of the brain and running forward. Philips looked down at the envelope. The name was Katherine Collins, age twenty-one. The typed X-ray report glued to the envelope listed "seizure disorder" as the clinical information.

Taking Katherine Collins' X ray back to the small computer, he fed it to the scanner. Then he grabbed the remaining four envelopes and extracted a skull film from each. He began putting them on his viewer, but before his hand even left the edge of the first film, he knew he'd found yet another case. His eyes were now very sensitized to picking up the subtle changes. Ellen McCarthy, age twenty-two, clinical information: headaches, visual disturbance, and weakness of right extremities. The other films were normal.

Using a matched pair of lateral skull films from Ellen McCarthy's envelope, that had been taken at slightly different angles, Philips switched on the light in his stereo viewer. Looking through the eyepiece, he had great difficulty perceiving any speckling at all. What he could see seemed to be superficial, in the cerebral cortex rather than deeper in the nerve fibers of the white matter. That was somewhat disturbing information. The lesions of multiple sclerosis were usually in the white matter of the brain. Tearing off the printout from the computer, Philips read the report. At the top of the page was a THANK YOU referring to when Philips had inserted the film. This was followed by a girl's name and a fictitious phone number. It was more of Michaels' humor.

The report itself was just as Philips expected. The densities were described and as it had with Lynn Anne Lucas, the computer asked again to be advised as to the significance of the unprogrammed abnormalities.

Almost simultaneously Denise returned from the ER and Randy arrived with fifteen more envelopes. Philips gave Denise a resounding kiss. He told her that thanks to her suggestion he'd found two more cases, both young women. He took the new films from Randy and was about to start on them, when Denise put her hand on his shoulder.

"The ER is quiet now. An hour from now, who knows?"

Philips sighed. He felt like a child with a new toy being asked to abandon it for the night. Reluctantly he put the envelopes down and told Randy to pull the rest of the films from the second list and stack them on his desk. Then if he had any time left he could begin pulling the films from the main list, and stack them against the back wall, behind the worktable. As an afterthought Martin asked Randy to call Medical Records and have the hospital charts of Katherine Collins and Ellen McCarthy sent up to his office.

Glancing around the room Martin said, "I wonder if I'm forgetting anything."

"Yourself," said Denise with exasperation. "You've been here for eighteen hours. Good gravy, let's go."

Since the Towers was part of the medical center, it was connected to the hospital by a well-lit and cheerfully painted basement tunnel. Power and heat traveled the same route, concealed in the tunnel's ceiling, behind acoustical tiles. As Martin and Denise walked hand in hand they passed first under the old medical school and then the new medical school. Farther on they passed branching tunnels leading to the Brenner

Pediatric Hospital and the Goldman Psychiatry Institute. The Towers was at the end of the tunnel and represented the current limit of the cancerous spread of the medical center into the surrounding community. A flight of steps led directly into the lower foyer of the apartment house. A guard behind a bullet-proof glass recognized Philips and buzzed them in.

The Towers was a posh residential address inhabited mostly by MDs and other professionals from the medical center. A few other professors from the university lived there as well but they generally found the rents on the expensive side. Of the physicians, most were divorced, although there was a rising contingent of young turks with their aggressively career-minded wives. There were almost no children except for weekends when it was Dad's turn with the kids. Martin also knew there were quite a few psychiatrists, and he'd noticed not an insignificant number of gays.

Martin was one of the divorced. It had happened four years previously after six years of matrimonial suburban stalemate. Like most of his colleagues Martin had married during his residency as a kind of reaction against his demanding academic life. His wife's name was Shirley and he had loved her, at least he thought he'd loved her. He'd been shocked at the time when she upped and left him. Luckily they'd had no children. His reaction to the divorce had been depression, which he'd dealt with by working even longer hours, if that was possible. Gradually as time passed he was able to view the experience with the necessary detachment to realize what had happened. Philips had been married to medicine, his wife had been the mistress. Shirley had picked the year he'd

138

been appointed Assistant Chief of Neuroradiology as the time to leave because she'd finally understood his value system. Before his selection his excuse to his wife for his seventy hours per week was that he was shooting to become the Assistant Chief. Once he got the position his excuse for the same work week was that he *was* the Chief. Shirley had seen the light even if Philips hadn't. She had refused to be married and alone and so she left.

"Have you come to any conclusion about Marino's missing brain?" asked Denise, bringing Martin back to the present.

"No," said Philips. "But Mannerheim must have been responsible in some way."

They were waiting for the elevator beneath a huge, gaudy chandelier. The carpet was burnt orange with interlocking gold circles.

"Are you going to do anything about it?"

"I don't know what I can do. I sure wouldn't mind finding out why it was removed."

The nicest aspect of Philips' apartment was the view of the river and the graceful curve of the bridge. Otherwise it was very unremarkable. Philips had moved suddenly. He'd rented the apartment by telephone and had hired a rental firm to furnish it. And that's what he got—furniture: a couch; a couple of end tables; a coffee table; a couple of chairs for the living room; a dinette set; and a bed with matching side table for the bedroom. It wasn't much, but it was only temporary. The fact that Philips had been living there for four years didn't occur to him.

Martin was not a drinker but tonight he wanted to relax so he splashed some scotch over ice. To be polite he held the bottle up for Denise but she shook her head as he'd expected. She only drank wine or an occasional gin and tonic, and certainly not while she was on call. Instead she got herself a tall glass of orange juice from the refrigerator.

In the living room Denise listened to Martin's chatter, hoping that he'd burn himself out quickly. She was not interested in talking about research or missing brains. She was remembering his admission of affection. The possibility of his being serious excited her and it allowed her to admit her own feelings.

"Life can be amazing," Martin was saying. "In a single day it can take such wonderful twists."

"What are you referring to?" Denise asked, hoping he was going to talk about their relationship.

"Yesterday, I had no idea we were so close to producing the X-ray reading program. If things go ..."

Exasperated, she got up and pulled him to his feet and began pulling at his shirttails telling him that he should relax and forget the hospital. She looked up into his bemused face with a teasing smile, so that no matter what happened it wouldn't be awkward.

Philips agreed that he was wound up and said he'd feel better if he took a quick shower. It wasn't quite what she had in mind, but he encouraged her to come into the bathroom and keep him company. She watched him through the shower glass, which was frosted on one side and beveled on the other. The image of Philips' naked body was fractured and softened in a curiously erotic way as he twisted and turned under the jet of water.

Denise sipped her orange juice while Martin tried to carry on a conversation over the din of the water. She couldn't hear a word, which she thought was just as well. At the moment she preferred watching rather than listening. Affection welled up inside of her, filling her with warmth.

Finished, Martin turned off the water and, grabbing his towel, stepped out of the shower. To Denise's disgust he was still talking about computers and doctors. Annoyed, she snatched the towel and began to dry his back. When she was finished she turned him back around.

"Do me a favor," she said as if she were angry, "and shut up."

Then she grabbed his hand, and pulled him out of the bathroom. Confused at her sudden outburst, Philips allowed himself to be led into the darkened bedroom. There in full view of the silent river and the dramatic bridge, Denise threw her arms around his neck and passionately kissed him.

Martin responded instantly. But before he could even undress Denise, her beeper filled the room with its insistent sound. For a moment they just held each other, postponing the inevitable, and enjoying their closeness. Without saying it, they both knew that their relationship had reached a new plateau.

It was 2:40 A.M. when a city ambulance pulled into the receiving area of the Medical Center. There were already two similar ambulances parked there, and the new one backed up between them until its bumper thumped the rubber guard. The engine choked and died before the driver and the passenger alighted from the cab. With their heads bowed against the steady April rain, they trotted back and leaped up on the platform. The thinner of the two swung open the rear door of the ambulance. The other more muscular man reached in and pulled out an empty stretcher. Unlike the other ambulances this one was not bringing an emergency. It had come to pick up a patient. Not an uncommon occurrence.

The men lifted the stretcher from each end and, like an ironing board, its legs dropped down. Instantly the stretcher was converted into a narrow but functional gurney. Together they pushed through the automatic sliding door of the emergency room and looking neither right nor left, turned down the main corridor and took an elevator to Neurology West on the fourteenth floor. There were two RNs and five LPNs assigned to the floor for the shift, but one of the nurses and three of the aides were on their break, so Ms. Claudine Arnette, RN, was in charge. It was to her that the thinner man presented the transfer documents. The patient was being moved to a private room at New York Medical Center, where her own doctor had admitting privileges.

Ms. Arnette checked the papers, swore under her breath because she had just finished her paper work on the admission and signed the form. She asked Maria Gonzales to accompany the men down to room 1420. Then she went back to her narcotic check before her own break. Even in the reduced light she'd noticed that the driver had amazingly green eyes.

Maria Gonzales opened the door to room 1420, and tried to awaken Lynn Anne. It was difficult. She explained to the ambulance attendants that they'd received a phone call order for a double dose of sleep medication as well as phenobarbital because of the possibility of seizure. The men told Maria it didn't matter, and they positioned the stretcher and arranged the blankets. With a smooth, practiced maneuver, they lifted the patient and settled her with the blankets. Lynn Anne Lucas never even woke up.

The men thanked Maria, who had already begun to strip Lynn Anne's bed. Then they wheeled her out into the hallway. Ms. Arnette didn't look up when they passed the nurses' station and got back on the elevator. An hour later the ambulance pulled away from the Med Center. There was no need for the siren or rotating light. The ambulance was empty.

8

Moments before the alarm was due to sound, Martin pressed in the knob on the clock and lay there, looking up at the ceiling. His body was so used to waking at five-twenty-five that he rarely needed assistance, no matter what time he went to sleep. Marshaling his strength, he rose quickly and donned his jogging clothes.

The nighttime rain had saturated the air with moisture, and a stringy fog hung over the river, making the stanchions of the bridge appear as if they were supported by vaporous clouds. The dampness deadened the sound so that the early-morning traffic did not interrupt his thoughts, which were mostly about Denise.

It had been years since he had felt the excitement of romantic love. For a couple of weeks he hadn't even recognized the reason for his insomnia and odd mood swings, but then when he found himself remembering what Denise wore each day, the reality finally dawned on him with a mixture of cynicism and delight. The cynicism came from having watched several of his colleagues who were also forty plus make fools of themselves with new, young loves. The delight came from the relationship itself. Denise Sanger wasn't just a young body to be used to deny the inevitability of time. She was a fascinating combination of mischievous inventiveness and penetrating intelligence. The fact that she was so pretty was like icing on the cake. Philips had to admit that he was not only crazy about her, but was also becoming dependent upon her as a means of rescue from the self-fulfilling prophecy his life had become.

When he reached the 2.5-mile mark, Philips turned and headed back. There were more joggers now, some of whom he recognized; but he tended to ignore them as they did him. His breathing became a little heavier but he continued to maintain a strong smooth pace all the way to his apartment.

Philips knew that as much as he'd liked medicine, he'd used it as an excuse for not expanding any other parts of his life. The shock of his wife's flight had been the biggest single cause of this realization. What to do about it was another issue. For Martin, research had become the potential salvation. While he continued his grueling day-to-day commitments, he'd expanded his research hoping that it would eventually win some freedom for him. He didn't want to give up clinical medicine, just loosen the strangle-hold it had on his life. And now that Denise had come along, he was even more committed. He vowed he would not make the same mistake again. If things worked out between them, Denise was going to be his wife in the full sense of the word. But to do that his research had to succeed. By 7:15 he had showered, shaved, and was at his office door. When he went inside he stopped, amazed. Overnight the room appeared as if it had been transformed into a dump for old X rays. Randy Jacobs with his usual efficiency had pulled a great percentage of the films he'd requested. The envelopes from the master list were stacked in precarious piles behind the worktable. Those from the second, smaller list were stacked by Philips' alternator. Lateral skull films had been taken from each of the envelopes of the latter group and mounted on the viewing screens.

Philips experienced a new wave of enthusiasm and sat down in front of the alternator. He immediately began scanning the films for abnormalities similar to those he'd seen with Marino, Lucas, Collins, and McCarthy. He'd gotten through almost half when Denise walked in.

She looked exhausted. Her normally shiny hair seemed oily and her face was pale with dark circles under her eyes.

She gave him a quick hug and sat down. Looking at her wan expression he suggested she take a few hours off for a nap. He'd see her in the angiography room when she felt like returning. Meaning, of course, he'd start the case.

"Hold on," said Denise. "No special concessions for the boss's mistress. It's my turn to be in the cerebral angiography room and I'll be there whether I've slept or not."

Martin realized he'd made a mistake. Denise would never be anything but professional about her work. He smiled and patted her hand, telling her he was glad she felt the way she did.

Somewhat mollified, she said, "I'll just run and shower. I'll be back in thirty minutes."

Philips watched Denise leave, then spun to his viewing screen. In the process his eyes swept over his desk and noted something new in the chaos. Walking over he found two hospital charts and a note from Randy. The note merely told him that the rest of the X rays would be pulled the following evening. The charts were those of Katherine Collins and Ellen McCarthy.

Philips carried them over to the chair in front of the viewer, opening Collins' first. It took only a few minutes to glean the essential information, namely: Katherine Collins was a twenty-one-year-old white female with diffuse neurological symptoms, extensively worked up by neurology without a confirmed diagnosis. In the differential diagnosis, multiple sclerosis was being considered.

Philips carefully read through the whole chart. As he got to the end he noticed that Collins' visits and laboratory tests abruptly stopped about one month ago. Up until that time there had been increasingly frequent entries and some of the latter notes indicated that she was due back for follow-up. Apparently she never showed up.

Taking the other chart, which was considerably smaller, Philips read about Ellen McCarthy. She was a twenty-two-year-old female whose neurological history involved two seizures. She was in the process of being worked-up when her entries abruptly stopped. That was two months ago. Philips even found a note saying that the patient had been scheduled for another EEG with a sleep sequence the following week. It had never been done. Her work-up had not been completed and no differential diagnosis was listed in the chart.

Helen arrived and came in with her usual handful of problems, but before she said anything she presented Martin with a fresh cup of coffee and a doughnut she'd brought from Chock Full O' Nuts. Then she got down to business. Ferguson had called again and said that the supplies had to be out of the room in question by noon or they were going to be out on the street. Helen paused for a response.

Martin had no idea what to do with all the equipment. The department was already crammed into a space half the size they needed. Just to be rid of the problem, even temporarily, he told Helen to bring everything into his office and stack it against the wall. He said he'd think of something by the end of the week.

Satisfied, she went on to the problem with the technicians who wanted to get married. Philips told her to let Robbins handle it. Helen patiently explained that Robbins was the one who had presented the problem to her in order to have Philips handle it.

"Damn," said Martin. There was really no solution. It was too late to train new technicians before they left. If he fired them, they'd get new jobs easily while Philips would have trouble finding replacements. "Find out exactly how long they plan to be away," he said trying to stifle his exasperation. He hadn't taken a vacation himself in two years.

Turning to the next page of her notes, Helen told Philips that Cornelia Rogers from Typing had called in sick again making it the ninth day absent this month. She'd managed to be ill for at least seven days each month for the five months she'd been working for neuroradiology. Helen asked what Philips wanted to do about it.

Philips wanted to have the girl beat up, quartered, and thrown into the East River. "What would you like to do?" he asked, controlling himself.

"I think she should be given notice."

"Fine, you handle it."

Helen had one last comment before heading for the door: Philips had to give a 1 P.M. lecture on the CAT scanner to the current group of medical students. She was about to leave when Philips stopped her. "Listen, do me a favor. There's an in-patient named Lynn Anne Lucas. See that she gets scheduled this morning for a CAT scan and polytomography. If there's any trouble, just say it's a special request of mine. And tell the technicians to give me a call just before they do the procedures."

Helen wrote down the message and left. Martin went back to the two charts. It was encouraging that both young women had neurological symptoms, especially since multiple sclerosis was specifically listed as a possibility in Katherine Collins' case. In the case of Ellen McCarthy, Philips checked to see how often seizures were a part of the clinical picture of multiple sclerosis. Less than ten percent, yet they did occur. But why had both girls been suddenly lost to follow-up? Martin couldn't help worrying that he was going to have difficulty getting them in for X rays if they had transferred their care someplace else, maybe even to another city.

Just then Helen buzzed him to say that the resident was ready for him in the cerebral angiography room. Philips put on his lead apron with the faded Superman logo, picked up Collins' and McCarthy's charts and walked out of his office. Stopping at Helen's desk, he asked her to track the two patients down and encourage them to come in for some free diagnostic X rays. He wanted Helen not to frighten the young women, but to make sure they understood it was important.

Downstairs he found Denise waiting for him. She

had showered, washed her hair, and changed her clothes; it had been a miraculous thirty-minute transformation. She no longer looked tired and her light brown eyes sparkled above her surgical mask. Philips would have loved to have touched her, but instead let his eyes linger for an extra second on hers.

She had already done enough angiograms so that he just acted as her assistant. There was no conversation as she deftly handled the catheter, threading it up inside the patient's artery. Philips watched carefully, ready to make suggestions if he thought they were needed. They weren't. The patient was Harold Schiller, who'd been CAT scanned the day before. As Philips had guessed, Mannerheim had ordered a cerebral angiogram probably in preparation to operate, although clearly the case was inoperable.

An hour later the case was all but done.

"I tell you," whispered Martin, "you're getting better than I and you've only been doing it a few weeks." Denise blushed but Martin knew she was pleased. Leaving her to finish, he told her to buzz when the next case was ready to go. He wanted to finish scanning the skull films on his alternator, then begin to set up running the old films through Michaels' computer. He reasoned that if he could run a hundred a day he could go through the whole master list in a month and a half. He also thought that he could give Michaels the discrepancies as they surfaced so that perhaps by the time he finished, Michaels would have the bugs out of the program. If that were the case, they'd have something to present to the unsuspecting medical world by July.

But as Philips rounded the corner outside his office, Helen ambushed him with disappointing news. She'd had no luck with any of his requests. Lynn Anne Lucas could not be CAT scanned or X-rayed because she'd been transferred during the night to New York Medical Center. As far as Katherine Collins and Ellen McCarthy were concerned, she'd traced both of them to the university. They were both listed as undergraduates. However, Collins could not be reached because she'd allegedly run away a month ago and was considered a missing person. Ellen McCarthy, on the other hand, was dead. She'd had a fatal auto accident on the West Side Highway two months ago.

"Jesus Christ!" said Philips. "Tell me you're joking."

"I'm sorry," said Helen. "That's the best I could do."

Philips shook his head in disbelief. He'd been so sure that he'd get at least one case out of the three to examine. He stepped into his office and stared blankly at the far wall. His compulsive personality wasn't accustomed to dealing with such reversals.

He pounded his fist against his open hand so that the sound echoed in the room. Then he paced, trying to think. Collins was out. If the police couldn't find her, how could he. McCarthy? If she'd been killed she must have been taken to a hospital. But which? And Lucas . . . at least she'd been taken to New York Medical Center where he had a good friend, instead of Bellevue. If it had been Bellevue, he would have had to give up.

Philips told Helen to see if she could find out why Lynn Anne had been transferred and then asked her to put a call through to Dr. Donald Travis at New York Medical Center. He also asked her to see if the police knew where Ellen McCarthy had been taken after her accident.

Still distracted, Philips forced himself to concentrate on the skull films in front of him. They were all normal in respect to their texture. When he went out to Helen's desk, she had little good news. Dr. Travis was tied up and would have to call back. She hadn't been able to find out much about Lucas because the nurse on duty at the time went home at 7 A.M. and could not be reached. The only positive information she had was that Ellen McCarthy had been taken back to the Med Center after her accident.

Before Philips could ask her to track down that lead, a maintenance man appeared with an enormous trolley piled with boxes, paper, and other debris. Without a word, he pushed it into Philips' office and began unloading the material.

"What the hell?" asked Philips.

"That's the supplies from the storeroom you said to have put in here," explained Helen.

"Shit," said Philips as the man stacked the supplies along the wall. Philips had the uncomfortable feeling that events were slipping out of his control.

Sitting down amidst the chaos, Philips dialed Admitting. He felt his mood deteriorating further as the phone rang interminably on the other end of the line.

"Have a moment?" called William Michaels. He'd leaned in through Philips' open door, his cheerful grin in direct contrast to Martin's scowl. Then his eyes swept around the room in total disbelief.

"Don't ask," said Philips, anticipating some smart comment.

"My God," said Michaels. "When you work, you don't mess around."

At that point someone finally answered the phone in Admitting, but it was a temporary receptionist who transferred Martin to someone else. That person only handled admissions, not discharges or transfers, so Philips was switched again. Only then did he learn that the person he had to speak to was on a coffee break, so he hung up, frustrated with bureaucracy, saying, "Why didn't I become a plumber?"

Michaels laughed, then asked how Philips was doing with their project. Philips told him that he'd had most of the X rays pulled, indicating the pile with his hand. He told Michaels that he thought he could run them all in a month and a half.

"Perfect," said Michaels. "The sooner the better, because the new memory storage and association system we've been working on is proving better than we'd dreamed. By the time you finish we'll have a new central processor to handle the debugged program. You have no idea how good it's going to be."

"Quite the contrary," said Philips, getting up from the desk. "I have a pretty good idea. Let me show you what the program picked up."

Martin cleared a viewing screen and put up Marino's, Lucas', Collins', and McCarthy's X rays. With his index finger, then the piece of paper with the hole in it, Philips tried to show the abnormal densities on each.

"They look all the same to me," admitted Michaels.

"That's just the point," said Philips. "That's how good this system is." Just talking with Michaels rekindled Martin's excitement.

Just then the phone rang and Philips picked it up. It was Dr. Donald Travis from New York Medical Center. Martin explained his problem about Lynn Anne Lucas but purposefully left out the radiologic abnormality. Then he asked Travis if he would arrange to have a CAT scan and some special X rays done on the patient. Travis agreed and hung up. Immediately the phone buzzed and Helen told Philips that Denise was ready for the next angiogram.

"I got to be going anyway," said Michaels. "Good

luck with the films. Remember, it's up to you now. We need this information as soon as you can give it to us."

Philips lifted his apron off its hook and followed Michaels out of the office.

9

One of the large fluorescent light fixtures directly over Kristin Lindquist was malfunctioning so that it flickered at a rapid frequency and emitted a constant buzzing sound. She tried to ignore it, but it was difficult. She hadn't felt right ever since she'd awakened that morning with a slight headache and the quivering light intensified her discomfort. It was a steady dull pain and Kristin noticed that physical exertion did not make it worse as was the case with her usual headaches.

She looked at the naked male model on the platform in the center of the room, then down at her work. Her drawing looked flat, two-dimensional and without feeling. Normally she liked her life drawing class. But this morning she was not enjoying herself and her work reflected it.

If only the light would stop flickering. It was driving her crazy. With her left hand she shielded her eyes. That made it better. Using a fresh piece of charcoal, she began to draw a base for her figure to rest on. She started with a perpendicular line, pulling the fresh charcoal straight down the paper. When she lifted the marker she was surprised no line had resulted. Looking at the end of the charcoal she could see a flattened area where it had rubbed against the paper. Thinking it was a defective piece, Kristin turned her head slightly to make a mark with the charcoal in the corner of the paper. As she did so she noticed that the perpendicular line she had just drawn appeared in the periphery of her vision. She looked back and the line disappeared. Rotating her head slightly caused the line to appear. Kristin did it several times to make sure she wasn't hallucinating. Her eye couldn't perceive the perpendicular line when her head was perfectly aligned with it. If she rotated her head in either direction the line appeared. Weird!

Kristin had heard of migraine headaches, and although she'd never had a migraine, she guessed she was experiencing one. After putting down her charcoal and stacking her materials in her locker, Kristin explained to the instructor that she was not feeling well and left for her apartment.

Walking across the campus, Kristin experienced the same dizziness that she'd noticed on her way to class. It seemed that the world would abruptly rotate just a fraction of a degree to make Kristin's step feel slightly off-balance. It was accompanied by an unpleasant although vaguely familiar odor and a slight ringing in her ears.

One block from campus, Kristin's apartment was a third-floor walk-up, which she shared with her roommate, Carol Danforth. As Kristin climbed the stairs she felt a heaviness in her legs which made her wonder if she were getting the flu.

The apartment was empty. Carol was undoubtedly at class. In one way that was good because Kristin guessed she needed some undisturbed rest, but she would have appreciated Carol's sympathy. She took two aspirins, slipped out of her clothes, climbed into bed, and put a cold cloth over her head. Almost immediately she felt better. It was such a sudden reversal that she just lay there, concerned that if she moved the strange symptoms would recur.

When the phone by her bed rang she was pleased because she wanted to talk to someone. But it wasn't one of her friends. It was the GYN clinic calling to tell her that her Pap smear was abnormal.

Kristin listened, trying to keep herself calm. They told her not to be concerned because abnormal Pap smears were not that uncommon, especially when associated with the slight erosion she had on her cervix, but to be on the safe side they wanted her to return to the clinic that afternoon to repeat it.

Kristin tried to protest, mentioning her migraine headache. But GYN was insistent, saying the sooner the better. They had an opening that afternoon and Kristin could be in and out in no time.

Reluctantly Kristin agreed to come. Maybe something really was wrong with her and if that were the case she had to be responsible. But she dreaded going alone. She tried calling her boyfriend, Thomas, but of course he wasn't in. Kristin knew it was irrational, but she couldn't help feeling there was something evil about the Med Center.

Martin took a deep breath before entering Pathology. When Philips had been a medical student, that service had been his *bête noire*. His first autopsy had been an ordeal that he had not been prepared for. He

had assumed it was going to be like first-year anatomy, where the cadaver bore as little resemblance to
a human being as a wooden statue. The odor had
been unpleasant but at least it had been chemical.
Besides, anatomy lab had been characterized by
pranks and jokes, relieving any tension. Not so with
pathology. The autopsy had been on a ten-year-old
boy who had died from leukemia. His body was pale,
but supple and all too life-like. When the corpse had
been rudely opened, then gutted like a fish, Martin's
legs had turned to rubber and his lunch came up in
his mouth. He'd avoided vomiting by turning his
head, but his esophagus burned from the acid of his
own digestive juices. The professor had droned on,
but Philips had heard nothing. He had stayed but he
had suffered, and his heart had gone out to that lifeless boy.

Now Philips pushed open the doors to Pathology.
The environment was a far cry from what he'd experienced as a medical student. The department had been
moved to the new medical-school building and
housed in an ultramodern setting. Instead of small
and somber spaces with high ceilings and marble
floors where footsteps echoed unnaturally, the new
pathology area was open and clean. The predominant
materials were white Formica and stainless steel. Individual rooms had been replaced by areas demar-
cated by shoulder-height dividers. The walls were
covered with colorful prints of Impressionist
paintings, particularly Monet.

The receptionist directed Martin to the autopsy
theater where Dr. Jeffrey Reynolds was helping the
residents. Martin had hoped to catch Reynolds in his
office, but the receptionist insisted that Philips could
go into the theater because Dr. Reynolds did not

mind interruptions. Philips wasn't worrying about Reynolds, he was concerned about himself. Nonetheless, he followed the receptionist's pointing finger.

He should have known better. In front of him on a stainless steel table, like a side of beef, was a corpse. The autopsy had just begun with a Y-shaped incision across the chest and down to the pubis. The skin and underlying tissues had been flopped back revealing the rib cage and the abdominal organs. At the moment of Philips' entry, one of the residents was loudly clipping through the ribs.

Reynolds saw Philips and walked over. In his hand he held a large autopsy knife like a butcher knife. Martin glanced around the room to keep from looking at the procedure in front of him. The area resembled an operating room. It was new and modern and completely tiled so that it could be easily cleaned. There were five stainless steel tables. On the rear wall were a series of square refrigerator doors.

"Greetings, Martin," said Reynolds, wiping his hands on his apron. "I'm sorry about that Marino case. I would have liked to have helped you."

"I understand. Thanks for trying. Since there wasn't going to be a post, I tried to run a CAT scan on the corpse. It was surprising. Do you know what I found?"

Reynolds shook his head.

"There was no brain," said Philips. "Somebody removed the brain and sewed her back up so you practically couldn't tell."

"No!"

"Yeah," said Philips.

"God. Can you imagine what kind of blowup that could cause if the press got a hold of it, much less the family? They were definite about no autopsy."

"That's why I wanted to talk to you," said Philips.

There was a pause.

"Wait a minute," said Reynolds. "You don't think Pathology was involved."

"I don't know," admitted Philips.

Reynolds' face reddened, and veins appeared on his forehead. "Well I can assure you. The body never came up here. It went directly to the morgue."

"What about Neurosurgery?" asked Philips.

"Well, Mannerheim's boys are crazy, but I don't think that crazy."

Martin shrugged, then told Reynolds the real reason he'd stopped by was to inquire about a patient by the name of Ellen McCarthy who'd arrived dead at the ER about two months previously. Philips wanted to know if she'd been autopsied.

Reynolds snapped off his gloves and pushed his way through the doors into the main portion of the department. Using Pathology's terminal for the main computer, he typed in Ellen McCarthy's name and unit number. Immediately her name appeared on the computer screen followed by the date and number of the autopsy as well as cause of death: head injury resulting in massive intracerebral hemorrhage and brain-stem herniation. Reynolds quickly located a copy of the autopsy report and handed it to Philips.

"Did you do the brain?" asked Philips.

"Of course we did the brain!" said Reynolds. He grabbed back the report. "You think we wouldn't do the brain on a head-injury case?" His eyes rapidly scanned the paper.

Philips watched him. Reynolds had gained nearly fifty pounds since they'd been lab partners in med school and a fold of skin on the back of his neck concealed the top of his collar. His cheeks bulged out and just beneath the skin there was a fine network of tiny red capillaries.

"She might have had a seizure before the auto accident," said Reynolds, still reading.

"How could that be determined?"

"Her tongue had been bitten multiple times. It's not certain, just presumptive . . ."

Philips was impressed. He knew that such fine points were usually only picked up by forensic pathologists.

"Here's the brain section," said Reynolds. "Massive hemorrhage. There is something interesting though. A section of the cortex of the temporal lobe showed isolated nerve-cell death. Very little glial reaction. No diagnosis was advanced."

"How about the occipital area?" asked Philips. "I saw some subtle X-ray abnormalities there."

"One slide taken," said Reynolds, "and that was normal."

"Just one. Damn, I wish there had been more."

"You might be in luck. It indicates here the brain was fixed. Just a minute."

Reynolds walked over to a card catalogue and pulled out the *M* drawer. Philips felt some mild encouragement.

"Well, it was fixed and saved but we don't have it. Neurosurgery wanted it so I guess it's up in the neurosurgical lab."

After stopping to watch Denise flawlessly and efficiently perform a single-vessel angiogram, Philips headed over to surgery. Dodging patient traffic in the holding area, he walked up to the OR desk.

"I'm looking for Mannerheim," said Philips to the blond nurse. "Any idea when he'll be out of surgery?"

"We know exactly."

"And what time will that be?"

"Twenty minutes ago." The other two nurses laughed. Apparently things were going smoothly in the OR for them to be in such good moods. "His residents are closing. Mannerheim's in the lounge."

Philips found Mannerheim holding court. The two visiting Japanese doctors were standing on either side of him smiling and bowing at irregular intervals. There were five other surgeons in the group, all drinking coffee. Mannerheim was holding a cigarette in the same hand as his cup. He'd given up smoking a year ago, which meant he didn't buy any cigarettes, but borrowed them from everybody else.

"So you know what I told this smart-ass lawyer?" said Mannerheim, gesturing dramatically with his free hand. "Of course I play God. Who do you think my patients want screwing around inside their brains, a garbage man?"

The group roared with approval, and then began to disperse. Martin approached Mannerheim and looked down on him.

"Well, well, our helpful radiologist."

"We try to please," said Philips pleasantly.

"Well, I can tell you I did not appreciate your little joke on the phone yesterday."

"It wasn't meant to be a joke," said Philips, "I'm sorry that my comment seemed out of place. I didn't know Marino was dead and I'd noticed some very subtle abnormalities on her film."

"You're supposed to look at the X rays before the patient dies," said Mannerheim nastily.

"Look, what I'm interested in discussing is that Marino's brain was removed from her corpse."

Mannerheim's eyes bulged and his full face turned

a dull red. Taking Philips by the arm he led him away from the two Japanese doctors.

"Let me tell you something," he snarled, "I happen to know that you moved and X-rayed Marino's body last night without authorization. And I can tell you this, I don't like anybody fucking around with my patients. Especially my complications."

"Listen," said Martin, shaking his arm free from Mannerheim's grasp. "My only interest is some strange X-ray abnormalities that could result in a major research breakthrough. I have no interest in your complications."

"You'd better not. If there was something irregular done to Lisa Marino's body, it would be on your head. You're the only one known to have taken the body from the morgue. Keep that in mind." Mannerheim waved a threatening finger in Philips' face.

A sudden fear of professional vulnerability made Martin hesitate. As much as he hated to admit it, Mannerheim had a point. If it became known that Marino's brain had been removed, the burden would be on him to prove that he didn't do it. Denise, with whom he was having an affair, was his only witness.

"All right, let's forget Marino," he said. "I found another patient with the same X-ray picture. An Ellen McCarthy. Unfortunately she'd been killed in an auto accident. But she was posted here at the Med Center and the brain was fixed and turned over to Neurosurgery. I would like to get ahold of that brain."

"And I'd like you to stay out of my hair. I'm a busy man. I'm taking care of real patients, not sitting on my ass looking at pictures all day."

Mannerheim turned and started away.

Philips felt a surge of fury. He wanted to shout, "You arrogant provincial bastard." But he didn't. That was what Mannerheim expected, maybe even wanted. Instead Martin went for the surgeon's known Achilles' heel. In a calm, understanding voice Martin said: "Dr. Mannerheim, you need a psychiatrist."

Mannerheim whirled, ready for combat, but Philips was already out the door. To Mannerheim, psychiatry represented the absolute antithesis of everything he stood for. For him it was a morass of hyperconceptual nonessence, and to be told he needed one was the worst insult he could absorb. In a blind rage the surgeon crashed through the door into the dressing area, tore off his bloodstained OR shoes and threw them the length of the room. They crashed into a bank of lockers and skidded under the sinks.

Then he snatched the wall phone and made two loud phone calls. First he called the Director of the hospital, Stanley Drake, then he called the Chief of Radiology, Dr. Harold Goldblatt, insisting to each that he wanted something done about Martin Philips. Both men listened in silence: Mannerheim was a powerful individual within the hospital community.

Philips was not the kind of person who got angry very often, but by the time he reached his office, he was steaming.

Helen looked up when he appeared. "Remember you've got the medical-student lecture in fifteen minutes."

Philips mumbled under his breath as he walked by her. To his surprise Denise was sitting in front of his alternator studying McCarthy's and Collins' charts. She looked up when he came in. "How about a bite of lunch, old man?"

"I don't have time for lunch," snapped Philips, throwing himself into his chair.

"You're in a wonderful mood."

Leaning his elbows on the desk, he covered his face with his hands. There was a moment of silence. Denise put the charts down and stood up.

"I'm sorry," said Martin through his fingers. "It's been a trying morning. This hospital is capable of erecting unbelievable barriers to any enlightened inquiry. I might have stumbled onto an important radiological find, but the hospital seems determined to discourage me from looking into it."

"Hegel wrote: 'Nothing great in the world has been accomplished without passion,'" Denise said with a twinkle. Her undergraduate major had been philosophy and she'd discovered that Martin enjoyed her ability to quote some of the great thinkers.

Philips finally took his hands from his face and smiled. "I could have used a little more passion last night."

"Leave it to you to interpret the word in that context. That's hardly what Hegel meant. Anyway, I'm going to have some lunch. You sure you can't join me?"

"Not a chance. I've got a lecture with the medical students."

Denise started toward the door. "By the way, as I was going through those charts of Collins and McCarthy I noticed both had several atypical Pap smears." Denise paused at the door.

"I thought their GYN exams were normal," said Philips.

"Everything was normal except the Pap smears on both patients. They were atypical, meaning they weren't frankly pathological, just not perfectly normal."

"Is that uncommon?"

"No, but it's supposed to be followed up until the test is normal. I didn't see any normal reports. Well, it's probably nothing. Just thought I'd mention it. Bye!"

Philips waved but stayed at his desk, trying to recall Lisa Marino's chart. It seemed to him that he remembered the Pap smear being mentioned there as well. Leaning out into the hall, Philips caught Helen's attention: "Remind me to head down to Gynecology Clinic this afternoon."

At 1:05 P.M., armed with his carousel labeled "CAT Scanner Introductory Lecture," Philips entered the Walowski Memorial Conference room. It was a far cry from the rest of the Department of Radiology, which was utilitarian and crammed into inadequate space. The conference room was inordinately plush, looking more like a Hollywood screening room than a hospital auditorium. The chairs were upholstered with a soft corduroy and arranged in tiers, giving each an unobstructed view of the screen. When Philips entered, the room was already filled.

He put his carousel on the projector and mounted the podium. The students quickly settled into their chairs, giving him their attention. Philips dimmed the lights and flipped on the first slide.

The lecture was polished. Philips had given it many times. It began with the origin of the concept of the CAT scanner by Mr. Godfrey Hornsfield of England, followed by a chronological recounting of its development. Philips very carefully emphasized that although an X-ray tube was used, the picture that resulted was really a mathematical reconstruction after a computer had analyzed the information. Once the students understood that basic concept, he felt the major point of the lecture had been accomplished.

As he talked, Martin's mind began to wander. He was so familiar with the material that it made no difference. His admiration of the people who had developed the CAT scanner included a touch of jealousy. But then he realized that if his own research proved out, he was going to be catapulted into the scientific limelight. His work might have even a more revolutionary impact on diagnostic radiology. It would certainly put him in contention for a Nobel prize.

In the middle of a sentence describing the CAT scanner's ability to pick up tumors, Philips' beeper went off. Turning up the lights, he excused himself and ran to the phone. Philips knew Helen would not page him except in an emergency. But the operator told him it was an outside call, and before he could protest, he was connected to Dr. Donald Travis.

"Donald," said Martin, putting his hand around the receiver. "I'm in the middle of a lecture, can I call you back?"

"Hell no!" yelled Travis. "I've wasted a good portion of my morning looking for your mythical middle-of-the-night transfer."

"You can't find Lynn Anne Lucas?"

"No. In fact, there hasn't been any God-damn transfer from the Med Center for the last week."

"That's strange. I was distinctly told New York Medical Center. Look, I'll speak to Admitting, but please check once more, it's important."

Philips hung up the phone, but let his hand remain on the receiver for a moment. Dealing with bureaucracy was almost as bad as dealing with the likes of Mannerheim. Heading back to the podium, he tried to pick up the pieces of the lecture, but his concentration was completely broken. For the first time since he began teaching, he claimed a false emergency and wound up the lecture.

Back at his office, Helen apologized for the interruption, saying that Dr. Travis was insistent. Philips told her it was all right and she followed him into his office reeling off his messages. She said that the Director of the hospital, Stanley Drake, had called twice and wanted a call back as soon as possible. She said that Dr. Robert McNeally had called from Houston, asking if Dr. Philips would chair the Neuroradiology section at the annual radiology convention in New Orleans. She said he needed an answer within the week. She started to go on to the next topic, when Philips abruptly raised his hand.

"That's enough for now!" said Philips.

"But there's more."

"I know there's more. There's always more."

Helen was taken aback. "Are you going to call Mr. Drake?"

"No. You call him and tell him I'm too busy to call him today and I'll speak to him tomorrow."

Helen had the sense enough to know when to leave her boss alone.

Standing on the threshold of his office, Philips looked around the room. The mess made by the stacks of skull films had been removed and in their place were the morning's angiograms. At least his head technician, Kenneth Robbins, had things under control.

Work was Philips' stability. So he sat down, picked up the microphone, and began to dictate. He had come to the last angiogram when he realized someone had entered the office and was standing behind him.

for everyone's benefit. I'm just asking you to be reasonable."

"Thank you," said Philips, standing up. "Thank you for stopping by. I appreciate your comments, and I'll give them deep thought." Philips hustled Drake out of his office, then closed his door.

As he replayed the conversation, he had trouble believing it had happened. Through the door he could hear Drake talking with Helen, so he knew he hadn't been dreaming. But more than anything to date, it made him determined to be free of the departmental rat race. More than ever he knew that his research had to succeed.

With an increased sense of motivation, Philips picked up the master list of skull films taken over the last ten years. Checking the unit numbers with the stack of films, he quickly determined the order in which they had been stored. He took the first envelope, crossed the name off the list, then pulled out the X rays. He took two matching lateral skull films, replacing the rest. After giving the computer the necessary information, he fed one of the films into the laser scanner. The other went up on his viewer. The old X-ray report was placed next to the print-out console.

Like most compulsive personalities, Martin was a listmaker. He had noted down Marino, Lucas, Collins, and McCarthy when the phone rang. It was Denise, saying that the first afternoon angiogram was all ready to go. Philips thought for a moment, then said that his presence was superfluous and suggested she go ahead with the study as long as she felt comfortable. As he had suspected, she was pleased with the vote of confidence.

Going back to his list, Philips crossed off Collins. After Marino he wrote, "morgue see Werner." Philips had a strong feeling that the diener knew what had happened to Lisa Marino's body. After McCarthy, Philips wrote, "neurosurgical lab." That left Lucas. He was confident from his conversation with Travis that she was not at New York Medical Center, unless she had been admitted under an alias, but that hardly made sense, so he wrote, "night charge nurse Neuro 14 West" after her name.

Then he picked up the phone and called Admitting again. It took thirty-six rings for someone to answer. Once again the person Philips had to talk to was unavailable. Philips left his name and a request to be called back.

By that time the computer had finished its run. Philips read the report with excitement, comparing it to the old reading, and then checking the film itself. The computer not only picked up everything mentioned on the report, it even found some mild bone thickening and opacity in the frontal sinuses that had been missed on the original reading. Looking at the film, Philips had to agree with the computer. It was amazing.

He was repeating the procedure with the next film, when Helen stuck her head in the door saying in an apologetic voice that the "big boss" wanted to see him as soon as possible.

Dr. Harold Goldblatt's office was situated at the far end of the department, in a wing of the building that stuck out into the central courtyard like a small rectangular tumor. Everyone knew when they'd entered his domain because the floor was carpeted and the walls changed to paneled mahogany. It reminded Philips of one of those downtown law firms whose letterhead had as many names as a page in the phone directory.

174

He knocked on the heavy wood door. Goldblatt was sitting behind his massive mahogany desk. The room had windows on three sides and the desk faced the door. There was more than a casual resemblance to the Oval Office. Goldblatt revered the trappings of power, and after a lifetime of Machiavellian maneuvering, he had become an international figure in radiology. At one time he had been good at neuroradiology; now he was an institution, and his professional knowledge was dated and therefore limited. Although Martin was privately cynical about Goldblatt's understanding of such innovations as the CAT scanner, he still admired the man. He had been a major force in elevating radiology to its current prestigious status.

Goldblatt stood up to shake Philips' hand and motioned him to a chair facing the desk. Goldblatt was a vigorous sixty-four years old. He still dressed the way he had when he'd graduated from Harvard in 1939. His suit was a boxy three-piece affair with baggy, cuffed trousers, hemmed about an inch above his ankles. He wore a thin bow tie, tied by hand and therefore crooked and asymmetrical. His hair was almost white and cut in a modified crew cut, which allowed a little bit of length over the ears. He peered at Martin over the tops of wire-rimmed Ben Franklins.

"Dr. Philips," began Goldblatt, sitting down. He put his elbows on his desk, clasping his hands together in a solid embrace. "Bringing up cadavers who are barely cold from the morgue to the department in the middle of the night is not my idea of normal practice."

Philips agreed that it sounded preposterous, and as an explanation, not an excuse, he told Goldblatt first about the X-ray reading program that he and William

175

Michaels had developed, and then about the abnormal density the computer program had picked up on Lisa Marino's X ray. He told Goldblatt that he needed more films to characterize the abnormality. He said that he felt it imperative to follow up on the discovery because it could be used to launch the concept of a computer X-ray analyzer.

After Philips had spoken, Goldblatt smiled benignly, nodding, "Listening to you, Martin, makes me wonder if you know exactly what you are doing."

"I believe I do." Goldblatt's comment surprised Philips, and it was difficult not to take offense.

"I don't mean on the technical side of your endeavor. I mean with regard to the implication of your work. Frankly, I don't think the department can support a project whose goal is to alienate the patient even further than he is already from the physician. You're proposing a system whereby a machine replaces the radiologist."

Martin was stunned. He was not prepared to face a charge of heresy from Goldblatt. He'd expected that only from some of the marginally competent radiologists of whom Philips knew there were far too many.

"You have a promising future," continued Goldblatt, "and I'd like to help you keep it. I'm also committed to preserving the integrity of the department here at the Medical Center. It's my feeling that you should alter your research proclivities in a more acceptable direction. In any case, you may not X-ray any more cadavers without authorization. That shouldn't have to be said."

Philips had a sudden insight. Mannerheim must have gotten to Goldblatt. There was no other explanation. But Mannerheim was a prima donna who didn't like to share the spotlight with anyone. Why was he now working with Goldblatt and probably Drake? It didn't make sense.

"One last point," said Goldblatt, forming a steeple with his fingers. "It has been brought to my attention that you have formed some sort of liaison with one of the residents. I do not think the department can condone this kind of fraternization."

Philips abruptly stood up, his eyes narrowed, the muscles of his face tense. "Unless professional performance is compromised," he said slowly, "my personal life is none of the department's business."

He turned and walked out the office. Goldblatt called after him, saying something about the department's image, but Philips did not stop.

He passed Helen without a glance, although she stood up, message pad in her hand. He slammed his door, sat down in front of the alternator, and picked up his microphone. It was best to work and allow a little time to pass before confronting his feelings. The phone rang and he ignored it. Helen answered it and buzzed. Philips went to the door and in pantomine asked Helen who it was. Dr. Travis, she said.

Travis told Martin that there was definitely no Lynn Anne Lucas at New York Medical Center. He'd searched the hospital, investigating every conceivable way the transfer could have been screwed up. He then asked Philips what he'd learned from the Admitting Department.

"Not much," said Philips lamely. He was embarrassed to say he had not checked after putting Travis to so much effort. As soon as he hung up he called Admitting. Persistence paid off and finally he got to speak with the woman in charge of discharges and transfers. He asked her how a patient could leave the hospital in the middle of the night.

"Patients are not prisoners," said Admitting. "Was the patient admitted through the ER?"

"Yes," said Philips.

"Well, that's common," said the woman. "Often ER admissions are transferred after they have been stabilized, if the private physician does not have privileges here."

Philips grunted understanding, then asked for the details concerning Lynn Anne Lucas. Since the data-processing computer used by Admissions was keyed by unit number or date of birth, the woman said she'd have to get the unit number from the ER record before she could get any information. She'd call back as soon as she could.

Martin tried to go back to dictating, but it was difficult to concentrate. Right in front of his nose were Collins' and McCarthy's hospital charts. He remembered Denise's comment about the Pap smears. What he knew about gynecology in general and Pap smears in particular was negligible. Putting on his long white coat and taking Katherine Collins' chart, Philips left his office. Passing Helen, he told her he'd be back shortly and instructed her to page him only in an emergency.

The first step was the library. Passing several outpatients in foul-weather gear, Philips decided to use the tunnel. The new medical-school building was reached by taking the same right fork that Philips used to get to his apartment. It was just beyond the stairs that led up to the old medical school, which had been abandoned two years previously when the new facilities had been completed.

The old building was supposed to have been renovated to provide sorely needed space for the burgeoning clinical departments like radiology, but owing to enormous cost overruns, money had run out when the new school neared completion. After two years even a portion of the new building was still waiting for additional funding. So the old medical-school project had been indefinitely postponed and the clinical departments had to wait.

The new school was a far cry from Philips' student experience: particularly the library. Money had been no object, which was surely the reason the old medical school lay mostly abandoned. The foyer was spacious and carpeted with two mirror-imaged, curved staircases, which swept up to the floor above.

The library's card catalogue was under the lip of the balcony that formed the mezzanine. Philips got the call number of a standard gynecology text. Although he was interested in reading about the Pap smear, or Papanicolaou Smear, he wasn't interested in an exhaustive textbook of cytology. He was already aware of the efficacy of the test; as cancer-screening procedure, it was probably the best and most reliable. He'd even performed it himself, as a student, so he knew it was extremely easy, just a light scrape of the cervical surface with a tongue depressor, then smear the material on a glass slide. What he couldn't remember was the classification of the results, and what was supposed to be done if the report came back "atypical." Unfortunately the textbook wasn't too helpful. All it said was that any suspicious cervix should be followed up with a Schiller's test, which was an iodine-staining technique of the cervix—to determine abnormal areas, or a biopsy, or colposcopy. Philips had no idea what colposcopy was and had to use the index. It turned out to be a procedure whereby a microscope-like instrument was used to examine the cervix.

The thing that surprised Philips the most was learning ten to fifteen percent of new cases of cervical cancer occurred in twenty to twenty-nine year olds. He'd had the mistaken impression that cervical cancer was a problem of an older age group. There couldn't have been any better argument in favor of the annual gynecological examination.

Martin returned the text and made his way to the university's GYN clinic. He remembered that this portion of the service had been out of bounds for medical students, which had been like dangling meat in front of hungry animals since the women were usually cute college coeds. The patients available to the medical students were the old multiparous clinic regulars, and the contrast made the college coeds all look as if they were *Playboy* centerfolds.

Philips felt distinctly out of place as he approached the receptionist. When he stopped in front of her, she batted her eyes and sucked in a deep breath to elevate her flat chest. Martin stared at her because something seemed very strange about her face. He averted his gaze when he realized it was just that her eyes were unusually close set.

"I'm Dr. Martin Philips."

"Hi, I'm Ellen Cohen."

Involuntarily Philips glanced back at Ellen Cohen's eyes. "I'd like to talk with the doctor in charge."

Ellen Cohen again fluttered her eyelids. "Dr. Harper is examining a patient at present, but he'll be out soon."

In any other department Philips probably would have walked directly back into the examining area. Instead he turned to face the waiting room, feeling as self-conscious as he remembered he'd been at age twelve waiting for his mother in a hair salon. There were half-a-dozen young women sitting staring at him. The moment they caught his eye, they turned back to their magazines.

Martin sat down in a chair immediately adjacent to the receptionist's desk. Stealthily Ellen Cohen slid her paperback novel off the desk and dropped it into one of her drawers. When Philips happened to glance in her direction, she smiled.

Philips let his mind drift back to Goldblatt. The nerve of the man to think that he had the right to dictate Philips' personal life, or even his research, was astounding. Perhaps if the department funded Philips' research there might be some justification, but it didn't. Radiology's contribution was Martin's time. Funding that had been needed for hardware and programming fees, which had been considerable, came from sources available through Michaels' Department of Computer Science.

Suddenly Martin realized that a patient had approached the receptionist and was asking the meaning of an atypical Pap smear. She seemed to speak with effort, and she leaned weakly on the receptionist's desk.

"That, dearie," said Ellen Cohen, "is something you'll have to ask Ms. Blackman about." The receptionist immediately sensed Philips' attention. "I'm not a doctor," she laughed, mostly for his benefit. "Sit down. Ms. Blackman will be out shortly."

Kristin Lindquist had had all the frustration she could deal with that day.

"I was told that I'd be seen immediately," she said, and went on to tell the receptionist that she'd experienced a headache, dizziness, and changes in her vision that morning, so that she really could not wait like she had the day before. "Please tell Ms. Blackman right away that I'm here. She'd phoned me and promised there would be no delay."

Kristin turned and made her way over to a chair across from Philips. She moved slowly, like a person unsure of her balance.

Ellen Cohen rolled her eyes when she caught Philips', suggesting that the girl was unreasonably demanding, but she did get up to find the nurse. Martin turned to look at Kristin. His mind was busy making associations between atypical Pap smears and vague neurological symptoms. Kristin had closed her eyes so Philips could look at her without making her feel self-conscious. He guessed she was about twenty. Quickly Philips opened Katherine Collins' chart and rapidly flipped through the pages until he'd found the initial neurological note. Headache, dizziness, and visual symptoms were described as the presenting complaints.

He looked back at Kristin Lindquist. Could this woman in front of him be another case with the same radiological picture? Philips felt it was possible. With all the difficulties he'd encountered trying to get more X rays on the other patients, the idea of finding a new case was enormously seductive. He could take all the proper X rays right from the beginning.

Needing no more encouragement, he walked over and tapped Kristin on the shoulder. She jumped in surprise and brushed a wisp of blond hair from her face. The fear in her expression gave her a particularly vulnerable appearance and Martin suddenly became aware of the girl's beauty.

Choosing his words carefully, Martin introduced himself, saying he was from the Department of Radiology, and that he'd overheard her describe her symptoms to the receptionist. He told her that he had seen

X rays on four girls with similar problems and felt it might be to her advantage to have an X ray. He was careful to emphasize that it was purely precautionary and that she should not be alarmed.

For Kristin, the hospital was full of surprises. On her first visit the day before she'd been kept waiting for hours. Now she was confronted by a doctor who was apparently soliciting patients.

"I'm not very fond of hospitals," she said. She wanted to add doctors, but it seemed too disrespectful.

"To tell you the truth, I feel the same way," said Philips. He smiled. He'd taken an immediate liking to this attractive young woman and he felt protective. "But an X ray wouldn't take long."

"I still feel ill and I think it would be best if I get home as quickly as possible."

"It will be quick," said Philips. "I can promise you that. One film. I'll take you over myself."

Kristin hesitated. On the one hand she detested the hospital. On the other hand she still felt ill and she was susceptible to Philips' concern.

"How about it?" he said persistently.

"All right," said Kristin finally.

"Wonderful. How long will you be here at the clinic?"

"I don't know. They said not long."

"Good. Don't leave without me," said Martin.

Within minutes Kristin was called. Almost simultaneously another door opened and Dr. Harper emerged.

Philips recognized Harper as one of the residents he'd seen on occasion in and around the hospital. He'd never met the man but his polished head was hard to forget. Philips got up and introduced himself.

There was an awkward pause. As a resident, Harper did not have an office and since both examining rooms were occupied, there was no place to talk. They ended up in the narrow corridor.

"What can I do for you?" asked Harper, somewhat suspiciously. It was bizarre for the Assistant Director of Neuroradiology to be visiting Gynecology, since their interests and expertise lay at opposite ends of the medical spectrum.

Philips began his questioning in rather vague terms, expressing an interest in the way the clinic was manned, how long Harper had been there, and whether he enjoyed it. Harper's responses were abrupt and his small eyes darted over Philips' face as he explained that the university's clinic was a two-month elective rotation for a senior resident, adding that it had become a symbolic stepping-stone for being asked to join the staff following completion of the residency.

"Look," Harper said after a pause, "I've got a lot of patients to see." Martin realized that instead of making the man relax, his questions were making him more ill-at-ease.

"Just one more thing," said Philips. "When a Pap smear is reported as atypical, what's usually done?"

"That depends," said Harper warily. "There're two categories of atypical cells. One is atypical but not suggestive of tumor, whereas the other is atypical and suggestive of tumor."

"Whether it's in either class, shouldn't something be done? I mean, if it's not normal, it should be followed up. Isn't that right?"

"Yeah," said Harper evasively. "Why are you asking me these questions?" He had the distinct feeling he was being backed into a corner.

"Just out of interest," said Martin. He held up Collins' chart. "I've come across several patients who'd had atypical Pap smears in this clinic. But reading the GYN notes, I can't find any reference to Schiller's test, thoughts about a biopsy, or colposcopy . . . just repeat smears. Isn't that . . . irregular?" Philips eyed Harper, sensing his discomfort. "Look, I'm not here casting any blame. I'm just interested."

"I couldn't say anything unless I saw the chart," said Harper. He'd intended the comment to end the conversation.

Philips handed Collins' chart to Harper and watched as the resident opened it. When Harper read the name, "Katherine Collins," his face became tense. Martin watched curiously as the man rapidly flipped through the chart, too quickly to read anything adequately. When he got to the end, he looked up and handed it back.

"I don't know what to say."

"It is irregular, isn't it?" asked Martin.

"Put it this way: It's not the way I'd handle it. But I've got to get back to work now. Excuse me." He pushed past Philips, who had to press up against the wall to give him room to go by.

Surprised at the precipitous end to the conversation, Martin watched the resident hurry into one of the examining rooms. Philips had not intended his questions to be taken personally and he wondered if he had sounded more accusatory than he realized. Still the resident's response when he had opened Katherine Collins' chart had been strange. Philips had no doubt about that.

Believing there was no point in trying to talk further with Harper, Martin went back out to the receptionist and inquired after Kristin Lindquist. Ellen

Cohen at first acted as if she hadn't heard the question. When Philips repeated it, she snapped that Miss Lindquist was with the nurse and would be out shortly. Having not liked Kristin initially, the receptionist hated her even more now that Philips seemed interested in her. Unaware of Ellen Cohen's jealousies, Martin just felt incredibly confused about the university's GYN clinic.

A few minutes later, Kristin came out of the examining room, aided by a nurse. Martin had seen the nurse before, probably in the cafeteria, remembering her thick black hair, which she wore piled on her head in a tight bun.

He stood up as the woman approached the desk and heard the nurse instruct the receptionist to give Kristin an appointment in four days. Kristin looked very pale.

"Miss Lindquist," Martin called. "Are you finished?"

"I think so," said Kristin.

"How about that X ray?" asked Philips. "Do you feel up to it?"

"I think so," managed Kristin, again.

Suddenly the black-haired nurse strode back to the desk. "If you don't mind my asking, what kind of X ray are you talking about?"

"A lateral skull film," said Martin.

"I see," said the nurse. "The reason I ask is that Kristin has had an abnormal Pap test and we'd prefer she avoid abdominal or pelvic films until her Pap smear status is normal."

"No problem," said Philips. "In my department we're only interested in the head." He'd never heard of such an association between Pap smears and diagnostic X rays, but it sounded reasonable.

The nurse nodded, then left. Ellen Cohen slapped

an appointment card in Kristin's waiting hand before turning and pretending to busy herself with her typewriter. "California slut," she muttered under her breath.

Martin guided Kristin away from the bustle of the clinic and led her through a connecting door into the hospital proper. Once the fire door had been passed, the scene looked very pleasant in contrast to the clinic. Kristin was surprised.

"These are private offices for some of the surgeons," explained Philips as they walked down a long carpeted hall. There were even oil paintings on the freshly painted walls.

"I thought the whole hospital was old and decayed," said Kristin.

"Hardly." An image of the subterranean morgue flashed through Philips' mind, immediately merging with his recent vision of the GYN clinic. "Tell me, Kristin, as a patient, how do you find the university's clinic?"

"That's a difficult question," said Kristin. "I hate gynecology appointments so much that I don't think I can give a fair answer."

"How does it compare with your past experience?"

"Well, it is terribly impersonal, at least it was yesterday when I saw the doctor. But today I only saw the nurse and it was better. But then again I didn't have to wait today like I did yesterday, and all they did was draw more blood and recheck my vision. I didn't have another exam. Thank God."

They reached the elevator area and Philips pressed the button.

"Ms. Blackman also had the time to explain my Pap smear. Apparently it wasn't bad. She said it was only Type II, which is common and almost reverts to normal spontaneously. She told me it was probably caused by cervical erosion and that I should use a weak douche and avoid sex."

Martin was momentarily nonplussed at Kristin's forthrightness. Like most physicians, he was surprisingly unaware that his being a doctor encouraged people to make their secrets accessible.

Arriving in X-ray, Philips sought out Kenneth Robbins and put Kristin in his hands for the single lateral skull film he wanted. Since it was after four, the department was relatively quiet and one of the main X-ray rooms was empty. Robbins took the X ray and disappeared into the darkroom to load the film into the automatic developer. While Kristin waited, Martin stationed himself at the slot in the main hall where the film would emerge.

"You look like a cat watching a mouse hole," said Denise. She'd come up behind Philips and surprised him.

"I feel like one. Down in GYN I found a patient with similar symptoms to Marino and the others and I'm holding my breath to see if there's the same radiological picture. How did your angiograms go this afternoon?"

"Very well, thank you. I appreciate your letting me work on my own."

"Don't thank me. You earned it."

At that moment the tip of Kristin's X ray appeared, then oozed out of the roller, dropping into the holding bin. Martin snatched it up and put it on the viewer. His finger scanned back and forth in an area approximately over Kristin's ear.

"Damn," said Philips. "It's clear."

"Oh come on!" protested Denise. "Don't tell me you actually want the patient to have the pathology."

"You're right," said Martin. "I don't mean to wish it on anyone. I just want a case that I can X-ray properly."

Robbins stepped out of the darkroom. "You want any more films, Dr. Philips?"

Martin shook his head, took the X ray and walked into the room where Kristin was waiting. Denise followed.

"Good news," said Philips, waving the film. "Your X ray is normal." Then he told Kristin that perhaps they should repeat it in a week if her symptoms persisted. He asked her for her phone number and gave her his direct-dial number in case she had any questions.

Kristin thanked him and tried to stand. Immediately she had to support herself by grabbing the X ray table as a wave of dizziness hit her. The room seemed to spin in a clockwise direction.

"Are you all right?" Martin asked, holding her arm.

"I think so," said Kristin, blinking. "It was that same dizziness. But it's already gone." What she didn't say was that she again smelled the familiar obnoxious odor. It was too bizarre a symptom for her to share. "I'll be all right. I think I'd better get home."

Philips offered to get her a taxi but she insisted she was all right. As the elevator door closed she waved and even managed a smile.

"That was a very clever way to get an attractive young woman's phone number," said Denise, as she walked back to Philips' office. Rounding the corner, Martin was relieved when he saw that Helen had left. Denise took one look in his room and gasped in disbelief. "What the hell?"

"Don't say anything," said Philips, making his way through the debris to his desk. "My life is disintegrating and smart comments are not going to help."

He picked up the messages Helen had left. As he had expected, there were calls marked important from Goldblatt and Drake. After staring at them for a minute, he allowed the two pieces of paper to waft in a gentle spiral into his large institutional wastebasket.

Then he turned on the computer and fed in Kristin's skull film.

"Well! How's it going?" said Michaels, appearing at the doorway. He could tell from the litter that little had changed since the morning visit.

"Depends on what you're referring to," said Philips. "If you mean the program, the answer is fine. I've only run a few films, but so far it is performing with an accuracy of about a hundred-ten percent."

"Wonderful," said Michaels, clapping his hands.

"It's more than wonderful," said Philips. "It's fantastic! It's the only thing around here that has been going right. I'm just sorry I haven't had more time to work on it. Unfortunately, I'm behind on my regular work. But I'm going to stay here for a while tonight and run as many films as I can." Philips saw Denise turn and look at him. He tried to read her expression but the noisy clatter of the typewriter rapidly spewing out the report captured his attention. Michaels saw what was happening and he came up behind Philips to look over his shoulder. From Denise's perspective, the two of them looked like proud parents.

"It's reading a skull film I just took on a young woman," Martin said. "Her name is Kristin Lindquist. I thought maybe she'd have the same abnormality as those other patients I described to you. But she doesn't."

"Why are you so committed to this one abnormality?" asked Michaels. "Personally, I'd rather see you spending your time on the program itself. There will be time for this kind of investigative fun later."

"You don't know doctors," said Martin. "When we release this little computer on the unsuspecting medical community it's going to be like confronting the Medieval Catholic Church with Copernican astronomy. If we could present a new radiological sign that the program had discovered, it would make acceptance much easier."

When the print-out typewriter paused, Philips tore off the report. His eyes scanned the sheet rapidly, then riveted on one central paragraph. "I don't believe it." Martin grabbed the film and put it back up on his viewer.

With his hands blocking out most of the X ray, Philips isolated a small area at the back of the skull. "There it is! My God! I knew the patient had the same symptoms. The program remembered the other cases and was able to find this very small example of the same abnormality."

"And we thought it was subtle on the other films," said Denise looking over Philips' shoulder. "This just involves the tip of the occipital pole, not the parietal or temporal region."

"Maybe it's just earlier in the progress of the disease," suggested Philips.

"What disease?" asked Michaels.

"We don't know for certain," said Martin, "but several of the patients who showed this same density abnormality were suspected of multiple sclerosis. It's a shot in the dark."

"I don't see a thing," admitted Michaels. He put his face very close to the X ray, but it was no use.

"It's a textural quality," said Martin. "You have to be aware of what the normal texture is before you can appreciate the difference. Believe me, it's there. The program is not making it up. Tomorrow I'll get the patient back and cone down right over the area. Maybe with some better films you'll be able to see it."

Michaels admitted that his appreciation of the abnormality was not critical. After turning down an offer of dinner in the hospital cafeteria, Michaels excused himself. At the door he again begged Martin to spend more time running old films through the computer, saying there was a good chance the program would pick up all sorts of new radiologic signs, and if Philips took time to follow up each one, the program would never get debugged. With a final wave, Michaels departed.

"He's eager, isn't he," said Denise.

"With good reason," said Martin. "He told me today that to handle the program they have designed a newer processor that has a more efficient memory. Apparently it's going to be ready shortly. When it is, I'll be the only one holding them up."

"So you're planning to work tonight?" asked Denise.

"Of course." Martin looked at her and for the first time noticed how tired she was. She'd gotten almost no sleep the night before and had worked all day.

"I was hoping you'd be interested in coming over to my apartment for a little dinner and perhaps finish what we had started last night."

She was being deliberately erotic and Martin was an easy target. Sexual expression would be a wonderful way to deal with the frustrations and exasperations of the day. But he knew he had to do some work and Denise was too important to just be used as he had the nurses when he was an intern needing to diffuse his tension.

"I've got to catch up a little," he said at last. "Why

don't you go home early. I'll call and perhaps come over later."

But Denise insisted on waiting while he went over all the angiograms and the day's CAT scans, which had been dictated by the neuroradiology fellows. Even if his name did not appear on the reports, Philips checked everything done in the department.

It was a quarter to seven when they scraped back their chairs and stood up to stretch. Martin turned to look at Denise, but she hid her face.

"What's the matter?"

"I just don't like you to see me when I look so awful."

Shaking his head in disbelief, he reached out and tried to lift her chin, but she shook off his hand. It was amazing how within seconds of switching off the viewer she had changed from an engrossed academician to a sensitive woman. As far as Martin was concerned she appeared tired but as appealing as ever. He tried to tell her, but she wouldn't believe it. She kissed him quickly, then said she was going home for a long bath, and that she hoped to see him later. Like a bird in flight, she left.

It took Martin a few moments to collect himself. Denise had the power to short-circuit his brain. He was in love and he knew it. Getting out Kristin's telephone number he dialed, but there was no answer. He decided to take a file of correspondence to proofread while he ate dinner in the cafeteria.

It was nine-fifteen when Martin cleared up the last of the dictation and correspondence. During the same time he had been able to run twenty-five more old films through the flawlessly functioning computer. Meanwhile Randy Jacobs was making frequent trips back and forth from the file room. He'd been returning the completed envelopes, but since he'd pulled several hundred additional ones, Philips' office was even more jumbled and disorganized than before.

Using the phone at his desk, Philips again tried Kristin's number. She answered on the second ring.

"I'm a little embarrassed," he said, "but looking at your X ray more closely, I think there is a very small area that needs closer examination. I was hoping you'd be willing to come back, like tomorrow morning?"

"Not in the morning," said Kristin. "I've missed classes two days in a row. I'd rather not miss more."

They agreed on three-thirty. Martin assured her that she would not have to wait. When she arrived she was supposed to come directly to Philips' office.

Hanging up, Martin leaned back in his chair and let the day's problems wash over him. The conversations with Mannerheim and Drake were exasperating, but at least they were consistent with the personalities of the two men. The conversation with Goldblatt was different. Philips had not expected such an attack from someone who had been his mentor. Martin was quite sure that Goldblatt had been responsible for his being named Assistant Chief of Neuroradiology four years ago. So it didn't make sense. If hostility to the computer work was behind Goldblatt's conduct, they were in for more trouble than either Philips or Michaels had anticipated. The thought made Martin sit up and search for the list he'd made of the patients with the potentially new radiologic sign. Corroboration of the new diagnostic technique had assumed greater importance. He found the list and added Kristin Lindquist's name.

Even allowing for Goldblatt's dislike of the new computer unit, his behavior still did not make sense.

It suggested collusion with Mannerheim and Drake, and for Goldblatt to be siding with Mannerheim, if that were the case, something out of the ordinary had to be going on. Something very bizarre.

Philips sat up and snatched his list: Marino, Lucas, Collins, McCarthy and Lindquist. After McCarthy he had written "Neurosurgical lab." If Mannerheim could be devious, so could he. Philips walked out of his dim office into the brightness of the corridor. Toward the fluoroscopy rooms he saw what he was looking for: the cleaning carts of the janitorial staff.

Having accustomed himself to working long hours, Martin had had numerous opportunities to become acquainted with the cleaning crew. On several occasions they had cleaned his office with him in it, joking that he secretly lived under his desk. It was an interesting group composed of two men in their middle twenties, one white and one black, and two older women, one Puerto Rican, the other Irish. Philips wanted to speak to the Irish woman. She'd worked for the center for fourteen years and was their nominal supervisor.

Philips found the crew inside one of the fluoroscopy rooms having their coffee break. "Listen, Dearie," said Martin to the woman. Dearie was her nickname, because it was how she addressed everyone else. "Can you get into the Neurosurgical Research lab?"

"I can get into everything in this hospital except the narcotics cabinets," said Dearie proudly.

"Wonderful," said Martin. "I'm going to make you an offer you can't refuse." He went on to say that he wanted to borrow her passkey for fifteen minutes to get a specimen from the Neurosurgical lab which he wanted to X-ray. In return she could have a free CAT scan!

It dook Dearie a full minute to stop laughing. "I'm not supposed to give this out, but considering who you are. . . . Just have it back before we leave Radiology. That gives you twenty minutes."

Philips used the tunnel to get to the Watson Research Building. The elevator was waiting in the deserted lobby and he got right in and pressed his floor. Although Martin was in the middle of a busy medical center within a populous and sprawling city, he felt isolated and alone. Research was done between eight and five, and the building was vacant. The only sound was the wind hissing in the elevator shaft as the car sped upward.

The doors opened and he stepped out into a poorly illuminated foyer. Passing through a fire door he found himself in a long hallway that ran the length of the building. To conserve energy nearly all the lights were out. Dearie hadn't given him a key, she'd given him her whole brass ring of keys and it jangled in the silence of the empty building.

The Neurosurgical lab was the third door on the left, close to the other end of the corridor, and as Martin got closer, he felt himself tense. The door to the lab was metal with a central frosted pane of glass. After glancing over his shoulder, he slipped the passkey into the lock. The door swung open. Philips quickly stepped in and closed the door. He tried to laugh at his own sense of suspense, but it didn't do any good. His nervousness had increased out of proportion to what he was doing. He decided he'd make a lousy burglar.

The light switch made an inordinately loud snap when he turned it on. Banks of fluorescent light bathed the huge lab. Two central counter tops ran down half of the room, complete with sinks, gas jets, and overlying shelves of laboratory glassware. At the far end was an animal surgical area, which looked like a modern operating room in three-quarter size. It had operating lights, a small operating table, and even an anesthesia machine. There was no separation between the operating area and the lab except that the operating area was tiled. All in all it was an impressive setup and stood as tribute to Mannerheim's ability to obtain research grants.

Philips had no idea where a brain specimen would be stored, but he thought there might be a collection, so he only looked in the larger cabinets. He drew a blank but noticed there was another door down near the surgical area. It had a clear glass panel with embedded wire mesh and he leaned against the window, peering into a dark room beyond. Just beyond the door he could see a series of bookshelves containing glass jars; a whole group of which held brains immersed in preserving fluid.

With every second that passed Martin's anxiety continued to increase. The moment he saw the brains, he wanted to find McCarthy's and leave. He pushed open the door and began quickly scanning the labels. A strong animal smell assaulted his nose and in the darkness to the left he caught a glimpse of cages. But the jars held his interest; each was labeled with a name, a unit number and a date. Guessing that the date was the death of the patient, Philips walked quickly down the long row of jars. Since the only light was that which came through the glass panel in the door, he had to lean closer to the jars with each step. McCarthy's was at the very far end of the room near an exit door.

Reaching up to grasp the specimen, Philips was devastated by a bloodcurdling scream that reverberated around the small room. It was immediately followed by a crash of metal against metal. Philips' legs buckled as he spun around to defend himself, his shoulder hitting the wall. Another scream shattered the air, but an attack did not materialize. Instead Martin found himself staring into the face of a caged monkey. The animal was in an absolute rage. His eyes were burning black coals. His lips were drawn back exposing his teeth, two of which had broken when he had tried to bite through the steel bars of his prison. From the top of the monkey's head protruded a group of electrodes like multicolored spaghetti.

Philips realized he was looking at one of the animals Mannerheim and his boys had turned into a screaming monster. It was well known in the Med Center that Mannerheim's latest interest was finding the exact location in the brain associated with rage reaction. The fact that other researchers felt that there was not one single center had not deterred Mannerheim at all.

As Philips' eyes adjusted to the dim light, he could see many cages. Each contained a monkey with all varieties of head mutilation. Some had the entire back of their skulls replaced by Plexiglas hemispheres through which passed hundreds of embedded electrodes. A few were docile as if they had been lobotomized.

Philips pushed himself back to a standing position. Keeping an eye on the raging animal who continued to scream and noisily shake his cage, Philips lifted the jar containing McCarthy's partially dissected brain. Behind it was a group of slides bound by a rubber band. Philips took those as well. He started to leave when he heard the outer door of the lab open and close, followed by muffled noises.

Martin panicked. Balancing the jar, the slides, and the ring of keys, he opened the back door of the animal room. In front of him the fire stairs plunged down in an endless series of retreating angles. Philips paused at the top stair and realized that fleeing was not the answer. Catching the door before it clicked shut, he returned to the lab.

"Doc Philips," said a startled security man. His name was Peter Chobanian. He was on the Med Center's intermural basketball team and had had several late-night conversations with Philips. "What are you doing up here?"

"Needed a snack," said Martin with a straight face. He held up the specimen jar.

"Ahhh," said Chobanian, looking away. "Before I worked here I thought only psychiatrists were nuts!"

"Seriously," said Philips, walking ahead on rubbery legs. "I'm going to X-ray this specimen. I was supposed to pick it up today but didn't . . ." He nodded to the other security man whom he didn't know.

"You oughtta let us know when you're coming up here," said Chobanian. "Some of the microscopes have been walking outta this building and we're trying to tighten up."

Philips got one of the evening radiology technicians to come over to Neuroradiology between ER trauma cases to offer an opinion. Philips had tried unsuccessfully to take an X ray of McCarthy's partially dissected brain, which he had put on a paper plate. No matter what Philips did, the X rays were bad. On all the films it was difficult to make out the internal structure. He'd tried reducing the kilovoltage, but it didn't help. The technician took one look at the brain and turned green. After he left, Martin finally decided what the problem was. Even though the brain had been in formaldehyde, the internal structure must have decomposed enough to blur any radiological definition. Plopping the brain back into its jar, Philips took it and the pack of slides up to Pathology.

The lab wasn't locked up but it was deserted. If someone wanted to steal microscopes, this is where they should come, thought Philips. He opened the door to the autopsy room. No one there either. Walking down the long central table supporting a whole line of microscopes, each with its dictation unit next to it, Philips remembered the first time he had looked at his own blood. He recalled his terror that the slide would be leukemic. Medical school had been a time for imaginary diseases and Martin had contracted almost all of them.

Toward the back of the room he found a Bunsen burner busily boiling a beaker of water. Putting down the jar and the slides, he waited. It wasn't long. A grossly overweight pathology resident waddled in. He wasn't expecting company because he was zipping his fly as he came through the door. His name was Benjamin Barnes.

Philips introduced himself and asked if Barnes would do him a favor.

"What kind of favor? I'm trying to get this autopsy done so I can get my ass out of here."

"I've got a few slides. I wonder if you would take a quick look at them?"

"There's plenty of scopes here. Why don't you help yourself?"

It was a presumptuous way to treat a staff man even if he was from another department, but Martin forced himself to suppress his irritation. "It's been a few years," he said, "Besides, it's a brain and I was never good at brain."

"It would be better to wait for Neuropath in the morning," said Barnes.

"I'm interested in a quick impression now," Martin said.

Philips had never found fat people to be jolly, and the pathologist was confirming his impression.

Barnes reluctantly took the slides and placed one under the scope. He scanned around, then put in another. It took about ten minutes to go through the group.

"Interesting," he said. "Here, take a look at this." He moved aside so Philips could see.

"See that open area?" asked Barnes.

"Yeah."

"Used to be a nerve cell there."

Philips looked at Barnes.

"All these slides with the red-grease-pencil marks have areas where the neurons are either missing or in bad shape," said the resident. "The curious thing is that there's very little if any inflammation. I don't have any idea what it is. I'd have to describe it as 'multifocal, discrete neuron death,' etiology unknown."

"You don't even want to guess the cause?" asked Philips.

"Nope."

"What about multiple sclerosis?" asked Philips.

The resident made a strange face, wrinkling his forehead. "Maybe. Occasionally there's some gray matter lesions in multiple sclerosis, even though the lesions usually are all white matter. But they don't look like this. There'd be more inflammation. But to be sure I'd have to do a myelin stain."

"How about calcium?" asked Philips. Philips knew there weren't too many things that affected X-ray density, but calcium was one of them.

"I didn't see anything that suggested calcium. Again, I'd have to do a stain."

"One other thing," said Philips. "I'd like to have some slides made from the occipital lobe." He patted the top of the glass jar.

"I thought you only wanted me to look at the slides," said Barnes.

"That's right. I don't want you to look at the brain, just section it." Martin had had a bad day and he wasn't in a mood to deal with a lazy pathology resident.

Barnes had sense enough not to say anything else. He picked up the glass jar and waddled into the autopsy room. Philips followed. With a scoop, Barnes took the brain out of the formaldehyde and put it on the stainless steel counter next to the sink. Brandishing one of the large autopsy knives, he allowed Philips to point to the area he wanted. Barnes then took several half-inch slices and put them in paraffin.

"The sections will be done tomorrow. What kind of stains do you want?"

"Everything you can think of," said Philips. "And one last thing. Do you know the diener who works nights down in the morgue?"

"You mean Werner?"

Philips nodded.

"Vaguely. He's a little weird but he's reliable and a good worker. He's been there for years."

"Do you think he's on the take?"

"I don't have any idea. What could he be on the take for?"

"Anything. Pituitary glands for growth hormone; gold teeth; special favors."

"I don't know. But I guess it wouldn't surprise me."

After the unsettling experience in the Neurosurgical lab, Philips felt particularly ill-at-ease as he followed the red line toward the morgue in the subbasement. The huge, dark, cavern-like room outside of the morgue looked like the perfect setting for some gothic horror. The quartz window in the door of the incinerator glowed in the darkness like the eye of a cyclopean monster.

"For God's sakes, Martin. What the hell is wrong with you?" said Philips, trying to fortify his waning confidence. The morgue looked exactly as it had the evening before. The bulbless hooded light fixtures hanging down on their wires gave the scene a weird unearthliness. There was a faint odor of decay. The door to the refrigerator was ajar and a bit of its interior light spilled out along with a current of cold mist.

"Werner!" called Philips. His voice echoed in the old tiled room. There was no response. Philips stepped into the room and the door closed insistently behind him. "Werner!" The silence was only broken by a dripping faucet. Tentatively Philips advanced to the refrigerator and glanced within. Werner was struggling with one of the corpses. It had apparently fallen from its gurney because Werner was lifting the naked, stiff cadaver and awkwardly trying to reposition it on the movable stretcher. He could have used some help but Philips stayed where he was and watched. When Werner succeeded in getting the body onto the gurney, Martin stepped into the refrigerator.

"Werner!" Martin's voice sounded wooden.

The diener flexed his knees and lifted his hands like a jungle creature about to attack. Philips had startled the man.

"I want to talk to you," said Philips. He had decided to be authoritative, but his voice sounded weak. Surrounded by the dead, his defenses dissolved. "I understand your position and I don't want to cause any trouble, but I need some information."

Recognizing Philips, Werner relaxed, but he didn't move. His breath came in short puffs of condensed vapor.

"I have to find Lisa Marino's brain. I don't care who took it or for what reason. I just want a chance to look at it for a research project."

Werner was like a statue. Except for his visible breaths he was like one of the dead.

"Look," said Martin. "I'll pay." He had never bribed anyone in his life.

"How much?" said Werner.

"A hundred dollars," said Philips.

"I don't know anything about Marino's brain."

Philips looked at the frozen features of the man. Under the circumstances he felt impotent. "Well, give me a call in X ray if you suddenly remember." He turned and walked out, but in the corridor he found himself running to the bank of elevators.

Entering the outer foyer of Denise's apartment building, Philips scanned the nameplates. He knew approximately where hers was, but there were so many, that he always had to search a little. After pushing the black button he waited with his hand on the front doorknob for the buzzer to let him in.

Inside the building it smelled as if everyone had

sautéed onions for their dinner. Philips started up the stairs. There was an elevator, but if it wasn't already waiting in the lobby it took too long to arrive. Denise only lived on the third floor and Philips didn't mind climbing the stairs. But on the last flight, he began to realize how tired he was. It had been a long grueling day.

Denise had again metamorphosed. She no longer looked tired and she said she'd taken a short nap after her bath. Her shining hair had been released from its barrette and cascaded from her head in gentle waves. She was dressed in a pink satin camisole with matching tap pants that left just the right amount to the imagination. Some of Martin's fatigue lifted. He was always amazed by her ability to drop her efficient hospital personality, though he understood that she was confident enough in her intellectual abilities that she could indulge her feminine fantasies. It was a rare and wonderful balance.

They embraced at the door, and then without speaking they walked arm in arm into the bedroom. Martin pulled her down onto the bed. At first she just acquiesced, enjoying his eagerness, but then she joined, her passion matching his until they both spent themselves in mutual fulfillment.

For some time they lay together, just enjoying the closeness and wishing to retain in their minds the pleasure they gave to each other. Finally Martin propped himself up on an elbow so he could trace his finger down her finely crafted nose and across her lips.

"I think this relationship is getting entirely out of hand," he said, smiling.

"I agree."

"I've shown symptoms for a couple of weeks, but

it's only been over the last two days that I'm sure of the diagnosis. I'm in love with you, Denise."

For Denise the word had never had more meaning. Martin had not mentioned love before, even when he told her how much he cared for her.

They kissed lightly. The words hadn't been necessary but they added a new dimension of closeness.

"Admitting my love for you," said Martin after a few moments, "scares me in one way. Medicine destroyed my previous relationship and I worry it could do it again."

"I don't think so."

"I do. It has a way of holding one hostage by ever increasing demands."

"But I understand those demands."

"I'm not so sure you do. Not yet," said Martin. He was aware the comment sounded condescending but he knew at this point in Sanger's career it would be impossible to convince her that running a department made day-to-day medicine as much of a rat race as most other businesses. Besides, Goldblatt's challenge to their relationship was very much in Philips' mind, so the worry was not hypothetical.

"I think I understand more than you think," said Denise. "I think you've changed since your divorce. Back then I think you had a kind of macho belief you could get most of your fulfillment from your career. Now I think that's changed. I believe you realize that the greater part of your satisfaction is going to come from your own interpersonal relationships."

There was a silence. Martin was stunned at his transparency as well as Denise's clairvoyance. Denise broke the silence. "The only thing I can't understand is if you're interested in having more of a life outside the hospital, why not ease up on your research?"

"Because it can be the key to my freedom," said Martin holding her close. "You have become my promise for fulfillment and research has the power of giving me what I want from medicine as well as more time with you."

They kissed, secure in their newly expressed affection for each other. But as they lay there in each other's arms, they began to feel their fatigue and knew they should go to sleep.

Denise went to brush her teeth, while Martin let his mind drift back to Lynn Anne's mysterious disappearance. Glancing at the closed bathroom door, he decided to make a quick call to the hospital, reminding the nurse Lynn Anne had been admitted through the ER, then immediately transferred. The nurse recalled the case because the transfer had come right after she'd finished all the admission paper work. Martin asked if she remembered where the patient had been sent, but the nurse said she did not. Philips thanked her and hung up.

In bed he curled up against Denise's back, but had trouble falling asleep. He began telling her about his disturbing experience with the monkeys with the electrodes in their heads, and asked if she thought the information Mannerheim obtained was worth the sacrifice. Denise, on the verge of sleep, just grunted, but Martin's overstimulated mind jumped back to his visit to the university's GYN clinic.

"Hey, have you ever been to the GYN clinic in the hospital?" He pushed himself up on his elbow rolling Denise over on her back. The movement awakened her.

"No. I haven't."

"I visited there today and the place gave me a strange feeling."

"What do you mean?"

"I don't know. It's hard to say, but then again I haven't been in too many GYN clinics."

"They're really fun," said Denise sarcastically, and turned back on her side away from Martin.

"Would you do me a favor and check it out?"

"You mean as a patient?"

"I don't care. I'd like to know your opinion about the personnel."

"Well I'm a bit late on my annual checkup. I suppose I could have it done there. In fact, I'll call tomorrow."

"Thanks," said Martin, finally settling himself to sleep.

10

It was after seven when Denise woke up and grabbed for the clock. She was horrified at the time. Being so accustomed to Martin getting up before six, she didn't set the alarm when he slept over. Throwing back the covers, she dashed into the bathroom to jump into the shower. Philips opened his eyes in time to catch her bare back heading down the hallway. It was a wonderful image to start the day.

Oversleeping had been Philips' deliberate gesture of defiance to his old life, and he stretched luxuriously in the warm bed. He thought about going back to sleep but then decided showering with Denise was a better idea.

In the bathroom, he found she was almost finished and in no mood to kid around. Entering the shower stall he got in her way and she petulantly reminded him that she had to present the X rays at the CPC at 8:00 A.M.

"Why don't we make love again?" crooned Martin. "I'll give you a doctor's excuse for being late."

Denise draped her wet washcloth over Martin's head, and stepped out onto the bath mat. While she dried herself she spoke to Philips over the sound of the water. "If you finish at a decent hour, I'll make some dinner tonight."

"I'm not accepting any bribes," shouted Martin. "I'm going to see what Pathology says about my sections on McCarthy's brain, and I'm hoping to take some polytomes and a CAT scan on Kristin Lindquist. Besides, I've got to run a bunch of old skull films through the computer. Today research is going to get top billing."

"I think you're stubborn," said Denise.

"Compulsive," said Martin.

"When do you want me to go to the GYN clinic?"

"As soon as possible."

"Okay. I'll make it for tomorrow."

While Sanger used the hair dryer, conversation was impossible. Philips got out of the shower and shaved with one of her disposable razors. The two of them had to do a complicated dance in the confines of the small bathroom.

As Denise leaned close to the mirror to put on her eye makeup she asked, "What do you think is causing the density variation on those X rays?"

"I really don't know," said Philips, trying to tame his thick blond hair. "That's why I've got the section in Pathology."

Denise leaned back to assay her efforts. "It seems that answering that question would be the first step rather than associating the abnormality with a specific disease like multiple sclerosis."

"You're right," said Philips. "The multiple sclerosis idea originated from the charts. It was a stab in the dark. But you know something? You've just given me another idea."

Philips entered the old medical-school building from the tunnel. The entrance from the street had long since been sealed off. As he climbed the stairs to the lobby, he felt a surprising sentimentality for that time in his life when the future held nothing but promise. When he reached the familiar dark wood doors with the worn red leather panels, he paused. The carefully lettered sign saying MEDICAL SCHOOL had been desecrated by a crude board nailed haphazardly across it. Below, held in place with thumbtacks, was a cardboard sign which read, "Medical School located in the Burger Building."

Beyond the venerable old doors, the decor deteriorated. The old foyer had been demolished, its oak wainscoting sold at auction. The renovation funds had dried up even before the demolition had been completed.

Martin followed a path cleared of debris that ran around what had been an information booth, and started up the curved staircase. Looking down the length of the foyer he could see the barred entrance from the street. The doors had been chained together.

Philips' destination was the Barrow Amphitheatre. When he arrived he noticed a new sign that read DE-PARTMENT OF COMPUTER SCIENCE: DIVISION OF ARTIFI-CIAL INTELLIGENCE. Philips opened the door and, walking up to the iron piping that formed the railing, looked down into the semi-circular auditorium. The seats had been removed. Arranged in intervals on the various tiers were all sorts of components. Down in the pit were two large units constructed similarly to the small processor that had been brought to Philips' office. A young man in a short-sleeved white coat was working on one of them. He had a soldering gun in one hand and wire in the other.

"Can I help you?" he shouted.

"I'm looking for William Michaels," yelled Philips.

"He's not here yet." The man put down his tools and worked his way up toward Philips. "Would you like to leave a message?"

"Just tell Mr. Michaels to give Dr. Philips a call."

"You're Dr. Philips. Nice to meet you. I'm Carl Rudman, one of Mr. Michaels' graduate students." Rudman stuck his hand out through the railing. Philips grasped it, looking out over the impressive equipment.

"Quite a setup you have down here." Martin had never visited the computer lab before and had not imagined that it was so extensive. "It gives me a strange feeling to be in this room," he admitted. "I went to med school here and back in sixty-one, I took microbiology in this amphitheater."

"Well," said Rudman. "At least we're putting it to good use. We probably wouldn't have gotten any space if they hadn't run out of money for the med-school renovation. And this place is perfect for computer work because there's never any people."

"Are the microbiology labs still intact behind the amphitheater?"

"They sure are. In fact, we're using them for our memory research. The isolation is perfect. I'll bet you don't realize how much spying goes on in the computer world."

"You're right," said Philips as his beeper began its insistent sound. He switched it off and asked, "Do you know anything about the skull-reading program?"

"Of course. That's our prototype artificial intelligence program. All of us know a great deal about it."

"Well, maybe you can answer my question. I wanted to ask Michaels if the subroutine dealing with densities can be separately printed."

"Sure can. Just ask the computer. That thing will do just about everything but polish your shoes."

By eight-fifteen Pathology was in full swing. The long counter top with its line of microscopes was packed with residents. Frozen sections had begun arriving fifteen minutes earlier from surgery. Martin found Reynolds in his small office in front of an elaborate microscope fitted with a thirty-five-millimeter camera on the top so he could photograph whatever he was looking at.

"You got a minute?" asked Philips.

"Sure. In fact I already looked at those sections you brought up last night. Benjamin Barnes brought them in to me this morning."

"He's a pleasant fellow," said Martin sarcastically.

"He is cantankerous, but an excellent pathology resident. Besides, I like having him around. He makes me feel skinny."

"What did you find on the slides?"

"Very interesting. I want someone from Neuropath to look at them because I don't know what it is. Focal nerve cells have either dropped out or are in bad shape with dark, disintegrating nuclei. There's little or no inflammation. But the most curious thing is that the nerve-cell destruction is in narrow columns perpendicular to the surface of the brain. I've never seen anything like it."

"How about the various stains. What did they show?"

"Nothing. No calcium or heavy metals if that's what you mean."

"Then there's nothing that you could see that would show up on an X ray?" asked Philips.

"Absolutely not," answered Reynolds. "Certainly not the microscopic columns of cell death. Barnes said you mentioned multiple sclerosis. Not a chance. There were no myelin changes."

"If you had to hazard a diagnosis, what would you say?"

"That would be tough. Virus, I guess. But I wouldn't feel confident. This stuff looks bizarre."

When Philips got to his office Helen was waiting with a virtual ambush. She jumped up and tried to bar entrance with a handful of telephone messages and correspondence. But Philips faked left and went around her to the right, grinning the whole time. The night with Denise had changed his whole outlook.

"Where have you been? It's almost nine o'clock." Helen began to give him his calls as he rummaged around on his desk for Lisa Marino's skull film. It was under the hospital charts, which were under the master skull-film list. With the X ray under his arm, Philips walked over to the small computer and turned it on. To Helen's annoyance he began keying in the information on the input typewriter. He instructed the machine to display the density sub-routine.

"Dr. Goldblatt's secretary called twice," said Helen, "and you're supposed to call the instant you arrive."

The output unit activated and asked Martin if he wanted a digital and/or analog display. Philips didn't know so he asked for both. The printout told him to insert the film.

"Also," droned Helen, "Dr. Clinton Clark, Chief of

Gynecology called, not his secretary, the doctor himself. And he sounded very angry. He wants you to call. And Mr. Drake wants a call too."

The printout leaped into action and began spewing out page after page of paper filled with numbers. Philips watched with mounting confusion. It was as if the little machine had had some sort of nervous breakdown.

Helen elevated her voice to compete with the rapid staccato typing. "William Michaels called and said he was sorry he wasn't in when you paid your surprise visit to the computer lab. He wants you to phone. The people from Houston called about your chairing the Neuroradiology section at the national meeting. They said they have to know by today. Let's see what else."

While Helen shuffled through her messages, Philips was lifting up the incomprehensible sheets of computer paper covered with thousands of digits. The printer finally stopped producing the numbers and then drew a schematic of the lateral skull where the various areas were letter-coded. Philips realized that by finding the proper letter code he could find the sheet corresponding to the areas he was interested in. But still the printout did not stop. It then produced a schematic of the various areas of the skull and the density values were printed in shades of gray. That was the analog printout and it was easier to look at.

"Oh yeah," said Helen. "The second angioroom is going to be out all day today while they install a new film loader."

At that point Philips was not listening to Helen at all. Comparing areas in the analog printout, Martin saw that the abnormal areas had an overall density less than the surrounding normal areas. This came as a surprise because even though the changes were subtle, he'd had the mistaken impression the density was greater. Looking at the digital readout, Philips understood why. In the digital form it was apparent that there were wide jumps between the values of neighboring digits, which was why on the X rays he had thought there might have been little flecks of calcium or some other dense material. But the machine was telling him that the abnormal areas were overall less dense or more lucid than the normal tissue, meaning the X rays could pass through more easily. Philips thought about the nerve-cell death he'd seen in Pathology, but clearly that wasn't enough to affect X-ray absorption. It was a mystery that Philips could not explain.

"Look at this," he said, showing the digital readout to Helen. Helen nodded and pretended to understand.

"What does it mean?" she asked.

"I don't know, unless . . ." Martin stopped in midsentence.

"Unless what?" asked Helen.

"Get me a knife. Any kind of knife." Philips sounded excited.

Helen got the one from the peanut butter jar by the coffee urn, marveling at her weird boss. When she returned to his office, she gagged, unprepared for what she saw. Philips was lifting a human brain out of a formaldehyde jar, and putting it on a newspaper, its familiar convolutions glistening in the light from the X-ray viewer. Fighting off a wave of nausea, Helen watched as Philips proceeded to cut a ragged slice from the back of the specimen. After returning the brain to the formaldehyde he headed for the door, carrying the slice of brain on the newspaper.

"Also, Dr. Thomas' wife is ready for you in the

myelogram room," said Helen, when she saw Philips was leaving.

Martin didn't answer. He went quickly down the hall to the darkroom. It took his eyes a few minutes to adjust to the dim red light. When he could see adequately, he took out some unexposed X-ray film, put the brain slice on top of it, and put both into an upper cabinet. Sealing the cabinet with tape, he added a sign: "Unexposed film. Do not open! Dr. Philips."

Denise called the GYN clinic when she got out of the CPC conference. Deciding she would be better able to evaluate the personnel if they did not know she was a physician she just indicated that she was part of the university community. She was surprised when the receptionist put her on hold. When the next person picked up, Denise was impressed with the amount of information the clinic requested prior to an appointment. They insisted on knowing about her general health, and even her neurological status, as well as her gynecological history.

"We'll be happy to see you," said the woman finally. "In fact, we have an opening this afternoon."

"I couldn't make that," said Denise. "How about tomorrow?"

"Fine," said the woman. "About eleven forty-five?"

"Perfect," said Denise. After she hung up she wondered why Martin seemed suspicious about the clinic. Her initial reaction was very positive.

Leaning closer to the myelogram X ray on his viewer, Philips tried to figure out exactly what the orthopedic surgeon had done to Mrs. Thomas' back. It appeared as if she'd had an extensive laminectomy involving the fourth lumbar vertebra.

At that moment Philips' office door burst open, and an angry Goldblatt stormed in. His face was flushed and his glasses clung to the very tip of his nose. Martin gave him a glance, then went back to his X rays.

Being snubbed added to Goldblatt's fury. "Your impudence is astounding," he growled.

"I believe you stormed in here without knocking, sir. I respected your office. I think I should be able to expect the same from you."

"Your recent behavior regarding private property doesn't warrant such courtesy. Mannerheim called me at the crack of dawn screaming that you'd broken into his research lab and stolen a specimen. Is that correct?"

"Borrowed it," said Philips.

"Borrowed it, Christ!" shouted Goldblatt. "And yesterday you just borrowed a cadaver out of the morgue. What the hell has gotten into you, Philips? Do you have a professional suicide wish? If that's the case, tell me. It will be easier on both of us."

"Is that all?" asked Philips with deliberate calm.

"No! It's not all!" shouted Goldblatt. "Clinton Clark tells me you were haranguing one of his best residents in the GYN clinic. Philips, are you going crazy? You're a neuroradiologist! And if you weren't such a good one you'd be outta here on your ear."

Philips remained silent.

"The trouble is," said Goldblatt, with a voice that was losing its angry edge, "you are an outstanding neuroradiologist. Look, Martin, I want you to keep a low profile for a little while, okay? I know Mannerheim can be a pain in the ass. Just stay out of his way. And Christ! Stay out of his lab. The guy doesn't like anybody in there, anytime, much less sneaking around at night."

For the first time since his arrival, Goldblatt allowed his eyes to roam around Philips' cluttered office. His jaw slowly dropped in amazement at the unbelievable disorder. Turning back to Philips, he eyed him silently for a full minute.

"Last week you were fine and doing a wonderful job. You've been groomed from the first to eventually run this place. I want you to return to that old Martin Philips. I don't understand your recent behavior and I don't understand the way this office looks. But I can tell you this, if you don't shape up, you'll be looking for another position."

Goldblatt spun on his heels and walked out of the room. Philips sat silently staring after him. He didn't know whether to be angry or laugh. After all his thoughts of independence, the idea of being fired was terrifying. As a result, Martin became a whirlwind of directed activity. He ran around the department and checked all the cases in progress giving certain suggestions when needed. He read all the morning films that had accumulated. Then he personally did a left cerebral angiogram on a difficult case, which definitely demonstrated the patient did not need surgery. Getting the medical students together he gave them a lecture on the CAT scanner which left them either dazzled or totally confused, depending on their degree of concentration. In between he kept Helen busy answering all the correspondence and messages that had accumulated over the last few days. And in addition to everything else, he had a clerk rearrange the mass of skull films in his office in a systematic way, so that by three in the afternoon he had also managed to run sixty of the old films through the computer and had compared the results to the old reading. The program was functioning superbly.

At three-thirty, he stuck his head out of his office and asked Helen if there'd been any calls from a Kristin Lindquist. She shook her head. Walking down to the X-ray rooms, Philips asked Kenneth Robbins if the young woman had shown up. The answer was no.

By four o'clock Philips had run another six films through the computer. Once again the machine suggested it was a better radiologist than was Philips by picking up a trace of calcification that suggested a meningioma tumor. Looking back at the film, Philips had to agree. He put the X ray aside to see if Helen could trace the patient down.

At four-fifteen Philips dialed Kristin Lindquist's number. It was answered on the second ring by her roommate.

"I'm sorry, Dr. Philips, but I haven't seen Kristin since before she left for the Metropolitan Museum this morning. She missed her eleven and one-fifteen classes, which is not like her."

"Would you try to locate her for me and have her give me a call?" said Philips.

"I'd be glad to. Frankly, I'm a little concerned."

At quarter-to-five Helen came into Philips' office with the day's correspondence for him to sign so she could post the letters on her way home. A little after five-thirty Denise stopped by.

"Looks like things are more under control," she said, looking around appreciatively.

"Just appearances," said Philips as the laser scanner snatched an X ray out of his hand.

He closed his office door and gave her a solid embrace. He didn't want to let go of her and when he finally did, she looked up and said, "Wow, what did I do to deserve this?"

"I've been thinking about you all day and reliving

last night." He wanted desperately to talk with her about the insecurities Goldblatt had evoked that morning, and tell her that he wanted her to stay with him for the rest of his life. The trouble was that he hadn't given himself any time to think, and while he didn't want to let go of her yet, he wanted to be alone, at least for a while. When she reminded him she had promised to make dinner, he hesitated. Seeing her hurt face he said, "What I was thinking is that if I can get a good enough head start running these old films, maybe we could drive out to the island Saturday night."

"That would be marvelous," said Denise, mollified. "Oh, by the way, I called GYN and made an appointment for tomorrow around noon."

"Good. Who'd you talk with?"

"I don't know. But they were very nice and seemed genuinely happy to accommodate me. Look, if you finish up early why don't you come over?"

Denise had been gone about an hour when Michaels arrived, delighted to see that Philips had finally started working on the program in earnest.

"It's exceeding all my expectations," said Martin. "There hasn't been a single false negative reading."

"Fabulous," said Michaels. "Maybe we're farther along than we'd guessed."

"It certainly looks like it. If this keeps up, we could have a functioning, commercially available system by early fall. We could use the annual radiology meeting to unveil it." Philips' mind raced ahead, imagining the impact. It made his professional insecurity that morning seem ridiculous.

After Michaels left, Philips went back to work. He'd developed a system of feeding the old X rays into the machine that speeded up the process. But as he worked he began to feel progressively more uncomfortable about Kristin Lindquist's absence. A growing sense of responsibility overtook his initial irritation at her apparent unreliability. It would be too much of a coincidence if something happened to this woman that precluded him from getting more X rays.

Around nine Martin dialed Kristin's number again. Her roommate answered it on the first ring.

"I'm sorry, Dr. Philips. I should have called you. But I cannot find Kristin anyplace. No one has seen her all day. I've even called the police."

Philips hung up, trying to deny reality by telling himself it couldn't happen. It was impossible . . . Marino, Lucas, McCarthy, Collins, and now Lindquist! No. It couldn't be. It was preposterous. Suddenly he remembered he hadn't heard from Admitting. Lifting the phone, he was surprised when it was answered after four rings. But the woman who was looking into the case had left at five and wouldn't be back until eight the next morning, and there was no one else who could help him. Philips slammed the receiver down.

"Damn!" he shouted, getting up from his stool and beginning to pace. Suddenly he remembered the section of McCarthy's brain he'd put in the cabinet.

At the darkroom, he had to wait for a technician to finish processing some ER films. As soon as he could, Martin opened the cabinet and retrieved the film and the now dried-up slice of brain. Not knowing what to do with the specimen, he ended up dumping it into the wastebasket. The unexposed film went into the developer.

Standing out in the hallway next to the slot where his film would emerge, Martin wondered if Kristin's disappearance could possibly be just another coincidence. And if it were not, what would it mean? More important, what could he do?

At that moment the X ray dropped into the holding bin. Martin expected the film to be totally dark, so that when he snapped it up on the viewer, he was shocked. "Holy Christ!" His mouth opened in disbelief. There was a lucent area the exact shape of the brain slice. Philips knew that there was only one possible cause. Radiation! The density abnormality on the X rays was from a significant amount of radiation.

Philips ran all the way down to Nuclear Medicine. In the lab next to the betatron he found what he needed: a radiation detector and a generous-sized, lead-shielded storage box. He could lift the box but it wasn't something he was interested in carrying so he put it on a gurney.

His first stop was his office. The jar with the brain was definitely hot so he donned some rubber gloves and put it into the lead box. He also found the newspaper he'd put the brain on and put that in the box. He even went out and found the knife he'd used to cut the brain and put that in the box as well. Then with the radiation detector he went around his room. It was clean.

Down in the darkroom, Philips got the wastebasket and dumped its contents into the box. Testing the wastebasket afterward, he was satisfied. Back in his office he took off the rubber gloves, threw them into the box, and sealed it. He checked the room again with the radiation detector and was pleased to find only an insignificant amount of radiation. His next step was to take the film out of the dosimeter he wore on his belt and prepare it for processing. He wanted to know exactly how much radiation he'd received from the brain specimen.

During all this feverish physical activity, Martin tried unsuccessfully to relate all the disparate facts: five young women, presumably all with significantly high levels of radiation in their heads and maybe other parts of their bodies . . . neurological symptoms suggestive of a condition like multiple sclerosis . . . all with gynecological visits and atypical Pap smears.

Philips had no explanation for these facts, but it seemed to him that the radiation must have been the central issue. He reasoned that high levels of general radiation could cause alterations in cervical cells and therefore an atypical Pap smear. But it was peculiar that all of the cases had had atypical smears. Once again it seemed difficult to explain a specific phenomenon by coincidence. Yet what else could be the explanation?

When the cleanup was completed, Philips wrote down Collins' and McCarthy's unit numbers and the dates of their GYN visits on his list. Then he hurried down the central corridor of Radiology and cut through the main X-ray reading room. At the elevators, he pushed the down button with a rising sense of urgency. He realized that Kristin Lindquist was a walking time bomb. For the radiation in her head to show up on a regular X ray, there had to be a very large amount involved. And to find her, Martin believed he would have to solve all the puzzling events of the last week. To his surprise he found Benjamin Barnes draped over his work stool. The pathology resident might not have a pleasant personality but Martin had to respect the man's dedication.

"What brings you up here two nights in a row?" asked the resident.

"Pap smears," said Philips with no preamble.

"I suppose you have an emergency slide for me to read," said Barnes sarcastically.

"No. I just want some information. I want to know if radiation can cause an atypical Pap smear."

Barnes thought for a moment before answering. "I've never heard of it from diagnostic radiology but certainly radiotherapy will affect the cervical cells and hence the Pap smear."

"If you looked at an atypical smear, could you tell if it was caused by radiation?"

"Maybe," said Barnes.

"Remember those slides you looked at for me last night?" continued Philips. "The brain sections. Could those nerve-cell lesions be caused by radiation?"

"I kinda doubt it," said Barnes. "The radiation would have to have been aimed with a telescopic sight. The nerve cells right next to the damaged ones looked fine."

Philips face went blank while he tried to put together the inconsistent facts. The patients had absorbed enough radiation to show up on a X ray, yet on a cellular level, one cell was totally knocked out while a neighbor was all right.

"Are Pap smear specimens saved?" he asked finally.

"I think so. At least for a while, but not here. They're over in the Cytology lab, which operates on bankers' hours. They'll be in in the morning after nine."

"Thanks," said Philips, sighing. He wondered if he should try to get into the lab right away. Perhaps if he called Reynolds. He was about to leave when he thought of something else. "When they read Pap smears, is the result in the chart just the classification, or do they describe the pathology?"

"I think so," said Barnes. "The results are stored on

tape. All you need is the patient's unit number and you can read the report."

"Thanks a lot," said Philips. "I know you're busy so I appreciate your time."

Barnes gave a slight nod of acknowledgment, then put his eyes back to his microscope.

The Pathology computer terminal was separated from the lab by a series of room dividers. Pulling up a chair, Martin sat down in front of the unit. It was similar to the terminal in Radiology with a large TV-like screen directly behind the keyboard. Taking out the list of five patients, Philips keyed in the name Katherine Collins, followed by her unit number and the code for Papanicolaou Smear. There was a pause, then letters appeared on the screen as if someone were typing. First it spelled out Katherine Collins very rapidly, followed by a slight pause. Then the date of the first Pap smear followed by:

Adequate smear, good fixation, and proper stain-ing. Cells show normal maturation and differ-entiation. Estrogen effect normal: 0/20/80. A few candida organisms seen. Result: negative.

Philips checked the date of the first smear while the machine spelled out the next report. The date corresponded to the first date Philips had written on the list. Looking back up at the computer screen, Philips' disbelieving eyes read that the second Pap smear on Collins was also negative!

Philips cleared the screen and rapidly entered Ellen McCarthy's name, her unit number, and the proper code. He felt his stomach tighten into a knot as the machine began to spell out the information. It was the same—negative!

As he went back downstairs, Martin felt stunned. In medicine he had learned to believe what he read in charts, especially in regard to laboratory reports. They were the objective data while the symptom of the patients and the impressions of the doctors were the subjective. Philips knew that there was a small chance there could be an error in laboratory tests just as he knew there was a possibility that he could miss or misinterpret something on an X ray. But the low probability of error was a far cry from deliberate falsification. That required some sort of conspiracy, and Philips took it very personally.

Sitting at his desk, Martin cradled his head in his hands and rubbed his eyes. His first impulse was to call the hospital authorities, but that meant Stanley Drake, and he decided against it. Drake's response would be to keep it out of the papers, cover it up. The police! Mentally he ran through a hypothetical conversation: "Hello, I'm Dr. Martin Philips and I want to report that something funny is going on at Hobson University Medical Center. Girls get Pap smears that are normal but are entered into the chart as atypical." Philips shook his head. It sounded too ridiculous. No, he needed more information before the police were involved. Intuitively he felt the radiation was connected even though it didn't make any sense. In fact, radiation might cause an atypical Pap smear and it seemed to Philips that if someone wanted to avoid discovery of the radiation, they might report atypical Paps as normal, but not vice versa.

Philips thought again about the diener. After their abortive meeting the previous evening, Martin had been convinced Werner knew more about Lisa Marino than he'd been willing to disclose. Perhaps one hundred dollars wasn't enough. Maybe Philips should offer more. After all, the affair was no longer an academic exercise.

Martin realized that trying to successfully confront Werner in the morgue was an impossibility. Surrounded with the dead, Werner was in his element, whereas Martin found the place totally unnerving and he knew he would have to be forceful and demanding if Werner was going to be made to talk. Philips glanced at his watch. It was twenty-five after eleven. Werner obviously worked the evening shift, four to midnight. Impulsively Martin decided he'd follow Werner home and offer him five hundred dollars.

With some trepidation he dialed Denise's number. It rang six times before a sleepy voice answered: "Are you coming over?"

"No," said Philips evasively. "I'm in the middle of something and I'm going to keep at it."

"There's a nice warm spot here for you."

"We'll make up for it this weekend. Sweet dreams."

Martin got his dark blue ski parka out of his closet and put on the Greek captain's cap he found in the pocket. It was April but the drizzly weather had brought in wind from the northeast and it was chilly.

He left the hospital through the emergency room, leaping from the platform to the puddle-strewn tarmac of the parking area. But instead of walking out to the street, he turned right, round the corner of the main hospital building and headed down a canyon formed by the north face of the Brenner Childrens Hospital. After fifty yards it opened up to the inner courtyard of the Med Center.

The hospital buildings soared up into the misty night like sheer cliffs forming an irregular cement valley. The Med Center had been built in spurts without the benefit of a rational overall plan. This fact was obvious in the courtyard, where buildings impinged upon the space with chaotic angles and buttresses. Philips recognized the small wing that housed Goldblatt's office, and using that as a landmark, was able to orient himself. It was only about twenty-five yards farther on that he found the unmarked platform that he knew led into the depths of the morgue. The hospital did not like to advertise that it dealt in death, and the bodies were stealthily excreted into the waiting black hearses far from the public eye.

Martin leaned up against the wall and thrust his hands into his pockets. While he waited he tried to review the complicated events he'd experienced since Kenneth Robbins had handed him Lisa Marino's X ray. It hadn't even been two days, yet it seemed like two weeks. The initial excitement that he'd felt seeing the strange radiologic abnormality had now changed to a hollow fear. He almost dreaded to find out what was going on in the hospital. It was like a sickness in his own family. Medicine had been his life. If it weren't for his immediate sense of responsibility about Kristin Lindquist, he wondered if he'd just forget what he knew. Goldblatt's tirade about professional suicide rang in his ears.

Werner emerged on schedule, turning to secure the door behind him. Philips leaned forward and shaded his eyes in the half-light to make sure it really was Werner. He had changed his clothes, and was now wearing a dark suit, white shirt, and tie. To Martin's surprise the diener looked like a successful merchant closing his boutique for the night. His gaunt face, which had appeared evil within the morgue, now gave the man an almost aristocratic cast.

Werner turned and hesitated a moment, stretching out an upturned palm to see if it was raining. Satisfied, he set off toward the street. In his right hand he carried a black briefcase. Over his flexed arm dangled a tightly clasped umbrella.

Following from a safe distance, Martin noticed Werner had a strange gait. It wasn't a limp; it was more like a hop as if one leg was much stronger than the other. But he moved quickly and at a steady pace.

Martin's hopes that Werner lived close to the hospital were dashed when the man rounded the corner on Broadway and descended the subway stairs. Quickening his step, Philips closed the gap, taking the stairs two at a time. At first he did not see Werner. Apparently the man had had a token. Philips hastily purchased one, and went through the turnstile. The IRT elevator was empty, so Philips jogged down the sloping passage toward the IND platform. As he rounded the corner, he caught sight of Werner's head just disappearing down the stairs to the downtown platform.

Pulling a newspaper out of a waste bin, Philips pretended to read. Werner was only thirty feet away, sitting on one of the molded plastic chairs, engrossed in a book on, of all things, "Opening Chess Moves." In the pasty white subway light, Philips could better appreciate the man's attire. His suit was dark blue, and Edwardian, cut in at the sides. His closely cropped hair had been freshly brushed; with his high-boned, suntanned cheeks, he looked like a Prussian general. The only thing that marred his appearance was his shoes. They were badly scuffed and in need of polish.

With the hospital shift just changing, the subway platform was crowded with nurses, orderlies, and technicians. When the downtown express thundered into the station, Werner boarded and Philips followed. The diener sat on the train like a statue with his book in front of him; his deeply set eyes darted back and forth across the pages. His briefcase, clasped between his knees, stood upright on the floor. Philips sat halfway down the car across from a handsome Spanish fellow in a polyester suit.

At each stop, Martin was ready to disembark, but Werner never budged. As they passed Fifty-ninth Street, Philips became concerned. Perhaps Werner was not going directly home. For some reason that possibility had never occurred to Philips. He was relieved when he finally followed the diener off at Forty-second Street. It was now no longer a question of whether Werner was going home or not. Now it was a question of how long was he going to spend wherever he was headed. Philips felt foolish and discouraged when he reached the street.

The night people were out in force. Despite the hour and the damp chill, Forty-second Street was ablaze with its garish sights. The nattily dressed Werner ignored the bizarre and grotesque people who jostled one another in front of the pornographic movie houses and bookstores. He seemed to be accustomed to the world's psychosexual perversions. For Philips it was different. It was as if the alien world willfully impaired his progress, forcing him to twist and turn and even step into the street occasionally to pass clotted groups of humanity while he kept Werner in sight. Ahead he saw Werner abruptly turn and enter an adult bookstore.

Martin stopped outside. He decided he'd give Werner an hour of this nonsense. If the diener did not go back to his apartment within that time, Philips would give up. Waiting, Martin soon discovered he was fair game for a host of solicitors, peddlers, and outright beggars. They were an insistent lot, and to avoid their entreaties, Philips changed his mind and entered the store.

Just inside, situated in a pulpit-like balcony near the ceiling, sat a lavender-haired, hard-looking woman who peered down at Philips. Her eyes, deeply set above dark circles, wandered over Martin's body as she assessed his suitability for admission. Averting his gaze, embarrassed for anyone to see him in such a location, he walked down the nearest aisle. Werner was not in sight!

A customer pushed past Philips with his arms limply at his sides so that his hands brushed across Philips' backside. It wasn't until the man was already past that Martin realized what had happened. It made him sick, and he almost shouted out, but the last thing he wanted to do was to call attention to himself.

He moved around the shop to make sure Werner couldn't be hidden behind one of the bookshelves or magazine racks. The lavender-haired woman in her crow's nest seemed to follow every movement Philips made, so to appear less suspicious he picked up a magazine, but he discovered it was sealed in plastic wrap and he put it back. On the cover were two men acrobatically coupling.

Suddenly, Werner emerged from a door in the back of the shop and walked past the startled Philips, who quickly turned away to fondle some pornographic video cassettes. But Werner looked neither right nor left. It was as if he were wearing blinders. He was out of the shop in seconds.

Martin delayed as long as he thought he could without losing Werner. He didn't want it too apparent that he was following the man, but as he exited, the woman in the balcony leaned over and watched him go out the door. She knew he was up to something.

Reaching the street, Philips caught sight of Werner getting into a taxi. Frightened that he might lose him after all his effort, Philips leaped from the curb and frantically waved for a cab. One stopped across the street and Philips dodged the traffic to jump in.

"Follow that Checker cab behind the bus," said Philips excitedly.

The cabby just looked at him.

"Come on," insisted Philips.

The man shrugged and put the car in gear. "You some sort of cop?"

Martin didn't answer. He felt the less conversation the better. Werner got out at Fifty-second and Second Avenue; Martin got out about one hundred feet back from the corner and ran up to the end of the block, looking after him. Werner entered a shop three doors away.

Crossing the avenue Martin looked over at the store. It was called "Sexual Aids." It was very different from the adult bookstore on Forty-second Street with a very conservative exterior. Glancing around, Philips noticed that it was situated among antique shops, fashionable restaurants, and expensive boutiques. Looking up he could tell the apartment buildings were all middle class. It was a good neighborhood.

Werner appeared at the door accompanied by another man who was laughing and had his arm over the diener's shoulder. Werner smiled and shook hands with the man before setting out, walking up Second Avenue. Philips fell in behind him, keeping a safe distance.

If he had had any inkling that following Werner

was going to entail all these stops, he wouldn't have done it. As it was, he kept expecting the odyssey to terminate. But Werner had other ideas. He crossed over to Third Avenue, making his way up to Fifty-fifth Street, where he entered a small building huddled in the shadow of a glass and cement skyscraper. It was a saloon that looked as if it stood in a 1920's photograph.

After debating with himself, Martin followed, afraid that he might lose Werner if he didn't keep him in view. To Philips' amazement the establishment was jammed with animated customers despite the hour, and he had to squeeze inside. It was a popular singles bar, again unfamiliar turf for Philips.

Scanning the crowd for Werner, Philips was shocked to see him immediately to his left. He was holding a mug of beer and smiling to a blond secretary. Philips pulled his hat a little lower on his head.

"What do you do?" asked the secretary, shouting to be heard over the din of voices.

"I'm a doctor," said Werner. "A pathologist."

"Really," said the secretary, obviously impressed.

"It's got its good and bad points," said Werner. "I usually have to work late, but maybe you'd like to have a drink sometime."

"I'd love it," shouted the woman.

Martin pushed up to the bar wondering if the girl had any idea what she was getting herself into. He ordered a beer, and worked his way over to the back wall, where he found a spot from which he could observe Werner. Sipping his drink, Martin began to appreciate the absurdity of the situation. After all his years of education, he was in a singles bar in the middle of the night, following a bizarre individual who looked frighteningly normal. In fact, when Phil-

ips glanced around he was impressed with how easily
Werner merged with the businessmen and lawyers.

After taking the secretary's phone number, the diener polished off his beer, gathered his belongings,
and caught another cab on Third Avenue. Martin had
a short argument with his taxi driver about following,
but it was solved by a five-dollar bill.

The ride passed in silence. Philips watched the city
lights until they were blurred by an abrupt down-
pour. The cab's windshield wipers hurried to keep
ahead of the rain. They crossed town on Fifty-sev-
enth; went diagonally north on Broadway from
Columbus Circle, then turned onto Amsterdam Avenue. Philips recognized Columbia University when
they passed it on the left. The rain let up as suddenly
as it had started. On One-hundred-forty-first they
turned right, and Philips sat forward and asked what
section of town they were in. "Hamilton Heights,"
said the driver, turning left on Hamilton Terrace, and
then slowing down.

Ahead, Werner's taxi stopped. Philips paid his fare
and got out. Although the cityscape on Amsterdam
Avenue had deteriorated as they'd gone north, Philips
now found himself in a surprisingly attractive neighborhood. The street was lined with quaint town
houses whose varying facades reflected about every
architectural school since the Renaissance. Most of
the buildings clearly had been renovated, others were
in the process. At the end of the street, facing down
Hamilton Terrace, Werner entered a white limestone-
fronted building whose windows were surrounded
with Venetian Gothic decoration.

By the time Philips got to the building, the lights
had gone on in the third-floor windows. Up close, the
town house was not in such good condition as it ap-

peared from afar, but its shoddiness did not detract from its overall effect; it gave Philips a feeling of tarnished elegance, and he was impressed by Werner's ability to provide for himself.

Entering the foyer, Philips acknowledged that he was not going to be able to surprise Werner by knocking directly on his door. As in Denise's apartment, there was a locked foyer with individual buzzers to the various apartments. Helmut Werner's name was third from the bottom.

Putting his finger on the buzzer, Philips hesitated, not sure if he wanted to go through with the whole thing. He wasn't even sure what he should say, but the thought of Kristin Lindquist gave him courage. He pressed the button and waited.

"Who is it?" Werner's voice, laden with static, issued from a tiny speaker.

"Dr. Philips. I've got some money for you, Werner. Big money."

There was a moment or two of silence and Martin could feel his pulse.

"Who else is with you, Philips?"

"No one."

A raucous buzz filled the once sumptuous foyer and Philips pushed through the door. He headed up the stairs for the third floor. Behind the sole door he could hear multiple locks being released. The door opened slightly so that a sliver of light cut across Philips' face. He could see one of Werner's deeply set eyes looking at him. The brow was raised in apparent surprise. A chain was then removed and the door swung open.

Martin stepped briskly into the room, forcing Werner to back up to avoid a collision. In the center of the room Martin stopped.

"I don't mind paying, my friend," he said with as much assertiveness as he could muster. "But I want to find out what happened to Lisa Marino's brain."

"How much you willing to pay?" Werner's hands were opening and closing rhythmically.

"Five hundred dollars," said Philips. He wanted the amount to sound enticing without being ridiculous.

Werner's thin mouth pulled back in a smile so that deep lines appeared in his hollow cheeks. His teeth were small and square.

"Are you sure you're alone?" asked Werner.

Philips nodded.

"Where's the money?"

"Right here." Philips patted his left breast.

"All right," said Werner. "What do you want to know?"

"Everything," said Philips.

Werner shrugged his shoulders. "It's a long story."

"I got the time."

"I was just going to eat. You want to eat?"

Philips shook his head. His stomach was a tense knot.

"Suit yourself." Werner turned and with his characteristic gait, went into the kitchen. Philips followed, allowing himself a quick glance at the apartment. The walls were some sort of red velvet, the furniture Victorian. The room had a sleazy, heavy elegance, which was enhanced by the low-level illumination coming from a single Tiffany lamp. On the table was Werner's briefcase. A Polaroid camera, which had apparently been in the case, lay next to it, along with a stack of photos.

The kitchen was a small room with a sink, a tiny stove, and a refrigerator, the likes of which Martin hadn't seen since his childhood. It was a porcelain-surfaced box with a cylindrical coil on top. Werner opened the refrigerator and removed a sandwich and a bottled beer. From a drawer beneath the sink, he got an opener and removed the cap from the beer, putting the opener back where he got it.

Holding up the beer, Werner said, "Would you care for a drink?"

Philips shook his head. The diener came out of the kitchen and Philips backed up. At the dining-room table Werner pushed his briefcase and Polaroid to one side, motioning Martin to sit. The diener took a long draught of beer, then burped loudly as he set the bottle down. The longer he delayed, the less confident Philips felt. He had lost his initial advantage of surprise. To keep his hands from trembling, he put them on his knees. His eyes were glued to Werner, watching every move.

"Nobody can live on a diener's salary," said Werner.

Philips nodded, waiting. Werner took a bite of his sandwich.

"You know I come from the old country," said Werner with his mouth full, "from Rumania. It's not a nice story because the Nazis killed my family and took me back to Germany when I was five years old. That was the age I started handling corpses in Dachau. . . ." Werner went on to tell his story in grisly detail, how his parents had been killed, how he'd been treated in the concentration camps, and how he was forced to live with the dead. The gruesome story went on and on and Werner did not spare Martin a single repulsive chapter. Philips tried on several occasions to interrupt the ghastly tale, but Werner persisted and Philips felt his fixity of purpose melt like wax before a hot coal.

"Then I came to America," said Werner, finishing his beer with a loud sucking sound. He scraped back his chair and went into the kitchen for another. Philips, numb from the story, watched him from the table. "I got a job with the medical school in the morgue," yelled Werner as he opened the drawer beneath the sink. Below the bottle opener were several large autopsy knives Werner had spirited out of the morgue when autopsies were still done on the old marble slab. He grasped one of them, and point first, slid the knife up inside the left sleeve of his jacket. "But I needed more money than the salary." He opened the beer bottle and replaced the opener. Closing the drawer, he turned and came back toward the table.

"I only want to know about Lisa Marino," said Martin, limply. Werner's life story had made Philips conscious of his physical fatigue.

"I'm coming to that," said Werner. He took a sip from the fresh beer, then put it on the table. "I started making extra money around the morgue when anatomy was more popular than it is now. Lots of little things. Then I hit on the idea of pictures. I sell them on Forty-second Street. I've been doing it for years." With one of his arms Werner made a gesture of introduction around his apartment.

Philips let his eyes roam the dimly lit room. He'd vaguely been aware the red velvet walls were covered with pictures. Now when he looked, he realized the pictures were lewd, gruesome photos of nude female corpses. Philips slowly turned his attention back to the leering Werner.

"Lisa Marino was one of my best models," said Werner. He picked up the pile of Polaroid shots on the table and dumped them in Philips' lap. "Look at them. They're bringing top dollar, especially on Second Avenue. Take your time. I've got to go to the bathroom. It's the beer; it goes right through me."

Werner walked around the stunned Philips and disappeared through the bedroom door. Martin reluctantly looked down at the sickeningly sadistic photos of Lisa Marino's corpse. He was afraid to touch them, as if the mental aberration they represented might rub off on his fingers. Werner had obviously misinterpreted Philips' interest. Perhaps the diener didn't know anything about the missing brain, and his suspicious behavior was only owing to his illicit trade in necrophilic photos. Philips felt the stirrings of nausea.

Werner had gone through the bedroom and into the bathroom. He ran the water at a rate that sounded like someone urinating and, reaching into his sleeve, he extracted the long slender autopsy knife. He grabbed it in his right hand like a dagger, then moved silently back through the bedroom.

Philips was sitting fifteen feet away, his back to Werner, his head bowed, looking at the photos in his lap. Werner paused just beyond the bedroom doorway. His slender fingers tightened around the worn wooden handle of the knife and he pressed his lips tightly together.

Philips picked up the pictures and lifted them in preparation of putting them face-down on the table. He got them as far as his chest when he was aware of motion behind him. He started to turn. There was a scream!

The knife blade plunged down just behind the right clavicle at the base of the neck, slicing through the upper lobe of the lung before piercing the right pulmonary artery. Blood poured into the opened bronchus, causing a reflex agonal cough, which sent the blood hurling from the mouth in a ballistic arc over the top of Philips' head, drenching the table in front of him.

Martin moved by animal reflex, jumping to the right and grabbing the beer bottle in the process. Spinning around, he was confronted by the sight of Werner staggering forward, his hand groping vainly to pull out a stiletto buried to the hilt in his neck. With only a gurgle issuing from his throat, his thrashing body fell forward onto the table before crashing in a heap on the floor. The autopsy knife Werner had been holding clattered as it hit the table and skidded off with a thump.

"Don't move, and don't touch anything," yelled Werner's assailant, who had come through the open door to the hallway. "It's a good thing we decided to put you under surveillance." He was the Spanish-American with the heavy mustache and polyester suit Philips remembered seeing on the subway. "The idea is to hit either a major vessel or the heart, but this guy wasn't going to give me any time." The man leaned over and tried to pull his knife from Werner's neck. Werner had collapsed with his head against his right shoulder and the blade was trapped. The assailant stepped over the twitching diener to give himself a better purchase on the weapon.

Philips had recovered enough from the initial shock to react as the man bent down by the table. Swinging the beer bottle in a full arc, Martin brought it down on the intruder's head. The man had seen the blow coming and, at the last minute, had turned slightly away so some of the force was dissipated on his shoulder. Still, it sent him sprawling on top of his dying victim.

In the grip of utter panic, Philips started to run,

still clutching the beer bottle. But, at the door, he thought he heard noises in the hallway below, making him afraid that the killer wasn't alone. Grabbing the doorjamb to reverse his direction, he dashed back through Werner's apartment. He saw that the killer had regained his feet but was still stunned, holding his head with both hands.

Martin rushed to a rear window in the bedroom and threw up the sash. He tried to open the screen but couldn't so he bashed it out with his foot. Once out on the fire escape, he plummeted down. It was miraculous he didn't stumble, because his exit was more like a controlled fall. On the ground, he had no choice of direction; he had to run east. Just beyond the neighboring building, he entered a vegetable garden in a vacant lot. To his right there was a hurricane fence that barred the way back to Hamilton Terrace.

The ground fell off sharply as he ran eastward and he found himself sliding and falling down a steep rock-strewn hill. The light was now behind him and he advanced into darkness. Soon he tumbled against a wire fence. Beyond it was a drop of ten feet into an automobile junkyard. Beyond that was the weakly illuminated expanse of St. Nicholas Avenue. Philips was about to scale the low fence when he realized it had been cut. He squeezed through the convenient opening and swung himself down the cement wall, dropping the last few feet blindly.

It wasn't a real junkyard. It was just a vacant area where abandoned cars had been left to rust. Carefully, Martin picked his way between twisted metal hulks toward the light on the avenue in front of him. At any second he expected to hear pursuers.

Once on the street, he could run more easily. He

wanted to put as much distance as possible between himself and Werner's apartment. Vainly, he looked for a police cruiser. He saw no one. The buildings on either side of him had deteriorated, and as Philips looked from side to side, he realized that many of the structures were burned out and abandoned. The huge empty tenements looked like skeletons in the dark misty night. The sidewalks were cluttered with trash and debris.

Suddenly, Philips realized where he was. He'd run directly into Harlem. The realization slowed his pace. The dark and deserted scene accentuated his terror. Two blocks farther on Martin saw a ragged group of street-tough blacks who were more than a little shocked at Philips' running figure. They paused in their drug-dealing to watch the crazy white fellow run past them, heading toward the center of Harlem.

Although he was in good shape, the strenuous pace soon exhausted him and Martin felt as if he was about to drop, each breath bringing a stabbing pain in his chest. Finally, in desperation, he ducked into a dark, doorless opening, his breath coming in harsh gasps while his feet stumbled over loose bricks. By holding on to the damp wall, he steadied himself. Immediately his nostrils were assaulted by the rank smell. But he ignored it. It was such a relief to stop running.

Cautiously, he leaned out and struggled to see if anyone had followed him. It was quiet, deathly quiet. Philips smelled the person before he felt the hand that reached out from the black depths of the building and grabbed his arm. A scream started in his throat, but when it escaped from his mouth it was more like the bleat of a baby lamb. He leaped out of the doorway, thrashing his arm as if it were in the grasp of a venomous insect. The owner of the hand was inadvertently pulled from the doorway and Martin found himself looking at a drug-sodden junkie, barely capable of standing upright. "Christ!" shouted Philips as he turned and fled back into the night.

Deciding not to stop again, Philips settled into his usual jogging pace. He was hopelessly lost, but he reasoned that if he kept going straight, he'd eventually have to run into some sort of populated area.

It had started to rain again, a fine mist that swirled around in the glow of the infrequent street lamps.

Two blocks farther Philips found his oasis. He'd reached a broad avenue and on the corner was an all-night bar with a garish neon Budweiser sign that blinked a blood-red wash over the intersection. A few figures huddled in nearby doorways as if the red sign offered some sort of haven from the decaying city.

Running a hand through his damp hair, Martin felt a stickiness. In the light of the Budweiser sign, he realized it was a splattering of Werner's blood. Not wishing to appear like he'd been in a brawl, he tried to wipe the blood off with his hand. After several passes, the stickiness disappeared and Philips pushed open the door.

The atmosphere in the bar was syrupy and thick with smoke. The deafening disco music vibrated so that Martin could feel each beat in his chest. There were about twelve people in the bar, all in a partial stupor, and all black. In addition to the disco music, a small color television was transmitting a 1930's gangster movie. The only person watching was the burly bartender, who was wearing a dirty white apron.

The faces of the customers turned toward Philips and a sudden tension filled the air like static electricity before a storm. Philips felt it instantly, even through his panic. Although Philips had lived in New York for almost twenty years, he'd shielded himself from the desperate poverty that characterized the city just as much as the ostentatious wealth.

Now advancing into the bar warily, he half-expected to be attacked at any moment. As he passed, the threatening faces swung around to follow his progress. Ahead of him, a bearded man turned on the bar stool and planted himself directly in Philips' path. He was a muscular black whose body glistened with sheer power in the muted light.

"Come on, Whitey," he snarled.

"Flash," snapped the bartender. "Ease off." Then, to Philips, he said: "Mister, what the fuck are you doin' here. You want'a get killed?"

"I need a phone," managed Philips.

"In the back," said the bartender, shaking his head in disbelief.

Philips held his breath as he stepped around the man called Flash. Finding a dime in his pocket, he then searched for the phone. He found one near the toilets but it was occupied by a fellow who was having an argument with his girlfriend. "Look, baby, whatta' you going and crying for?"

Earlier, in his panic, Martin might have tried to wrest the phone from the man, but now he was at least partially in control and he walked back into the bar and stood at the very end to wait. The atmosphere had relaxed a degree and conversations had recommenced.

The bartender demanded cash up front, then served him his brandy. The fiery fluid soothed his jangled nerves and helped focus his thoughts. For the first time since the unbelievable event of Werner's death, Martin was able to consider what had happened. At the moment of the stabbing he'd thought that he'd been a coincidental accessory and that the fight was between Werner and his assailant. But then the assailant had said something that suggested he'd been following Philips. But that was absurd! Martin had been following Werner. And Martin had seen Werner's knife. Could the diener have been about to attack him? Trying to think about the episode made Philips feel more confused, especially when he remembered he'd seen the assailant on the subway that night. Philips downed his drink and paid for another. He asked the bartender where he was and the man told him. The names of the streets meant nothing to Philips.

The black fellow who'd been arguing on the phone passed behind Philips and left the bar. Martin pushed off his stool, and taking his fresh drink, he headed back toward the rear of the room. He felt somewhat calmer and thought he could make a more intelligent case to the police. There was a little shelf below the phone and Philips put his drink there. Dropping in a coin, he dialed 911.

Over the sound of the disco and the TV he could hear the ringing on the other end of the line. He wondered if he should say anything about his discoveries and the hospital, but decided it would only add confusion to an already confused situation. He decided not to say anything about his medical concerns unless he was specifically asked what he was doing at Werner's apartment in the middle of the night. A bored husky voice answered.

"Division Six. Sergeant McNeally speaking."

"I want to report a murder," said Martin, trying to keep his voice even.

"Where about?" asked the sergeant.

"I'm not sure of the address, but I'll be able to recognize the building if I see it again."

"Are you in any danger right now?"

"I don't think so. I'm in a bar in Harlem ..."

"A bar! Right, mac," interrupted the sergeant. "How many drinks have you had?"

Philips realized the man thought he was a crank. "Listen. I saw a man get knifed."

"A lot of people get knifed in Harlem, my friend. What's your name?"

"Dr. Martin Philips. I'm staff radiologist at the Hobson University Medical Center."

"Did you say Philips?" The sergeant's voice had changed.

"That's right," said Martin, surprised at the sergeant's reaction.

"Why didn't you say that immediately. Look, we've been waiting for your call. I'm supposed to transfer you immediately to the Bureau. Hold on! If you get cut off, call me right back. Okay!"

The policeman didn't wait for a response. There was a click as Philips was put on hold. Pulling the receiver away from his ear, Martin looked at it as if it would explain the odd conversation. He was sure the sergeant had said that he'd been waiting for his call! And what did he mean by the Bureau? The Bureau of what?

A series of clicks was followed by the sound of someone else picking up the other end of the line. This voice was intense and anxious.

"All right, Philips, where are you?"

"I'm in Harlem. Who is this?"

"My name is Agent Sansone. I'm the Assistant Director of the Bureau here in the city."

"What Bureau?" Philips' nerves, which had begun

to settle, tingled as if he were connected to a galvanic source.

"The FBI, you idiot! Listen, we may not have much time. You've got to get out of that area."

"Why?" Martin was bewildered, but he sensed Sansone's seriousness.

"I don't have time to explain. But that man you clobbered on the head was one of my agents trying to protect you. He just reported in. Don't you understand? Werner's involvement was just a freak accident."

"I don't understand anything," shouted Philips.

"It doesn't matter," snapped Sansone. "What matters is getting you out of there. Hang on, I've got to see if this is a secured line."

There was another click while Philips was put on hold. Glaring at the silent phone, Philips' emotions were strung out to the point that he felt anger. The whole thing had to be a cruel joke.

"The line's not secure," said Sansone, coming back on the phone. "Give your number and I'll call you back."

Philips gave him the number and hung up. His anger began to fragment into renewed fear. After all, it was the FBI.

The phone jangled under Philips' hand, startling him. It was Sansone. "Okay, Philips. Listen! There is a conspiracy involving the Hobson University Medical Center, which we've been secretly investigating."

"And it involves radiation," blurted Philips. Things started to make sense.

"Are you certain?"

"Absolutely," said Philips.

"Very good. Listen, Philips, you're needed in this investigation, but we're afraid you might be under

surveillance. We've got to talk to you. We need someone inside the medical center, understand?" Sansone
didn't wait for Philips to respond. "We can't have
you come here in case you are being followed. The
last thing we want at this moment is to let them know
the FBI is investigating them. Hold on."

Sansone went off the line but Philips could hear a
discussion in the background.

"The Cloisters, Philips. Do you know the Cloisters?" asked Sansone, coming back on the line.

"Of course," said Martin, bewildered.

"We'll meet there. Take a cab and get out at the
main entrance. Send the cab away. It will give us a
chance to make sure you are clear."

"Clear?"

"Not being followed, for God's sake! Just do it,
Philips."

Philips was left holding a dead receiver. Sansone
hadn't waited for questions or acquiescence. His in-
structions weren't suggestions, they were orders. Philips couldn't but be impressed by the agent's utter
seriousness. He went back to the bartender and asked
if he could call a cab.

"Hard to get cabs to come to Harlem at night," said
the bartender.

A five-dollar bill made him change his mind and he
used the phone behind the cash register. Martin noted
the butt of a forty-five pistol in the same location.

Before a taxi driver would agree to come, Martin
had to promise a twenty-dollar tip and say his destination was Washington Heights. Then he spent a
nervous fifteen minutes before he saw the cab pull up
in front. Martin climbed in and the taxi squealed off
down the once fashionable avenue. Right after they'd

pulled away, the driver asked Martin to lock all doors.

They went over ten blocks before the city began to look less threatening. Soon they were in an area familiar to Philips and lighted store fronts replaced the previous desolation. Martin could even see a few people walking beneath umbrellas.

"Okay, where to?" said the driver. He was obviously relieved as if he'd rescued someone from behind enemy lines.

"The Cloisters," said Philips.

"The Cloisters! Man, it's three-thirty in the morning. That whole area will be deserted."

"I'll pay you," said Martin, not wishing to have an argument.

"Wait a minute," said the driver, stopping at a red light. He turned to look through the Plexiglas partition. "I don't want no trouble. I don't know what the fuck you're up to, but I don't want no trouble."

"There will be no trouble. I just want to be dropped off at the main entrance. Then you're on your way."

The light changed and the driver accelerated. Martin's comment must have satisfied him because he didn't complain anymore and Martin was glad of the chance to think.

Sansone's authoritative manner had been helpful. Under the circumstances, Philips felt he could not have made any decisions for himself. It was all too bizarre! From the moment Philips had left the hospital, he'd descended into a world not bound by the usual restraints of reality. He even began to wonder if his experiences had been imaginary until he saw Werner's bloodstains on his parka. In a sense, they were reassuring; at least Philips knew he had not gone mad.

Looking out the window, he stared at the dancing city lights and tried to concentrate on the improbable intervention of the FBI. Philips had had enough experience in the hospital to realize that organizations typically function for their own best interests, not those of the individual. If this affair, whatever it was, was so important to the FBI, how could Martin expect they'd have his best interests at heart. He couldn't! Such thoughts made him feel uneasy about the meeting at the Cloisters. Its remoteness disturbed him. Turning, he peered out the back of the taxi, trying to determine if he were being followed. Traffic was light and it seemed unlikely, but he couldn't be certain. He was about to tell the driver to change direction when he realized with a sense of impotence that there was probably no safe place to go. He sat tensely until they were almost at the Cloisters, then leaned forward and said:

"Don't stop. Keep driving."

"But you said you wanted to be dropped off," protested the cabby.

The taxi had just entered the oval cobblestoned area, which served as the main entrance. There was a large lamp over the medieval doorway and the light glistened off the wet granite paving.

"Just drive around once," said Philips, as his eyes scanned the area. Two driveways led off into the darkness. Some of the interior lights of the building could be seen above. At night the complex had the threatening aura of a Crusader's castle.

The cabby cursed but followed the circular road that opened up for a view of the Hudson. Martin couldn't see the river itself, but the George Washington Bridge with its graceful parabolas of lights stood out against the sky.

Martin swiveled his head around looking for any signs of life. There were none, not even the usual lovers parked next to the river. It was either too late or too cold or both. When they came full circle to the entrance, the taxi stopped.

"All right, what the fuck do you want to do?" asked the driver, looking at Philips in the rear-view mirror.

"Let's get out of here," he said.

The driver responded by spinning the wheels and accelerating away from the building.

"Wait. Stop!" yelled Martin, and the cabby jammed on the brakes. Philips had seen three tramps who'd stood and looked over the stone wall lining the entrance drive. They'd heard the screeching of the tires. By the time the taxi had stopped, they were thirty yards back.

"How much?" asked Martin, looking out the window of the cab.

"Nothing. Just get out."

Philips put a ten-dollar bill in the Plexiglas holder and got out. The taxi sped away the second the door was closed. The sound of the car died away quickly in the damp night air. In its wake was a heavy silence, broken only by the occasional hiss of cars on the invisible Henry Hudson Parkway. Philips walked back in the direction of the tramps. On his right, a paved path led off the road and dipped down through the budding trees. Philips could vaguely see that the path split with one fork twisting back and running beneath the arched roadway.

He made his way down it and looked beneath the overpass. There weren't three tramps; there were four. One was passed out, lying on his back and snoring. The other three were sitting, playing cards. There was a small fire going, illuminating two empty half-gallon wine jugs. Philips watched them for a while, wanting to be certain that they were what they appeared, just vagrants. He wanted to figure out some way of using these men as a buffer between himself and Sansone. It wasn't that he expected to be arrested, but his experience with institutions motivated him to investigate and have some idea what to expect, and the use of an intermediary was the only method he could think of. After all, even if it made sense, meeting at the Cloisters in the middle of the night was hardly normal procedure.

After watching for a couple more minutes, Philips walked in under the archway acting as if he were a little drunk. The three bums eyed him for a moment and, deciding he meant no harm, went back to their cards.

"Any of you guys want to earn ten bucks?" said Martin.

For the second time, the three derelicts looked up.

"Whatta we have to do for ten bucks?" asked the youngest.

"Be me for ten minutes."

The three bums looked at one another and laughed. The younger one stood up.

"Yeah, and what do I do when I'm you?"

"You go up to the Cloisters and you walk around. If anybody asks you who you are, you say, Philips."

"Let me see the ten bucks."

Philips produced the money.

"How about me?" said one of the older men, getting to his feet with difficulty.

"Shut up, Jack," said the younger. "What's your whole name, mister?"

"Martin Philips."

"Okay, Martin, you got a deal."

Taking off his coat and his hat, Philips made the man put them on, pulling the hat well down. Then Martin took the bum's coat and reluctantly put his arms into the sleeves. It was an old shabby chesterfield with a narrow velvet lapel. In the pocket was part of a sandwich without a wrapper.

Despite Martin's objections, the other two men insisted on coming along. They laughed and joked until Philips said the whole deal was off if they didn't shut up.

"Should I walk real straight?" asked the younger fellow.

"Yes," said Martin, who was having second thoughts about the masquerade. The path approached the courtyard below the main driveway. There was a steep incline just before the cobblestoned area with a bench at the top for tired pedestrians. The stone wall bordering the entrance ended abruptly at the intersection. Directly across was the main doorway to the Cloisters itself.

"Okay," whispered Martin. "Just walk over to that door, try to open it, then walk back, and the ten spot is yours."

"How do you know I'm not going to just run away with your hat and coat," said the younger fellow.

"I'll take the chance. Besides, I'd catch you," said Philips.

"What's your name again?"

"Philips. Martin Philips."

The tramp pulled Philips' hat even lower on his forehead so that he had to tilt his head back to see. He started up the incline but lost his balance. Martin gave him a shove in the small of the back and he pitched forward and catwalked on his hands and feet up to the level of the drive.

Martin inched up the incline until his eye line was just above the stone wall. The tramp had already crossed the roadway and had reached the cobblestones, the irregular surface momentarily causing him to lose his balance, but he caught himself before he fell. He skirted the central island, which served as a bus stop, and made his way over to the wooden door. "Anybody home?" he yelled. His voice echoed in the courtyard. He stumbled out into the center of the yard and shouted: "I'm Martin Philips."

There was no sound except a light patter of rain, which had just begun. The ancient monastery, with its roughhewn ramparts, gave the scene an unreal, timeless quality. Martin wondered again if he was the victim of a giant hallucination.

Suddenly, a shot shattered the quiet. The tramp in the courtyard was lifted off his feet and dashed to the granite paving. The effect was the same as a high velocity shell hitting a ripe melon. The entrance of the bullet was a surgical incision; the exit was a horrid tearing force that took away most of the man's face and scattered it over a thirty-foot arc.

Philips and his two companions were stunned. When they realized that someone had shot the tramp, they turned and fled, falling over each other down the precipitous incline that fell away from the monastery.

Never had Martin felt such desperation. Even when he'd run from Werner's, he hadn't experienced such fear. Any second he expected to hear the rifle again and feel the searing pain of a deadly bullet. He knew that whoever was after him would check the body in the courtyard and immediately realize the mistake. He had to get away.

But the rocky hillside was a danger in itself. Philips' foot snagged and he fell headlong, just missing an outcropping. As he pulled himself up, he saw a path veering off to the right. Pushing away the underbrush, he made his way toward it.

A second shot was followed by an agonizing scream. Philips' heart leaped into his mouth. Once clear of the forest he ran as fast as possible, hurling himself down the walkway into the darkness.

Before he realized what was happening, he had launched himself into the air at the top of a stairway. It seemed like an incredibly long time before he hit the ground again. Instinctively, he fell forward to absorb the shock, tucking his head under and doing a somersault, like a gymnast. He ended up on his back, and sat up, dazed. From behind, he could hear running footsteps on the walkway, so he forced himself to his feet. He ran on, struggling against dizziness.

This time, he saw the stairs in time, and slowed. He took the steps in threes and fours, then ran on with rubbery legs. The path intersected another, crossing at right angles. It came up so quickly that Martin had no time to decide whether to change his direction.

At the next intersection, Martin's path ended, forcing him to hesitate for a moment. Below and to the right he could see the forest ended. At the edge of the trees there was some sort of balcony with a cement balustrade. Suddenly, Philips heard footsteps again and this time it sounded like more than one person. There was no time to think. He turned and raced down to the balcony. Below him, stretching out about a hundred yards, was a cement playground with swings and benches and a central depression that was probably a wading pool in the summer. Beyond the playground was a city street and Martin saw a yellow cab go by.

Hearing the running steps draw closer, he forced himself down the wide cement stairs that descended from the side of the balcony to the playground. It was only then, hearing the pounding footsteps drawing closer, that he realized he could not get across the open area before whoever it was behind him reached the balcony. He'd be exposed.

Quickly he ducked into the dark recess beneath the balcony, mindless of the stench of old urine. At that moment, he heard labored feet reach the roof. He stumbled blindly back until he hit up against a wall. Turning, he allowed himself to slowly sink to a sitting position, trying to control his loud gasping for breath.

The columns supporting the balcony stood out against the dim image of the playground. A few lights could be seen in the city beyond. The heavy footsteps ran across the roof, then descended the stairs. Abruptly, a dark ragged figure whose frantic wheezing breath carried back to Martin was clearly silhouetted as the man stumbled out into the playground, heading for the street beyond.

A series of lighter steps sounded on the balcony above. Philips heard muffled words. Then silence. Ahead the figure was cutting diagonally across the wading pool.

The rifle spoke sharply above Philips and simultaneously the fleeing figure in the playground was sent crashing on its face. Once it hit the cement, it didn't move. The man had been killed instantly.

Martin resigned himself to fate. Further flight was impossible. He was cornered like a fox after a chase. All that was left was the coup de grace. If he hadn't been so exhausted, maybe he would have thought of resisting but, as it was, he just stayed still, listening to light footsteps cross the balcony and start down the stairs.

Expecting to see silhouetted figures appear momentarily within the frames of the columns in front of him, Philips waited, holding his breath.

11

Denise Sanger woke up in one instant. She lay there unmoving, scarcely breathing while she listened to the sounds of the night. She could feel the pulse at her temples, hammering away from the adrenaline that had been pumped into her system. She knew that she'd been awakened by some foreign noise but it was not repeated. All she could hear was the rumbling of her ancient refrigerator. Her breathing slowly returned to normal. Even her refrigerator, with a final thump, kicked off, leaving the apartment in silence.

Rolling over, wondering if perhaps she'd just had a bad dream, she realized she had to go to the bathroom. The pressure on her bladder slowly augmented until she could no longer ignore it. As distasteful as the idea was, she had to get up.

Pulling herself from the warm bed, Denise padded into the bathroom. Gathering up her nightgown in a bundle on her lap, she sat down on the cold toilet seat. She didn't turn on the light nor did she close the door.

The adrenaline in her system seemed to have inhibited her bladder and she was forced to sit for several minutes before she could urinate. She had just finished when she heard a dull thud that could have been someone hitting her wall from another apartment.

Denise strained her ears for any other sound but the apartment was quiet. Marshaling her courage, she moved silently down the hall until she had a view of her front door. She felt a sense of relief when she saw that the police lock was securely in place.

She turned and started back toward the bedroom. It was at that moment that she felt the draft along the floor and heard a slight rustle of some of the notes tacked to her bulletin board. Reversing her direction, she returned to the foyer and glanced into the dark living room. The window to the fire escape in the air well was open!

Denise tried desperately not to panic, but the possibility of an intruder had been her biggest fear since coming to New York. For almost a month after her arrival, she'd had great difficulty sleeping. And now with her window ajar her worst nightmare seemed to be unfolding. Someone was in her apartment!

As the seconds ticked by, she remembered that she had two phones. One by her bed, the other on the kitchen wall just ahead of her. In one step, she crossed the hall, feeling the aging linoleum under her feet. Passing the sink, she grabbed a small paring knife. A glint of meager light sparkled off its small blade. The tiny weapon gave Denise a false sense of protection.

Reaching past the refrigerator, she grasped the phone. At that instant, the old refrigerator compressor switched on and with a sound similar to a subway, chugged to life. Startled by the noise, her nerves already drawn out to a razor's edge, she panicked, letting go of the phone and starting to scream.

But before she could make a sound, a hand grabbed her neck and lifted her with great power, causing her strength to drain away. Her arms went flaccid and the paring knife clattered to the floor.

She was whisked around like a rag doll and rapidly propelled down the hall with her feet just touching the floor. Stumbling into the bedroom there were several flashes, a sensation of searing heat on the side of her head, and the sounds of a pistol with a silencer.

The bullets slapped into the mound of blankets on her bed. A final rude shove sent Denise to her knees as the blankets were yanked back.

"Where is he?" snarled one of the attackers. The other pulled open the closets.

Cowering by the bed, she looked up. Two men dressed in black with wide leather belts were standing in front of her.

"Who?" she managed in a weak voice.

"Your lover, Martin Philips."

"I don't know. At the hospital."

One of the men reached down and lifted her up high enough to throw her onto the bed. "Then we'll wait."

For Philips, time had passed as if in a dream. After the last rifle shot he'd heard nothing. The night had remained still except for an occasional car on the city street beyond the playground. He was aware that his pulse had slowed to normal, but he was still having trouble collecting his thoughts. Only now, as the rising sun imperceptibly brushed over the playground, did his mind begin to function again. As the dawn brightened he was able to make out more details in the landscape, like the series of concrete wastebaskets that were fashioned to look like the surrounding natural rock. Birds had suddenly convened on the area, and several pigeons wandered over to the sprawled body in the dry wading pool.

Martin tried moving his stiff legs. He gradually realized that the dead body out in the playground was a new threat. Someone would soon call the police and after last night Martin was understandably terrified of them.

Heaving himself to his feet, he steadied himself against the wall until his circulation returned. His body ached as he cautiously made his way back up the cement stairs, scanning the area. He could see the path down which he'd made his terrified plunge just hours before. Way off he could see someone walking his dog. It wouldn't be long before the body in the playground was discovered.

He descended the stairs and hurried toward the far corner of the park, passing close to the body of the derelict. The pigeons were feasting on bits of organic matter that had been sprayed by the bullet. Martin looked away.

Emerging from the park, he turned up the narrow lapels of the tramp's overcoat and crossed the street, which he saw was Broadway. There was a subway entrance on the corner but Martin was frightened of being trapped below the ground. He had no idea if the people who were after him were still in the area.

He stepped into a doorway and scanned the street. It was getting lighter every minute and the traffic was beginning to pick up. That made Philips feel better. The more people, the safer he should be, and he didn't see any men loitering suspiciously or sitting in any of the parked cars.

A taxi stopped at the traffic light directly in front of him. Martin dashed from the doorway and tried to open the rear door. It was locked. The driver turned around to look at Philips, then accelerated despite the red light.

Martin stood in the street bewildered, watching the cab speed into the distance. It was only as he walked back to the doorway and caught sight of his reflection in the glass that he realized why the cabby had pulled away. Martin appeared to be a veritable tramp. His hair was hopelessly disheveled, matted on the side with dried blood and bits of leaves. His face was dirty and sported a twenty-four-hour growth of whiskers. The tattered chesterfield coat completed the derelict image.

Reaching for his wallet, Philips was relieved to feel its familiar form in his back pocket. He took it out and counted the cash. He had thirty-one dollars. His credit cards would be useless under the circumstances. He kept out one of the fives and replaced the wallet.

About five minutes later another cab pulled up. This time Philips approached from the front so the cabby could see him. He'd made his hair as presentable as possible and opened the overcoat so that its shabby condition wasn't immediately apparent. Most important, he held up the five-dollar bill. The cabby waved him in.

"Where to, Mister!"

"Straight," said Philips. "Just go straight."

Although the cabby eyed Martin a little suspiciously in the rear-view mirror, he put the car in gear when the light changed, and drove down Broadway.

Philips twisted in the seat and looked out the back window. Fort Tryon Park and the small playground receded rapidly. Martin still wasn't sure where to go, but he knew he'd feel safer in a crowd.

"I want to go to Forty-second Street," he said finally.

"Why didn't you tell me before," complained the driver. "We could have turned on Riverside Drive."

"No," said Philips. "I don't want to go that way. I want to go down the East Side."

"That's going to cost about ten bucks, mister."

"It's okay!" said Martin. He took out his wallet and showed ten dollars to the driver, who was watching in the rear-view mirror.

When the car began to move again Martin let himself relax. He still could not believe what had happened in the last twelve hours. It was as if his whole world had collapsed. He had to keep stifling his natural impulse to go to the police for help. Why had they turned him over to the FBI? And why on earth would the Bureau want to annihilate him, no questions asked? As the car flashed down Second Avenue his sense of terror returned.

Forty-second Street provided the anonymity Philips needed. Six hours earlier the area had been alien and threatening. Now, the same aspects were comforting. These people wore their psychoses up front. They didn't hide behind a facade of normality. The dangerous people could be recognized and avoided.

Martin bought a large fresh orange juice and polished it off. He had another. Then he walked down Forty-second Street. He had to think. There had to be a rational explanation for everything. As a doctor, he knew that no matter how many disparate signs and symptoms there were in an illness, they could invariably be traced to a single disease. Nearing Fifth Avenue, Philips walked into the little park by the library. He found an empty bench and sat down. Pulling the dirty chesterfield around him, he made himself as comfortable as possible and tried to go over the events of the night. It had started at the hospital . . .

Martin woke with the sun almost overhead. He glanced around to see if anyone was watching him. There were lots of people in the park now, but no one seemed to be paying any attention to him. It had gotten warm and he was sweating heavily. When he stood up he was aware of his heavy ripe smell. Walking out of the park he glanced at his watch and was shocked to learn it was ten-thirty.

He found a Greek coffee house several blocks away. Balling up the old coat, he put it under the table. He was famished and he ordered eggs, home fries, bacon, toast and coffee. He used the tiny men's room but decided not to clean up. No one seeing him would ever guess he was a doctor. If he were being sought he couldn't have a better disguise.

As he finished his coffee he found the crumpled list he'd made of the five patients: Marino, Lucas, Collins, McCarthy, and Lindquist. Was it possible that these patients and their histories were related to the bizarre fact that he was being pursued by the authorities? But even so, why would they be trying to kill him; and what had happened to these women? Had they been murdered? Could the affair be somehow related to sex and the underworld? If so, how did radiation fit in? And why was the FBI involved? Maybe the conspiracy was national, affecting hospitals all across the country.

Getting more coffee, Martin was certain the answer to the puzzle lay in the Hobson University Medical

Center, but he knew that was the one place the authorities would expect him to go. In other words, the hospital was the most dangerous place for Martin, yet the only place where he had a chance to figure out what was happening. Leaving his coffee, Philips went back to use the pay phone. His first call was to Helen.

"Doctor Philips! I'm so glad you called. Where are you?" Her voice was strained.

"I'm outside the hospital."

"I guessed that. But where?"

"Why?" asked Martin.

"Just wanted to know," said Helen.

"Tell me," said Martin. "Has anybody been looking for me . . . like . . . the FBI?"

"Why would the FBI be looking for you?"

Martin was now reasonably certain that Helen was under observation. It was not like her to answer a question with a question, especially an absurd one about the FBI. Under normal circumstances she would have simply told Martin he was crazy. Sansone or one of his agents had to be there with her. Philips hung up abruptly. He would have to think of another way to get the charts and other information he wanted from his office.

Martin next called the hospital and had Dr. Denise Sanger paged. The last thing he wanted was for her to go to the GYN clinic. But she did not pick up her page and Martin was afraid to leave a message. Hanging up, he placed a final call to Kristin Lindquist. Kristin's roommate picked up on the first ring, but when Philips introduced himself and asked about Kristin the girl said she could not give him any information and that she'd prefer he didn't call. Then she hung up.

Back at his table, Philips spread the list of patients

in front of him. Taking out a pen he wrote: "strong radioactivity in the brains of young women (? other areas); Pap smears reported abnormal when they were normal; and neurological symptoms something like multiple sclerosis." Philips stared at what he'd written, his mind racing in crazy circles. Then he wrote: "Neurological—GYN—police—FBI," followed by "Werner necrophilia." There didn't seem to be any possible way all these things could be related, but it did seem as if GYN was in the middle. If he could find out why those Pap smears were reported abnormal, maybe he'd have something.

Suddenly a wave of desperation swept over him. It was obvious he was up against something bigger than he could possibly handle. His old world with the daily headaches no longer seemed so terrible. He would gladly put up with a little boring routine if he could go to bed at night with Denise in his arms. He wasn't a religious person, but he found himself trying to strike a bargain with God: if He would rescue him from this nightmare, Martin would never complain about his life again.

He looked down at the paper and realized that his eyes had filled with tears. Why would the police be after him, of all people? It didn't make sense.

He went back to the phone and tried again to reach Denise, but she wasn't answering her page. In desperation he called the GYN clinic and spoke to the receptionist.

"Has Denise Sanger had her appointment yet?"

"Not yet," said the receptionist. "We expect her any minute."

Martin thought quickly before he spoke. "This is Doctor Philips. When she arrives tell her that I canceled the appointment and that she should see me."

"I'll tell her," said the receptionist and Martin sensed she was genuinely bewildered.

Martin walked back to the small park and sat down. He found himself incapable of any sensible decision. For a man who believed in order and authority, not to be able to contact the police after being shot at seemed the height of irrationality.

The afternoon passed in fitful sleep and wakeful confusion. His lack of decision became a decision in itself. Rush hour started and reached its crescendo. Then the crowds began to dissipate and Martin went back to the coffee shop for dinner. It was a little after six.

He ordered a meatloaf plate and tried paging Denise while it was being prepared. Still she didn't pick up. When he was through he decided to try her apartment, wondering if the police knew enough about him to stake her out.

She picked up the phone on the first ring.

"Martin?" her voice was desperate.

"Yes, it's me."

"Thank God! Where are you?"

Martin ignored the question and said, "Where have you been? I've been paging you all day."

"I haven't been feeling well. I stayed at home."

"You didn't let the page operator at the hospital know."

"I know I . . ." suddenly Sanger's voice changed. "Don't come . . ." she yelled.

Her voice was choked off and Philips could hear a muffled struggle. His heart jumped in his throat. "Denise!" he shouted. Everyone in the coffee shop froze; all heads turned in Philips' direction.

"Philips, this is Sansone." The agent had picked up the phone. Martin could still hear Denise trying to shout in the background. "Just a minute, Philips," said Sansone. Then turning away from the phone he said, "Get her out of here and keep her quiet." Coming back on the line Sansone said, "Listen, Philips . . ."

"What the hell is going on, Sansone," cried Philips. "What are you doing to Denise?"

"Calm down, Philips. The girl is fine. We're here to protect her. What happened to you last night at the Cloisters?"

"What happened to me? Are you crazy? You people wanted to blow me away."

"That's ridiculous, Philips. We knew it wasn't you in the courtyard. We thought they'd already caught you."

"Who's they?" asked the bewildered Philips.

"Philips! I can't talk about these things over the phone."

"Just tell me what the fuck's going on!"

The people in the coffee shop were still motionless. They were New Yorkers and accustomed to all sorts of strange happenings, but not in their local coffee shop.

Sansone was cool and detached. "Sorry, Philips. You have to come here, and you have to come now. Being out on your own you are simply complicating our problem. And you already know there are a number of innocent lives at stake."

"Two hours," yelled Philips. "I'm two hours away from the city."

"All right, two hours, but not a second longer."

There was a final click and the line was dead.

Philips panicked. In one second his indecision was

swept away. He threw down a five-dollar bill and ran out on the street toward the Eighth Avenue subway.

He was going to the Medical Center. He didn't know what he was going to do once he got there but he was going to the hospital. He had two hours and he had to have some answers. There was a chance Sansone was telling the truth. Maybe they did think that he'd been taken by some unknown force. But Philips wasn't sure and the uncertainty terrified him. His intuition told him that Denise was now in jeopardy.

The uptown train had standing-room only, even though the rush hour peak was over, but the ride was good for Philips. It tempered his panic and allowed him time to use his essential intelligence. By the time he got off he knew how he was going to get inside the medical center and what he was going to do when he did.

Martin followed the crowd off the train to the street, and headed for his first destination: a liquor store. The clerk took one look at Martin's disheveled appearance, bounded from behind his register and tried to hustle Philips out. He relented when Martin held up his money.

It took him just thirty seconds to pick out and pay for a pint of whiskey. Turning off Broadway onto a side street, Martin found a small alley filled with trash barrels. There he removed the top to the whiskey, took a good slug and gargled. He swallowed a small amount but spat most out onto the ground. Using the whiskey like cologne he anointed his face and neck, then slid the half-empty bottle back into his coat pocket. Stumbling past most of the trash barrels, Philips picked one toward the back. It was filled with sand probably used for the sidewalk in the winter. He dug a shallow hole and buried his wallet, putting the rest of his cash into the same pocket as the whiskey.

His next stop was a small but busy grocery store. People gave him a wide berth as he entered. It was quite crowded and Philips had to push past some customers to find an area with a clear line of sight to the checkout registers.

"Ahhh," screamed Philips as he choked and stumbled to the floor taking a display of canned beans on special with him. He writhed as if in pain as the beans rolled in every direction. When a shopper bent down to ask if he was all right, Martin rasped, "Pain. My heart!"

The ambulance arrived in moments. Martin had an oxygen mask strapped to his face and a rhythm EKG connected to his chest during the short drive to Hobson University Medical Center. His essentially normal EKG had already been preliminarily analyzed by radio and it had been determined that no cardiac drugs were needed.

As the attendants pushed him into the ER Martin glimpsed several policemen standing on the platform, but they didn't give him so much as a glance. He was carried down to one of the main ER rooms and transferred to a bed. One of the nurses searched his pockets for identification while the resident took another EKG. Since the tracing was normal, the cardiac team began to disperse, leaving the intern to take over.

"How's the pain, partner?" he asked, bending over Philips.

"I need some Maalox," Martin growled. "Sometimes when I drink cheap stuff I need Maalox."

"Sounds good to me," said the doctor.

Philips was given Maalox by a hardened thirty-five-year-old nurse who did everything but slap him for the pitiful shape he was in. She took a short history and Martin gave his name as Harvey Hopkins. It'd been his roommate in college. The nurse then said they'd give him a chance to relax for a few minutes to see if his chest pain came back. She pulled the curtain around his bed.

Philips waited for several minutes, then he climbed off the end of the bed. On an ER cart against the wall he found a prep razor and a small bar of soap used to clean wounds. He also got several towels, and a surgical cap and mask. So armed he peeked out of the curtains.

As usual at that time of night, the ER was a hopeless sea of confusion. The sign-in line at the front desk almost reached the entrance and ambulances were arriving at regular intervals. No one even looked at Martin as he walked down the central corridor and pushed open the gray door across from the besieged main desk. There was only one doctor in the lounge and he was engrossed in an EKG when Philips walked through to the showers.

Rapidly he showered and shaved, leaving his clothes in the corner of the room. By the sinks he found a pile of surgical scrub gear, which was the favorite apparel of the emergency room staff. He put on a shirt and pants and the surgical hat to cover his wet head. He even tied on the mask. There were many times that hospital personnel used masks outside of the OR, especially when they were suffering from a head cold.

Regarding himself in the mirror, Philips was convinced that someone would have to know him very well to recognize him. He'd not only gotten inside the hospital but he looked like he belonged. As for Harvey Hopkins, ER patients were always walking out, Philips looked at his watch. He'd used up an hour.

Charging out of the lounge, Philips crossed the ER and ran past two more policemen. He used the back stairs behind the cafeteria to reach the second floor. He wanted a radiation detector, but decided it was too dangerous to fetch the one in his office and had to search around the radiotherapy section until he found another. Then he ran back down the stairs to the main floor and hurried into the clinics building.

The elevators there were old and required operators, who had already left for the day, so Martin had to climb four flights to GYN. He had decided on the subway, sandwiched between two very unhappy businessmen, that the radiation could have been connected to GYN, but now that he had arrived, radiation detector in hand, his resolve began to falter. He had no idea what he was looking for.

Passing the main GYN waiting room, Philips turned into the smaller university clinic. It had yet to be passed over by the cleaning crew, and the area was littered with overflowing ashtrays and papers. It all looked so innocent and normal in the meager light.

Philips checked the receptionist's desk but it was locked. Trying the two doors behind the desk he found the whole area to be secured. But the locks were simple ones, which required the key to be inserted in the doorknob itself. A plastic card from the top of the receptionist's desk sufficed to open one. Martin went in, closed the door and turned on the lights.

He was standing in the hallway where he'd talked with Dr. Harper. There were two examining rooms to the left and the lab or utility room to the right. Martin selected the examining rooms first. Monitoring the detector very carefully he went over each room, sticking the detector into every cabinet and recess and even going over the examining tables themselves. Nothing. The place was clean. In the lab areas he did the same thing starting with the countertop cabinets, opening drawers, peering into boxes. At the end of the room he went over the large instrument cabinets. It was all negative.

The first response came from the wastebasket. It was a very weak reading and totally harmless, but it was nonetheless radiation. Glancing at his watch, Philips noticed that time was slipping rapidly away. In one-half-hour he was going to have to call Denise's apartment. He decided that he'd present himself only after he'd made sure Sansone wasn't holding her.

With the positive reading in the wastebasket he decided to go over the lab one more time. He found nothing until he returned to the closet. The lower shelves were filled with linen and hospital gowns, while the upper shelves had a mixture of laboratory and office supplies. Below the shelves was a hamper filled with soiled linen, which registered another weak positive reading when he pushed the probe almost to the floor.

Martin emptied out the soiled linen and went over it with the detector. Nothing. Sticking the probe into the emptied hamper Philips again got a weak response near the base. He reached down and put his hand into the enclosure. The walls and floor of the hamper were painted wood and seemed solid. With his fist he struck the bottom and felt a vibration. Taking his time he hit it all around the periphery. When he got to the far corner the board tilted slightly, then fell back into place. Pushing in the same location Martin raised the floor of the hamper and looked beneath. Below were two shielded lead storage boxes with the familiar radiation warning logo.

The two boxes had labels indicating their origin from the Brookhaven Laboratories, which was a source of all sorts of medical isotopes. Only one of the labels was entirely legible. It contained 2-[18F]fluoro-2 deoxy-D-glucose. The other label was partially scraped off although it was also an isotope of deoxy-D-glucose.

Martin quickly opened the boxes. The first one with the legible label was moderately radioactive. It was the other box which had a significantly thicker lead shield that made the radiation detector go crazy. Whatever it was, it was very hot. Philips shut and sealed the container. Then he piled the linen back into the hamper and shut the door.

Martin had never heard of either one of the compounds, but the mere fact they were in the GYN clinic was reason enough to make them highly suspect. The hospital had extremely strict controls concerning radioactive material that was used for radiotherapy, some diagnostic work and controlled research. But none of these categories was applicable to the GYN clinic. What Philips had to know was what radioactive deoxy-glucose was used for.

Carrying the radiation detector, Philips descended the clinic stairs to the basement. Once in the tunnel system he had to slow his dash in order not to surprise the groups of medical students. But when he reached the new medical school he increased his pace, arriving at the library totally out of breath.

"Deoxy-glucose," he panted. "I need to look it up. Where?"

"I don't know," said the startled librarian.

"Shit," said Philips and turned and started toward the card catalogue.

"Try the reference desk," called the woman.

Reversing his direction, Philips went to the periodical section where the reference desk was staffed with a girl who looked about fifteen. She'd heard the commotion and was watching Martin's approach.

"Quick. . . ." said Philips. "Deoxy-glucose. Where can I look it up?"

"What is it?" The girl eyed Martin with alarm.

"Must be some sort of sugar, made from glucose. Look, I don't know what it is. That's why I need to look it up."

"I guess you could start with the Chemical Abstract and try the Index Medicines, then. . . ."

"The Chemical Abstract! Where's that?"

The girl pointed to a long table backed by bookshelves. Philips rushed over and pulled out the index. He was afraid to look at his watch. He found the reference as a subheading under glucose, giving him the volume and page number. When he found the article, he started to skim it but his frenzy turned the words into a meaningless jumble. He had to force himself to slow down and concentrate, and when he did he learned that deoxy-glucose was so similar to glucose, the biological fuel of the brain, that it was transported across the blood-brain barrier and picked up by the active nerve cells. But then, once inside the active nerve cells it could not be metabolized like glucose, and piled up. Down at the very bottom of the short article it said: ". . . radioactively tagged deoxy-glucose has shown great promise in brain research."

Martin snapped the book shut and his hands trembled. The whole affair was beginning to make sense. Someone in the hospital was conducting experiments in brain research on unsuspecting human subjects! "Mannerheim!" thought Martin, so enraged that he could taste the venom.

He was not a chemist, but he remembered enough to realize that if a compound like deoxy-glucose was made sufficiently radioactive, it could be injected into people and used to study its absorption in the brain. If it were very radioactive, which the stuff in the box in GYN was, then it would kill the brain cells that absorbed it. If someone wanted to study a pathway of nerve cells in the brain they could selectively destroy them with this method, and it was the destruction of nerve pathways in animal brains that had been the foundation of the science of neuroanatomy. To a sufficiently ruthless scientist it was just a step to adopt the same methods to humans. Philips shuddered. Only someone as egocentric as Mannerheim would be able to overlook the moral aspects.

Martin was crushed by his discovery. He had no idea how Mannerheim got Gynecology to participate, but they had to be in on the study. And the hospital administrator had to know something too. Why else would Drake defend Mannerheim, the prima donna neurosurgeon, the demigod of the hospital. Martin sagged under the appalling implications.

He knew that Mannerheim was heavily funded by the government; millions and millions of dollars of public money went into his research activities. Could that be the reason for the FBI's intervention? Had Martin been accused of endangering a major breakthrough funded by the government? The FBI might have no idea that the breakthrough involved human experimentation. Martin was no tyro when it came to organizational snafus when the right hand had no idea what the left hand was doing. But it was a sorry twist that the use of human sacrifice for medical research could be unknowingly protected by the government.

Slowly Martin turned his wrist to see the face of his watch. Five minutes to go before he had to call Denise. He was not sure if the agents would harm her, but after their treatment of the tramps he was not about to take any chances. He wondered what he could do. He knew something about what was going on . . . not everything, but something. He knew enough that if he could get some powerful person to intervene, the whole conspiracy might unravel. But who? It would have to be someone outside of the hospital hierarchy, but knowledgeable about the hospital and its structure. The Commissioner of Health? Someone in the Mayor's office? The Commissioner of Police? Martin was afraid that these people might have already been told so many lies about Martin that his warnings would fall on deaf ears.

Suddenly Philips thought of Michaels, the boy wonder. He could get to the Provost of the university! His word could be enough to stimulate an inquiry. It might work. Martin ran to one of the phones and got an outside line. As he dialed Michaels' number, he prayed that he'd be home. When the scientist's familiar voice answered, Martin could have cheered.

"Michaels, I'm in terrible trouble."

"What's wrong?" asked Michaels. "Where are you?"

"I don't have time to explain; I've uncovered some gigantic research horror here in the hospital, which the FBI seems to be protecting. Don't ask me why."

"What can I do?"

"Call the Provost. Tell him that there's a scandal involving human experimentation. That should be enough unless the Provost is involved. If that's the case, heaven help us all. But the most immediate problem is Denise. She's being held by the FBI in her apartment. Get the Provost to call Washington and have her released."

"What about you?"

"Don't worry about me. I'm all right. I'm in the hospital."

"Why don't you come here to my apartment?"

"I can't. I'm going up to the Neurosurgical lab. I'll meet you at your computer lab in about fifteen minutes. Hurry!"

Philips hung up and dialed Denise's apartment. Someone lifted the phone but did not talk.

"Sansone," Martin cried. "It's me, Philips."

"Where are you, Philips? I have the uncomfortable feeling you are not taking this situation seriously."

"But I am. I'm just north of the city. I'm coming. I need more time. Twenty minutes."

"Fifteen minutes," said Sansone. Then he hung up. Martin raced back from the library with a sinking feeling. Now he was even more sure that Sansone was holding Denise hostage in order to make him give himself up. They wanted to kill him and they'd probably kill her to get him. Everything rested on Michaels. He had to get to uninvolved authority. But Martin knew he needed more information to back up his allegations. Mannerheim undoubtedly had some kind of cover story. Martin wanted to see how many of the brain specimens in Neurosurgery were radioactive.

Martin took an empty elevator to the Neurosurgical floor in the research building. He'd dispensed with the surgical hat and nervously ran his fingers through his tangled hair. He only had minutes left before calling Denise's apartment.

The door to Mannerheim's lab was locked and Martin looked around for something to break the glass. A small fire extinguisher caught his eye. Detaching it from the wall, he threw it through the glass panel of the door. With his foot he knocked out some remaining shards, and then reached in and turned the handle.

At that exact moment the doors at the far end of the hall burst open and two men charged into the corridor, both carrying pistols. They were not hospital security; they were dressed in polyester business suits.

One of the men dropped to a crouch, grabbing his gun with both hands while the other shouted: "Freeze, Philips!"

Martin fell forward onto the broken glass inside the lab and out of view from the hall. He heard the dull thump of a silencer as a bullet ricocheted off the metal door frame. He scrambled to his feet and slammed the door, knocking a few more bits of glass from the broken pane.

Turning into the lab Martin heard heavy footsteps pounding down the hall. The room was dark, but he remembered its layout and rushed down between the counter-top room dividers. He got to the door to the animal room as his pursuers reached the outer door. One of the men hit the light switch, filling the lab with raw fluorescent glare.

Martin functioned in a frenzy. Inside the animal room, he grabbed the cage housing the monkey who had electrodes implanted in his brain turning him into a raging monster. The animal tried to grab Martin's hand and bite him through the wire mesh. Pushing with all his might, Martin got the cage over to the door of the lab. He could see his pursuers coming around the nearest counter top. Holding his breath Martin released the door to the cage.

With a shriek that rattled the laboratory glassware, the monkey launched itself from its prison. In a single jump it reached the shelves under the counter tops, scattering instruments in all directions. Startled by the appearance of the raging beast trailing wire electrodes, the two men hesitated. It was all the animal needed. Powered by its pent-up fury, the monkey leaped from the shelf onto the shoulder of Martin's nearest pursuer, tearing at the man's flesh with its powerful fingers, and sinking its teeth into his neck. The other man tried to help but the monkey was too fast.

Martin did not stay to observe the results. Instead he dashed across the animal room, passing the long rows of preserved brains, and entered the stairwell. Down he plunged, taking the stairs as quickly as possible, leaping to the landings, turning, down again in a dizzying effort.

When he heard the stairwell door crash open far above him he hugged the wall but did not slow his descent. He wasn't sure if he could be seen but he didn't stop to check. He should have known that Mannerheim's Neurosurgical lab would have been guarded. Martin heard loud running footsteps begin descending the stairs but they were many floors away, and he reached the basement and entered the tunnel without hearing any more pistol shots.

The ancient two-way hinges on the doors to the old medical-school building squeaked as Philips burst through. After sprinting up the curved marble stairs, Philips raced down the partially demolished corridor until he reached the old amphitheater entrance. Then he abruptly stopped. It was dark, which meant that

Michaels had yet to arrive. Behind him there was silence. He'd outrun his pursuers. But now the authorities knew he was in the medical center complex, and it would be only a matter of time before he was discovered.

Martin tried to catch his breath. If Michaels didn't arrive shortly he'd have to go over to Denise's apartment no matter how helpless he'd feel. Anxiously he pushed on the amphitheater door. To his surprise it opened. He stepped inside and was enveloped by the black coldness.

The silence was broken by a low-pitched electrical snap familiar to Philips from his days as a student. It was the sound the lighting system made when it was activated. And just as in those former days, the room filled with light. Seeing movement out of the corner of his eye, Martin looked down toward the pit. Michaels was waving up at him. "Martin. What a relief to see you!"

Philips grabbed the handrail in front of him to help propel him along the horizontal aisle that used to lead between tiers of seats when the amphitheater had been used as a lecture hall. Michaels had positioned himself at the base of the stairs and he waved Philips down.

"Did you get the Provost?" shouted Philips. Seeing Michaels gave him the first glimmer of hope he'd had for hours.

"Everything is okay," yelled Michaels. "Come on down here."

Martin started down the stairs which were narrow and criss-crossed with cables to the electronic components that stood where the seats had once been. Three men were waiting with Michaels. Apparently he'd already gathered help. "We have to do something about Denise instantly they . . ."

"It's been taken care of," yelled Michaels.

"Is she all right?" asked Martin, halting his progress for a moment.

"She's fine and she's safe. Just come on down here."

The closer Martin got to the pit the more equipment there was and the more difficult it was to avoid the wires. "I just barely got away from two men who shot at me up in Neurosurgery lab." He was still breathless and his voice came in spurts.

"You're safe here," said Michaels, watching his friend come down the stairs.

As he arrived at the edge of the pit, Martin lifted his eyes from the cluttered stairs, and looked into Michaels' face. "I didn't have time to find anything in Neurosurgery," said Martin. He could now see the other three men. One was the congenial young student, Carl Rudman, whom he had met on his first visit to the lab. The other two he didn't recognize. They were dressed in black jumpsuits.

Ignoring Martin's last comment, Michaels turned to one of the strangers: "Are you satisfied now? I told you I could get him here."

The man who had not taken his eyes from Philips said, "You got him here, but are you going to be able to control him?"

"I think so," said Michaels.

Martin watched this strange exchange, his eyes moving from Michaels to the man in the jumpsuit. Suddenly he recognized the face. It was the man who'd killed Werner!

"Martin," said Michaels softly, almost paternally. "I've got some things to show you."

The stranger interrupted. "Dr. Michaels, I can

guarantee that the FBI will not act precipitously. But what the CIA does is not under my control. I hope you understand that, Dr. Michaels."

Michaels spun around. "Mr. Sansone. I'm aware that the CIA is not your jurisdiction. I need some more time with Dr. Philips."

Turning back to Philips he said, "Martin, I want to show you something. Come on." He took a step toward the door connecting to the neighboring amphitheater.

Martin was paralyzed. His hands were gripping the brass railing that fringed the pit. Relief had become perplexity, and with the perplexity had come the deep rumbling of renewed fear.

"What is going on here?" he asked with a sense of dread. He spoke slowly, enunciating each word.

"That's what I want to show you," Michaels said. "Come on!"

"Where's Denise?" Philips didn't move a muscle.

"She's perfectly safe. Believe me. Come on." Michaels stepped back over to Philips and grabbed his wrist to encourage him to step down into the pit. "Let me show you some things. Relax. You'll see Denise in a few minutes."

Philips allowed himself to be led past Sansone and into the next amphitheater. The young student had gone in before them and switched on the light. Martin saw another amphitheater, whose seats had been removed. In the pit where he was standing was a huge screen made of millions of light-sensitive photoreceptor cells whose wires fed into a processing unit. From this first processor emerged a significantly smaller number of wires, which were gathered into two trunks that led into two computers. Wires from these computers led into other computers, which were cross-connected. The setup filled the room.

"Do you have any idea what you're looking at?" asked Michaels.

Martin shook his head.

"You're looking at the first computerized model of the human visual system. It's large, primitive by our current standards, but surprisingly functional. The images are flashed on the screen and the computers you see here associate the information." Michaels made a sweeping gesture with his hands. "What you are looking at, Martin, is akin to that first atomic pile they built at Princeton. This will be one of the biggest scientific breakthroughs in history."

Martin looked at Michaels. Maybe the man was crazy.

"We have created the fourth-generation computer!" said Michaels, and he slapped Philips on the back. "Listen. The first generation was merely the first computers that were not just calculators. The second generation came in with transistors. The third generation was microchips. We have given birth to the fourth generation, and that little processor you have in your office is one of our first applications. You know what we've done?"

Philips shook his head. Michaels was on fire with excitement.

"We've created true artificial intelligence! We've made computers that think. They learn and they reason. It had to come, and we did it!" Michaels grabbed Martin's arm and pulled him into the hall connecting the two old amphitheaters. There between the two-tiered lecture rooms was the door that led into the old Microbiology and Physiology labs. When Michaels opened it, Martin saw the inside had been reinforced with steel. Behind it was a second door. It too was re-inforced and secured. Michaels unlocked it with a special key and pulled it open. It was like stepping into a vault.

Martin staggered under the impact of what he saw. The old labs with their small rooms and slate-top experiment tables had been removed. Instead Philips found himself in a hundred-foot-long room with no windows. Down the center was a row of huge glass cylinders filled with clear liquid.

"This is our most valuable and productive preparation," said Michaels, patting the side of the first cylinder. "Now I know your first impression will be emotional. It was for all of us. But believe me, the rewards are worth the sacrifice."

Martin slowly began to walk around the container. It was at least six feet high and three feet in diameter. Inside, submerged in what Martin later learned was cerebrospinal fluid, were the living remains of Katherine Collins. She floated in a sitting position with her arms suspended over her head. A respiration unit was functioning, indicating that she was alive. But her brain had been completely exposed. There was no skull. Most of the face was gone except for the eyes, which had been dissected free and covered with contact lenses. An endotracheal tube issued from her neck.

Her arms had also been carefully dissected to extract the ends of the sensory nerves. These nerve endings looped back like strands of a spider web to connect with electrodes buried within the brain.

Philips made a slow complete circle around the cylinder. An awful weakness spread over him and his legs threatened to give way.

"You probably know," said Michaels, "that significant advances in computer science, like feedback, came from studying biological systems. It's really what cybernetics is all about. Well, we've taken the natural step and gone to the human brain itself, not studying it like psychology, which thinks of it as a mysterious black box." Suddenly, Philips remembered Michaels using the enigmatic term on the day he presented Martin with the computer program. Now he understood. "We've studied it like any other vastly complicated machine. And we've succeeded, beyond our dreams. We've discovered how the brain stores its information, how it accomplishes parallel processing of information rather than the inefficient serial processing of yesterday's computers, and how the brain is organized in a functionally hierarchial system. Best of all, we've learned how to design and build a mechanical system that mirrors the brain and has these same functions. And it works, Martin! It works beyond your wildest imagination!"

Michaels had nudged Philips to continue down the row of cylinders, looking in at the exposed brains of the young women, all at different levels of vivisection. At the last cylinder Philips paused. The subject was in the earliest state of preparation. Philips recognized the remains of the face. It was Kristin Lindquist.

"Now, listen," said Michaels. "I know it's shocking when you first see it. But this scientific breakthrough is so big that it is inconceivable to contemplate the immediate benefits. In medicine alone, it will revolutionize every field. You've already seen what our very preliminary program will do with a skull X ray. Philips, I don't want you to make any snap decisions, you understand?"

They'd finished the trip around the room, which was a marriage between a hospital and a computer installation. In the corner was what appeared to be a complicated lifesupport setup, like an intensive-care unit. Sitting in front of the monitors was a man in a long white coat. Michaels' and Philips' arrival had not disturbed his concentration.

Standing again in front of Katherine Collins, Philips found words for the first time: "What is going into this subject's brain?" His voice was flat, unemotional.

"Those are sensory nerves," said Michaels eagerly. "Since the brain is ironically insensitive to its own state, we've joined Katherine's peripheral sensory nerves up to electrodes so that she can tell us which sections of her brain are functioning at any given moment. We've constructed a feedback system for the brain."

"You mean this preparation communicates with you?" Philips was genuinely surprised.

"Of course. That's the beauty of this whole setup. We've used the human brain to study itself. I'll show you."

Outside of Katherine Collins' cylinder but in line with her eyes was a unit that resembled a computer terminal. It had a large upright screen and a keyboard, which was electrically attached to a unit within the cylinder as well as to a central computer on the side of the room. Michaels keyed a question into the unit and it flashed onto the screen. How are you feeling, Katherine?

The question vanished and in its place came: Fine, I'm eager to start work. Please stimulate me.

Michaels smiled and looked at Martin. "This girl can't get enough. That's why she's been so good."

"What did she mean, 'stimulate me'?"

"We planted an electrode in her pleasure center. That's how we reward her and encourage her to cooperate. When we stimulate her she has the sensation of one hundred orgasms. It must be sensational because she wants it constantly."

Michaels typed into the unit: "Only once, Katherine. You must be patient." Then he pushed a red button on the side of the keyboard. Philips could see Katherine's body arch slightly and shudder.

"You know," said Michaels, "it's been shown now that the reward system of the brain is the most powerful motivating force, even greater than self-preservation. We've even found a way to incorporate that principle in our newest processor. It makes the machines function more efficiently."

"Who ever conceived of all this?" asked Philips not sure he believed everything he was seeing.

"No one person can take credit or blame," said Michaels. "It all happened in stages. One thing led to another. But the two people most responsible are you and I."

"Me," said Martin. He looked like he'd been slapped.

"Yes," said Michaels. "You know I've always been interested in artificial intelligence; that's why I was interested in working with you initially. The problems you presented about reading X rays crystallized the whole central issue called 'pattern recognition.' Humans could recognize patterns, but the most sophisticated computers had inordinate difficulty. By your careful analysis of the methodology you used to evaluate X rays, you and I isolated the logical steps that had to be solved electronically if we were to duplicate your function. It sounds complicated, but it isn't. We needed to know certain things about how a human brain recognizes familiar objects. I teamed up with some physiologists interested in neuroscience and we initiated a very modest study using radioactive deoxy-glucose, which could be injected into patients who were then subjected to a specific pattern. We used the E charts frequently used by Ophthalmology. The radioactive glucose analog then made microscopic lesions in the subjects' brains by killing the cells that had been involved in recognizing and associating the E pattern. Then it was just a matter of mapping those lesions to determine how the brain functioned. The technique of selective destruction had been used for research on animal brains for years. The difference was that, using it on humans, we learned so much so quickly that it spurred us on to greater efforts."

"Why young women?" asked Martin. The nightmare was becoming a reality.

"Purely because of ease. We needed a population of healthy subjects who we could call back whenever we needed them. The Gynecology population suited our purpose. They ask very little about what's being done to them, and by merely altering the Pap smear report, we could get them to return as often as necessary. My wife has been in charge of the university's GYN clinic for years. She selected the patients and then injected the radioactive material in their bloodstream when she drew blood for their routine laboratory work. It was very easy." Martin had a sudden vision of the severe, black-haired woman in the GYN clinic. He had trouble associating her with Michaels, but then he realized that was far more believable than everything else he'd seen.

The screen in front of Katherine Collins came alive again: Stimulate me, please.

Michaels typed into the keyboard: "You know the rules. Later, when the experiments begin."

Turning to Martin, he said: "The program was so easy and so successful that it encouraged us to expand the goals of the research. But this happened gradually, over several years. We were encouraged to give huge doses of radiation to delineate the final associative areas of the brain. Unfortunately this caused some symptomology in a few of the patients, especially when we began work on the temporal lobe connections. This part of the work became very tricky because we had to balance the destruction we were causing with the level of tolerable symptoms for the subjects. If the subject got too many symptoms we had to bring them in, which initiated this stage of the research." Michaels gestured toward the row of glass cylinders. "And it's been here in this room that all the major discoveries have been made. But of course we never envisioned this when we started."

"What about these recent patients, like Marino and Lucas and Lindquist?"

"Ah, yes. They did cause a bit of a stir. They were the patients receiving the highest dose of radioactivity, and their symptoms came on so fast that some of them went to physicians before we could get to them. But the physicians never came close to a diagnosis, especially Mannerheim."

"You mean he's not involved?" asked Martin with surprise.

"Mannerheim? Are you joking? You can't have egotistical bastards like that involved in a project of this magnitude. He'd want credit for every little breakthrough."

Philips looked around the room. He was horrified and overwhelmed. It didn't seem possible that it could happen, especially right smack in the center of a university's medical center. "The thing that amazes

me most," said Martin, "is that you could get away
with this. I mean some poor bastard up in pharmacol-
ogy mistreats a rat and the animal league is on his
back."

"We've had a lot of help. You might have noticed
those men out there are FBI agents."

Philips looked at Michaels. "You don't have to remind me of that. They tried to kill me."

"I'm sorry about that. I had no idea what was going
on until you called me. You've been under surveillance for over a year. But they told me it was for
your protection."

"I've been under surveillance?" Martin was incredulous.

"We all have. Philips, let me tell you something.
The results of this research are going to change the
entire complexion of society. I'm not being dramatic.
When we first started, it was a small project, but we
had some very early results, which we patented. That
caused the big computer companies to shower us with
research money and help. They didn't care how we
were making our discoveries. All they wanted was the
results, and they competed with one another in giving
us favors. But then the inevitable happened. The first
major application for our fourth-generation computer
was the Defense Department. It has revolutionized
the whole concept of weaponry. Using a small artificial intelligence unit combined with a holographic
molecular memory-storage system, we designed and
built the first truly intelligent missile-guidance system. The army now has a prototype 'intelligent mis-
sile.' It is the biggest defense breakthrough since the
discovery of atomic power. And the government is
even less interested in the origin of our discoveries
than were the computer companies. Whether we liked

it or not, they blanketed us with the highest level of security they've ever amassed, even more than the Manhattan Project back when the atomic bomb was being created. Even the President couldn't have walked in here. So we've all been under surveillance. And those guys are a paranoid lot. Every day they thought that the Russians were about to storm the place. And last night they said you went berserk and were a security risk. But I can control them, to a point. A lot depends on you. You're going to have to make a decision."

"What kind of decision?" Martin said tiredly.

"You're going to have to decide if you can live with this whole affair. I know it is a shock. I confess I was not going to tell you how we were making our break-throughs. But since you learned enough to nearly be liquidated, you had to know. Listen, Martin. I am aware that the technique of experimenting on humans without their consent, especially when they must be sacrificed, is against any traditional concept of medical ethics. But I believe the results justify the methods. Seventeen young women have unknowingly sacrificed their lives. That is true. But it has been for the betterment of society and the future guarantee of the defense superiority of the United States. From the point of view of each subject, it is a great sacrifice. From the point of view of two hundred million Americans, it is a very small one. Think of how many young women willfully take their lives each year, or how many people kill themselves on the highways, and to what end? Here these seventeen women have added something to society, and they have been treated with compassion. They have been well cared for and have experienced no pain. On the contrary they have experienced pure pleasure."

"I can't accept this. Why didn't you just let them kill me?" said Philips in a tired voice. "Then you wouldn't have had to worry about my decision."

"I like you, Philips. We've worked together for four years. You're an intelligent man. Your contribution to the development of artificial intelligence was and can be enormous. The medical application, especially in the field of radiology, is the cover for this whole operation. We need you, Philips. It doesn't mean we can't do without you. None of us is indispensable, but we need you."

"You don't need me," said Philips.

"I'm not going to argue with you. The fact is, we do need you. Let me emphasize one other point. No more human subjects are needed. In fact this biological aspect of the project is soon to be closed down. We have obtained the information we needed and now it's time to refine the concepts electronically. The human experimentation is over."

"How many researchers have been involved?" asked Philips.

"That," said Michaels proudly, "is one of the beauties of the whole program. In relation to the magnitude of the protocol, the number of personnel has been very small. We have a team of physiologists, a team of computer people and several nurse practitioners."

"No physicians?" asked Philips.

"No," said Michaels with a smile. "Wait! That's not entirely correct. One of the neuroscience physiologists is an M.D.-Ph.D."

There was a silence for a few moments as the two men eyed each other.

"One other thing," said Michaels. "You, obviously and deservedly, will take full credit for the medical advances that will be instantly realized with the application of this new computer technology."

"Is that a bribe?" asked Philips.

"No. It's a fact. But it will make you one of the most celebrated medical researchers in the United States. You will be able to program the entire field of Radiology so that the computers will be able to do all the diagnostic work with one-hundred percent efficiency. That will be an enormous benefit to mankind. You yourself told me once that radiologists, even good ones, only function around seventy-five percent. And one last thing . . ." Michaels looked down and shifted his feet as if he was somewhat embarrassed. "As I said, I can only control the agents to a degree. If they think someone is a security risk, it's out of my hands. Unfortunately Denise Sanger is now involved. She doesn't know the specifics about this research, but she knows enough to jeopardize the project. In other words, if you choose not to accept this program, not only you, but Denise too, will be liquidated. I have no control over that."

At the mention of a threat against Denise, another emotion overwhelmed Philips' sense of moral outrage. Hatred welled up inside of him. Only with great difficulty did he hold himself back from striking out in a fit of blind fury. He was exhausted and every nerve was drawn to its breaking point. It took every ounce of strength to force his mind back to rational thought. When he did, he was overcome by a feeling of futility in the face of the sheer power and momentum behind the project. Philips might have been able to sacrifice himself but he could not sacrifice Denise. A sad feeling of resignation settled over him like a smothering blanket.

Michaels put his hand on Philips' shoulder. "Well,

Martin? I think I've told you everything. What do you say?"

"I don't think I have a choice," said Martin slowly.

"Yes you do," said Michaels. "But it's a narrow one. Obviously both you and Denise will stay under close surveillance. You will be given no chance to give the story to either Congress or the press. There are contingency plans for any eventuality. Your choice is merely between life for you and Denise or purposeless instant death. I hate to be so blunt. If you decide the way I hope you will, Denise will only be told that our research has had Defense Department application that you did not know about and that you became a mistaken security risk. She will be sworn to secrecy and that will be the end of it. It will be your responsibility to keep her from knowing the biological origins."

Philips took a deep breath, turning himself away from the row of glass cylinders. "Where is Denise?"

Michaels smiled. "Follow me."

Retracing their steps back through the double vault-like doors and past the amphitheaters, the two men walked down the rubble strewn corridor, turning into the old medical-school administrative office.

"Martin!" shouted Denise. She jumped up from a folding chair and rushed between two agents. Throwing her arms around Philips she burst into tears. "What has been happening?" she sobbed.

Martin couldn't speak. His pent-up emotions overflowed with joy at seeing Denise. She was alive and safe! How could he take responsibility for her death?

"The FBI tried to convince me you had become a dangerous traitor," said Denise. "I didn't believe it for an instant, but tell me it isn't true. Tell me this is all a bad dream."

Philips closed his eyes. When he opened them he found his voice. He spoke slowly, choosing his words with great care, because he knew Denise's life was in his hands; they had him shackled for the moment, but he would find a way to break their hold someday, even if it took years. "Yes," said Philips. "It's all a bad dream. It's all a terrible mistake. But it's over now."

Martin tilted Denise's face up and kissed her mouth. She kissed him back, secure that her feeling about him had been correct, that as long as she trusted him she would be safe. For a moment he buried his face in her hair. If individual life was important, then so was hers. For him more than anyone.

"It's over now," she repeated.

Philips glanced at Michaels over Denise's shoulder and the computer expert nodded approval. But Martin knew it could never be over . . .

SCIENTIST SHOCKS SCIENTIFIC COMMUNITY; SEEKS POLITICAL ASYLUM IN SWEDEN

STOCKHOLM (AP)—

Dr. Martin Philips, the physician whose research has recently propelled him into international celebrity status, disappeared yesterday afternoon under mysterious circumstances in Sweden. Scheduled for a lecture at 1 P.M. at the famed Carolinska Institute, the neuroradiologist failed to appear in front of a packed audience. Along with the celebrated scientist, his wife of four months, Dr. Denise Sanger, also disappeared.

Initial speculation suggested the couple sought seclusion from the attention that has been showered on them since Dr. Philips began unveiling his series of startling medical discoveries and innovations six months ago.

That idea was abandoned, however, when it was learned that the couple had had surprisingly massive Secret Service protection and that their disappearance definitely depended on Swedish authorities' cooperation.

Inquiries to the State Department have been met with strained silence, which has been made more curious when it was learned that the affair had unleashed feverish activity on many U.S. government levels, seemingly out of proportion to the event. International curiosity, already peaked, was honed to a razor's edge by the following prepared statement released late last night by the Swedish authorities:

Dr. Martin Philips has asked for and has been granted political asylum in Sweden. He and his wife have been placed in political seclusion. Within twenty-four hours a document written by Dr. Philips will be released for the international community outlining a gross abrogation of human rights perpetrated under the aegis of medical experimentation. Until now, Dr. Martin Philips has been constrained from voicing his opinions by a consortium of vested interests including the United States government. After the document has been released, Dr. Philips will hold a press conference by video under the auspices of Swedish TV.

Exactly what the "gross abrogation of human rights" involves is not known, although the strange sequence of events surrounding Dr. Philips' disappearance has stimulated serious speculation. Dr. Philips' area of expertise involves computer interpretation of medical images, which hardly seems open to gross violation of experimental ethics. However, the reputation of Dr. Philips (his winning this year's Nobel Prize in Medicine is considered inevitable by most reputable researchers) guarantees him a large and attentive audience. Obviously the affair had to deeply offend Dr. Philips' sense of morality for him to jeopardize his career by taking this drastic and dramatic step. It also suggests that the field of medicine is not immune to having its own Watergate.

AUTHOR'S NOTE

Human experimentation since World War II has created some difficult problems with the increasing employment of patients as experimental subjects when it must be apparent that they would not have been available if they had been truly aware of the uses that would be made of them.[1]

That comment was made by an esteemed Professor of Research in Anaesthesia, Harvard Medical School, at the outset of an article describing twenty-two examples of experiments which he felt violated medical ethics. He chose these examples from a group of fifty, and he cited a Professor in England, Dr. M. H. Pappworth, who had amassed a list of five hundred.[2] The problem is not an isolated, infrequent episode. It is endemic, spreading from the basic value system inherent in the physician/experimentor image spawned by the current research-oriented medical community.

Consider some examples . . .

One experiment which has been in the news in recent years and a subject of a television video essay by *Sixty Minutes* involved various U. S. Government agencies experimenting on unknowing servicemen in an attempt to determine the effects of hallucinatory drugs. Perhaps more disturbing and closer to the story line of *Brain* was an experiment in which live cancer cells were injected into elderly patients without their informed consent.[3] At the time of the study the researchers did not know if the cancers would take or not. Apparently they took it upon themselves to decide that the patients were already so old that it didn't matter!

There are numerous examples of radioactive materials being injected into unknowing, unsuspecting people, primarily institutionalized mental defectives, but even new-born babies have not been immune.[4] There is no way that these studies can be justified for the therapeutic benefit of the individuals and there is no doubt that these unknowing people were subjected to the risk of injury and disease, not to mention discomfort and pain. On top of that, the results of studies of this kind are often of little consequence, serving more to augment the bibliographies of the involved researchers than advance medical science. Many of these studies were knowingly supported by the U.S. Government agencies.

Another experiment involved the purposeful injection of seven to eight hundred mentally retarded children with infected serum in order to produce hepatitis.[5] This study apparently was approved and supported by the Armed Forces Epidemiological Board, among others. Consent was mentioned to have been obtained from the parents but the circumstances lead one to wonder how the consent was obtained and the degree to which it was "informed consent";

and, even so, did this consent by the parent protect the rights of the subjects? The question remains: would any of the researchers have allowed a mentally retarded member of their own family to participate, or in the other experiments mentioned, would the researchers have allowed a family member or themselves to be involved as subjects? I sincerely doubt it. The intellectual elitism that medicine and medical research fosters creates a sense of omnipotence and with it, a double standard.

It would be irresponsible to suggest that the majority of research involving humans in the United States is based on unethical standards, because it is definitely not true. However, the fact that there is a significant minority is frightening and demands attention from the public. The pressure for research within our academic medical centers is as strong as ever and the ensuing investigative enthusiasm and air of professional competition can cause people to lose sight of the negative consequences for patients. Besides, the confusion of values between patient/subject risk and possible societal benefit has not been unequivocally settled.[6] And the idea that patient consent will obviate abuses has proved to be false. Take for instance the case of fifty-one women used as subjects for a study of an experimental labor-inducing drug. They all signed consent forms but apparently under less than ideal conditions. An investigation of the study reported that many gave their consent during the duress of the admitting procedures or in the delivery room itself.[7] After the fact, the patients were interviewed and almost forty percent had no idea they'd been the subject of research even though they had purportedly given "informed consent." One of the subtle ways consent was obtained was by saying the study involved a "new" drug, not an "experimental" drug, the researcher knowing full well that the adjective "new" would imply that the experimental drug was better than the "old" drug.

Subterfuge need not be necessary to obtain consent. Subtle innuendos suggesting that the care of the individual will be less than maximum if the person does not "cooperate" is the most frequent ploy. Next in frequency is for the researcher to cleverly imply that the experimental procedure might benefit the individual even if that possibility is negligible. Finally there is the method by which the researcher fails to inform the potential subject that there are alternative and, frequently, established modes of therapy.

All this is not new. Lip service has been given to violations of medical ethics involving human experimentation for more than twenty years in the medical journals. The fact that it still exists to the extent that it does is a tragedy of major proportions. And now that the decade of the eighties has arrived with medicine beginning a new love affair with physics, the opportunities for abuse reach a new and horrifying potential. The center stage for the marriage of medicine and physics is neuroscience, and the chief actor will be the human brain, considered by many to be the most mysterious and amazing creation in the universe. The ethical and moral issues involving human experimentation have to be solved before . . .

. . . before fiction and fantasy become fact.

ROBIN COOK, M.D.

1. Beecher, H. K., "Ethics and Clinical Research," *New England Journal of Medicine,* vol. 274, 1966, pp. 1354-60.

2. Pappworth, M. H., *Human Guinea Pigs: Experimentation on Man,* Beacon Press, Boston, 1967.

3. Barber, B., "The Ethics of Experimentation With Human Subjects," *Scientific American,* vol. 234, no. 2, February 1976, pp. 25-31.

4. Pappworth, M. H., *op. cit.*

5. Veatch, R. M., *Case Studies in Medical Ethics,* Harvard University Press, 1977, pp. 274-77.

6. Jonas, H., "Philosophical Reflections on Experimenting with Human Subjects," *Experimentation with Human Subjects,* P. A. Freud, ed., George Braziller, 1969.

7. Barber, B., *op. cit.*